'Gunnar Staalesen is one of my very favourite Scandinavian authors. Operating out of Bergen in Norway, his private eye, Varg Veum, is a complex but engaging anti-hero. Varg means "wolf" in Norwegian, and this is a series with very sharp teeth' **Ian Rankin**

'The Norwegian Chandler' **Jo Nesbø**

'Razor-edged Scandinavian crime fiction at its finest' **Quentin Bates**

'Not many books hook you in the first chapter – this one did, and never let go!' **Mari Hannah**

'With its exploration of family dynamics and the complex web of human behaviour, Staalesen's novel echoes the great California author Ross MacDonald's Lew Archer mysteries. There are some incredible set-pieces including a botched act of terrorism that has frightening consequences, but the Varg Veum series is more concerned with character and motivation than spectacle, and it's in the quieter scenes that the real drama lies' Russel McLean *Herald Scotland*

'There is a world-weary existential sadness that hangs over his central detective. The prose is stripped back and simple … deep emotion bubbling under the surface – the real turmoil of the characters' lives just under the surface for the reader to intuit, rather than have it spelled out for them' **Doug Johnstone**, *The Big Issue*

'Norwegian master Staalesen is an author who eschews police procedural narratives for noirish private eye pieces … Staalesen dislikes Scandinavian parochial in his writing, and continues to work – bravely, some would say – in a traditional US-style genre, drawing on such writers as the late Ross MacDonald. Nevertheless, he is a contemporary writer; there is some abrasive Scandicrime social commentary here' **Barry Forshaw**, *Financial Times*

'In Staalesen's deft yet unhurried style, numerous plot threads are interwoven around the kernel of suspense established in the beginning … this masterful first-person narrative is very much character-driven, as Varg's tenacious personality drives his destiny and the events that lead up to the surprise-laden finale' **Crime Fiction Lover**

'Staalesen's greatest strength is the quality of his writing. The incidental asides and observations are wonderful and elevate the book from a straightforward murder investigation into something more substantial' **Sarah J. Ward, Crime Pieces**

'Staalesen's mastery of pacing enables him to develop his characters in a leisurely way without sacrificing tension and suspense' ***Publishers Weekly***

'Gunnar Staalesen was writing suspenseful and socially conscious Nordic Noir long before any of today's Swedish crime writers had managed to put together a single book page … one of Norway's most skillful storytellers' **Johan Theorin**

'An upmarket Philip Marlowe' **Maxim Jakubowski,** *The Bookseller*

'The prose is richly detailed, the plot enthused with social and environmental commentary while never diminishing in interest or pace, the dialogue natural and convincing and the supporting characters all bristle with life. A multi-layered, engrossing and skilfully written novel; there's not an excess word' **Tony Hill, Mumbling About Music**

'There is a strong social message within the narrative which is at times chilling, always gripping and with a few perfectly placed twists and turns that make it more addictive the further you get into it' **Liz Loves Books**

'With his cynical and witty asides, an unflinching attitude to those who would thwart his investigations, and his dogged moral determination, Veum is a hugely likeable and vivid character' **Raven Crime Reads**

'The characters and settings are brilliantly drawn and the novel pulls you in so that you keep turning the pages and race to the conclusion ... This isn't just a crime novel that you pick up, read and then cast aside. It is a life that you have been given a glimpse of so that you want to see more' **Live Many Lives**

'Staalesen proves why he is one of the best storytellers alive with a deft touch and no wasted words; he is like a sniper who carefully chooses his target before he takes aim' **Atticus Finch**

'The plot is compelling, with new intrigues unfolding as each page is turned ... a distinctive and welcome addition to the crime fiction genre' **Jackie Law, Never Imitate**

'A well-paced, thrilling plot, with the usual topical social concerns we have come to expect from Staalesen's confident pen ...' **Finding Time To Write**

'*We Shall Inherit the Wind* brings together great characterisation, a fast-paced plot and an exceptional social conscience ... The beauty of Staalesen's writing and thinking is in the richness of interpretations on offer: poignant love story, murder investigation, essay on human nature and conscience, or tale of passion and revenge' **Ewa Sherman, EuroCrime**

WHERE ROSES NEVER DIE

ABOUT THE AUTHOR

One of the fathers of Nordic Noir, Gunnar Staalesen was born in Bergen, Norway in 1947. He made his debut at the age of twenty-two with *Seasons of Innocence* and in 1977 he published the first book in the Varg Veum series. He is the author of over twenty titles, which have been published in twenty-four countries and sold over four million copies. Twelve film adaptations of his Varg Veum crime novels have appeared since 2007, starring the popular Norwegian actor Trond Espen Seim. Staalesen, who has won three Golden Pistols (including the Prize of Honour), lives in Bergen with his wife. The next instalment in the Varg Veum series – *No One Is So Safe in Danger* – will be published by Orenda Books in 2017.

ABOUT THE TRANSLATOR

Don Bartlett lives with his family in a village in Norfolk. He completed an MA in Literary Translation at the University of East Anglia in 2000 and has since worked with a wide variety of Danish and Norwegian authors, including Jo Nesbø and Karl Ove Knausgaard. He has previously translated *The Consorts of Death*, *Cold Hearts* and *We Shall Inherit the Wind* in the Varg Veum series.

Where Roses Never Die

GUNNAR STAALESEN

Translated from the Norwegian by Don Bartlett

**ORENDA
BOOKS**

Orenda Books
16 Carson Road
West Dulwich
London SE21 8HU
www.orendabooks.co.uk

First published in Norwegian as *Der hvor roser aldri dør* in 2012
First published in English by Orenda Books 2016

Reprinted 2016
3 5 7 9 10 8 6 4 2

The publication of this translation has been made possible through the
financial support of NORLA, Norwegian Literature Abroad.

Typeset in Arno by MacGuru Ltd
Printed and bound by CPI Group (UK) Ltd, Croydon CR0 4YY

SALES & DISTRIBUTION

In the UK and elsewhere in Europe:
Turnaround Publisher Services
Unit 3, Olympia Trading Estate
Coburg Road, Wood Green
London N22 6TZ
www.turnaround-uk.com

In USA/Canada:
Trafalgar Square Publishing
Independent Publishers Group
814 North Franklin Street
Chicago, IL 60610
USA
www.ipgbook.com

For details of other territories, please contact *info@orendabooks.co.uk*

To our good friend, Gary Pulsifer (1957–2016). We miss him already. This English edition of *Where the Roses Never Die* is dedicated to his memory. Thanks for everything, Gary!

Don, Gunnar and Karen

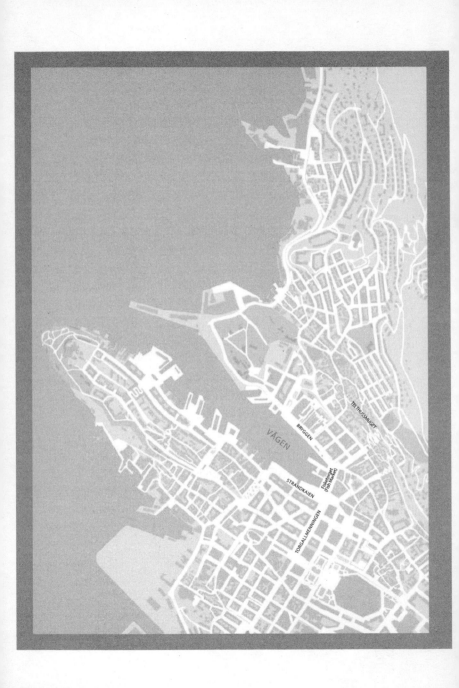

1

There are days in your life when you are barely present, and today was one of those. I was sitting behind my desk, half-cut and half-asleep, when I heard a shot from the other side of Vågen, the bay in Bergen. Not long afterwards I heard the first police sirens, although there was no reason to assume this would ever be a case that might involve me. By the time I had eventually staggered to my feet and made it to the window, it was all over.

Reading the newspapers the following day, I found out most of what had gone on, the rest I learned in dribs and drabs.

Afterwards they were universally referred to as the *Shell Suit Robbers*. There were just two customers in the exclusive jewellery shop in Bryggen when, at 15.23 on Friday, 7th December 2001, the door swung open and three heavily armed individuals, wearing balaclavas and dressed in what are informally known as BBQ suits, burst into the premises.

The two customers, an older woman and a younger one, cowered in the corner. In addition to the customers there were two female assistants in the shop. The owner was in the back room. He'd hardly had time to look up before one robber was standing in the doorway and pointing a sawn-off shotgun at him. He said in what was supposed to be English: 'Don't move yourself! The first person who presses an alarm button are shot!'

One of the robbers took up a position by the front door with an automatic weapon hanging down at thigh-height and kept lookout. The third opened a big bag, gave it to the assistant in front of the display cabinets and pointed a gun at her. He spoke in English too: 'Fill up!'

The assistant objected: 'They're locked!'

'Unlock!'

'But I'll have to get…' She motioned to the counter.

'Move, move, move!'

She cast a glance at the other assistant, who nodded resigned agreement. Then she opened a drawer behind the counter, took out a bunch of keys and went back to the display cabinets.

The robber in front of her directed a glance at the door: 'Everything OK?'

The robber posted there nodded mutely.

The robber by the office door intoned the same message: 'Move!'

The jewellery-shop owner shouted: 'You have no idea what you're doing! All our items are registered internationally. No one will buy the most expensive pieces.'

'Shut up!' The robber pointed to a safe in the wall. 'Open.'

'I haven't got…'

The robber rushed forward and held the rifle to his head. 'Open. If you…'

Sweat poured from the jeweller's forehead. 'Yes, alright … Don't…' He swivelled the office chair and rolled it towards the safe. 'I just have to … the code.' He put a finger to his brow to show how hard he was trying to remember.

'You know. Don't make me to laugh.'

'Yes, but when I'm nervous…'

'You soon have even more reason to be nervous if you…'

The robber tapped the safe door with the weapon, and the owner stretched out his right hand and with trembling fingers started to turn the lock and enter the code.

Inside the shop the older of the two assistants opened a display cabinet. She took out the watches one by one and carefully placed them in the bag, so slowly that the robber impatiently pushed her aside and began to scoop watches of all price ranges into the bag while shouting orders: 'Open the other cabinets! And you…' He looked at the assistant by the counter. 'All the drawers! At the bottom also.'

In the back room, the safe was open. The robber brutally shoved the jeweller out of the way and emptied the safe contents on to the work table. Papers and documents were sent flying to the floor. With a triumphant flourish, he held up a box of eight diamond-studded watches. The owner eyed him with an expression of despair.

The robber stuffed the box into a shoulder bag. Then he grabbed a wad of notes from the back of the safe and in they went too. 'Black money, eh?'

'Cash reserves,' the jeweller mumbled bitterly.

The robber backed towards the door and glanced out into the shop. 'Everything OK?'

The robber by the front door nodded. The other one was busy emptying the drawers from the counter. 'Just a moment.'

The robber who had been in the back room swung the sawn-off shotgun from the jeweller, to the two customers and finally to the older of the two assistants. 'Don't you move yourselves. The first person who presses the alarm button are shot.' He was still standing in the doorway with a view of the back room. 'Finished?' he said to the man behind the counter.

'That's it now.'

'Good.'

The robber by the front door leaned on the handle and glanced across the shop for instructions. The robber in the back room nodded, the front door was opened and with their weapons at the ready they dashed out.

That was when it happened.

None of the four women saw what went wrong. Other witnesses, on the pavement and around the quay on the other side of the street, could only relay fragments of what they thought they had observed. A passing motorist was convinced he had seen everything, 'from the corner of his eye', as he later put it.

As the robbers were making their getaway they must have collided with a man on the pavement. The man yelled, there was a second or two of silence, then further words were exchanged and a shot was fired, the man was hurled backwards and crashed on to the pavement, blood spurting from his chest, near his heart.

The three robbers hotfooted it across the street, sprinted along the harbour front and threw the bags into a small, white plastic boat waiting for them by the quay. An engine roared and the little boat, foam spraying over its bows, hurtled across Vågen, where eye-witnesses saw it disappear around the tip of Nordnes peninsula soon afterwards.

In the shop, the owner appeared from the back-room door. With sagging shoulders he said: 'I've rung the alarm.'

The younger of the two customers was the next to speak.

'That one by the door … I'm pretty sure … that one was a woman.'

Five minutes later the first police officers arrived, alerted by radio that a full-scale search was under way in the whole district.

The case was to become something of a mystery. I followed it only desultorily in the newspapers, and on radio and TV; first of all it was breaking news, then it was relegated to the back pages. There was more interest locally than nationally, but here too it wound up in semi-obscurity, as do most unsolved crimes, until something new is revealed and they become front-page news again.

The greatest mystery was how the robbers could have vanished. After the boat had powered round Nordnes peninsula it was never seen again. At the time in question, on a cold, blustery December day, there were not many people out walking in Nordnes Park, and no witnesses came forward, either from there or anywhere else along Puddefjorden. It did seem as if the thieves had literally vanished into thin air.

The police searched all the quays from Georgenes Verft, the ship-yard, and beyond, past Nøstet, Dokken and Møhlenpris, as far as Solheimsviken and from there to the Lyreneset promontory in Laksevåg, without turning up anything of any value. They went through the list of stolen boats in the region with a toothcomb. The ones they eventually found, they crossed off the list, but as late as March, three months after the robbery, there were still some that had not been located. It was the same story with the list of stolen cars. The general assumption was that the robbers must have come ashore somewhere in Nordnes or Laksevåg, transferred the booty to a car and driven off. Under such circumstances thieves often used a stolen vehicle and later set fire to it, after switching to their own cars. But no cars had been torched, to the police's knowledge, during that period – neither on the 7th December nor the following days.

What made the case especially serious was the murder. After a couple of days the dead man's name was released. Nils Bringeland was my age, fifty-nine years old, ran a little company in Bryggen and from all the indications seemed to have been no more than a casual passer-by. He left behind a partner and three children, two of them from an earlier marriage.

The case received broad media coverage, locally and nationally, for the first few days after the robbery. The shop owner, Bernhard Schmidt, was interviewed widely. He said his business had been run on the same premises for three generations since his grandfather, Wilhelm Schmidt, set it up from scratch in 1912. Bernhard Schmidt took the shop over from his father in 1965. There had been minor thefts, and in 1973 there was an attempted break-in through the backyard, but this was the first time in the company's history that they had experienced anything as dramatic as a robbery. He wouldn't divulge to the press the value of the items that had been stolen, but other sources speculated the figure lay somewhere between five hundred thousand and a million Norwegian kroner, perhaps even more. Neither the police nor the insurance company wished to comment on this aspect of the case.

The two female shop assistants were also interviewed, anonymously, but they had nothing of any importance to add, apart from the trauma of the experience. The younger of the two customers, Liv Grethe Heggvoll, appeared in the press with her full name. She and her mother had been in the shop looking for a fiftieth-birthday present, and they were as shocked as the shop employees by what they had witnessed. Asked by journalists whether she had noticed anything special about the robbers, she answered they had spoken English with what she considered was a Norwegian, or maybe an Eastern European, accent. 'What's more,' she added, 'I'm positive one of them was a woman.'

This information was later taken up by the police. They said it was too early to know whether this might have been an itinerant gang of professional robbers, but they were keeping all their avenues of inquiry open. As for the possibility of a woman being involved, they had no comment to make. The conspicuous get-ups – the so-called 'BBQ shell suits' – were discussed in several newspapers. The three suits were identical in colour and design: dark green with white stripes down the sleeves. Pictures of a similar style were everywhere, although the police refused to comment on whether they'd had any response from the general public.

As the investigation ground to a halt there was less and less to read about the case. There was no reason for me to give it a moment's thought. I had my own daily demons to fight at that time. I was on the longest and darkest marathon of my life, and it was still a long way to the tape.

2

The assignment I received on that Monday in March would perhaps turn out to be the most important I'd ever had, not least for my own sake. It was the first sign of light at the end of a tunnel that was much longer than I cared to admit.

The three years that had passed since Karin died had been like an endless wandering on the seabed. I had seen the most incredible creatures, some of them so frightening I had woken up bathed in sweat every time one appeared in my dreams. Enormous octopuses stretched out their long tentacles towards me, but they never managed to hold on to me. Monstrous monkfish forced me into jagged nooks and crannies, placed a knee on my crotch and emptied my pockets of valuables. Tiny fish floated by enticingly, their tails in the air, but were gone before I had managed to reach out a hand to grab them. A rare sea rose opened for me, drew me in and afterwards extracted its levy in the form of unpleasant after-effects and dwindling self-respect.

It was a life in darkness; I had difficulty seeing clearly down there. The only thing that kept me going was the consolation I found in all the bottles I stumbled over. None of them lay around long enough for green algae to form.

The millennium had passed and Doomsday had not arrived. Nostradamus had been wrong; so had St John and those who still believed in his revelations. Not even the IT experts who had prophesied the Y2K crisis had been proved right. No computer systems collapsed, the world continued on its wayward course with no further changes to our everyday lives, except that we had to write a '2' at the beginning of the year.

As for me, I spent the last days of 1999 delving into a hundred-year-old murder mystery, and when New Year's Eve came, like so many other Bergensians, I walked half-way up a mountain in pouring rain and watched the New Year rockets disappear from sight in the low cloud cover, never, it seemed, to return to earth again. Afterwards I trudged down to my flat in Telthussmauet, where I celebrated the arrival of a new millennium in the company of a bottle of aquavit.

The first two years of the new century passed more or less unnoticed, apart from the dramatic events of 11th September 2001 on the eastern seaboard of America. New Year 2002 didn't seem to be ringing in any great changes either, not in my life nor in the world beyond. It had just become even more burdensome to fly. An old lady with a heart defect and a tube of ointment in her hand luggage would create longer queues at the security check, and if she couldn't produce ID she was denied access to her plane. Apart from that, most things were the same.

The woman who came to see me that Monday in March was of the gentle sort. She tapped several times on the waiting-room door, then I heard her open it and venture in. I had plenty of time to screw on the top, put the bottle into a desk drawer, drain the glass, rinse it in the sink and place it tidily on the shelf under the mirror, before turning, walking to the door between the waiting room and the office, opening it wide, swaying in the doorway and saying, 'Yes?'

She met my eyes with trepidation. 'Are you … Veum?'

I nodded, stepped aside and ushered her in: 'This way.'

She was about my age, perhaps a bit younger, but I definitely put her in the late fifties. Her hair was lank, and it was some weeks since she had been to the hairdresser's. The grey was clearly visible at the roots of her hair, in the parting on the left of her head. Her choice of clothing didn't suggest she was out to make a winning first impression, either. She was wearing a classic, moss-green windproof jacket, brown trousers and flat shoes. The red in her scarf was the only colour to brighten her appearance. In her hand she was carrying a suede bag big enough to contain whatever she might need in terms of everyday accessories. Her skin was pale, her nose small, across the bridge a patch of freckles was just visible, and her face had a sad air about it, which immediately revealed she was struggling with a problem, perhaps several. But most of the people who came to visit me were. Why else would they come?

She glanced around shyly as she stepped into the office. I held out my hand and introduced myself properly. She told me her name: Maja Misvær.

I directed her to the client's chair. No one else apart from me had sat there for many weeks. I walked round the desk, slumped down into the swivel chair, unfurled the gentlest expression I could muster and asked: 'How can I help you?'

She looked at me gloomily, as if the word *help* didn't exist in her world. I could see my own face in hers, as though I was gazing into a mirror, the way it must have appeared to others over the last three years. Six months after Karin's death I had walked in the funeral cortege for my old school friend, Paul Finckel. One of my oldest friends, and best sources of information in Bergen's newspaper world, he had switched off his computer for good, without saving the contents for posterity. A newly employed colleague had taken it over before the corpse was cold. I felt my own demise had edged a step closer, like autumn announcing its arrival one frosty night in September. One by one they were leaving us, my old classmates. Soon there would only be a handful of us left. In the end, there would be none.

'D-do you remember a little girl called Mette?'

At first I didn't understand what she was talking about. 'Mette? I don't know that I...'

'She went missing in September 1977.'

Then a light came on. 'Ah, you mean *that* Mette.'

Two Bergen children had gone missing in the 1970s. Both disappearances had shaken the local community and had initially kept the media busy, before being put on a back burner. In fact, I had helped to solve one of the cases, the 1979 one, some eight years later. The other case had never, to my knowledge, been cleared up. It became known as 'The Mette Case'.

She nodded.

'But I don't quite remember ... when was it you said?'

'17th September 1977.'

I did some swift mental arithmetic: 1987, 1997, 2002. In six months the case would be time-barred, if someone had killed her, that is, and anything else was barely conceivable, bearing in mind how thorough the investigation had been. 'And Mette, she was … ?'

'Yes, she is my daughter.'

I noted the change of tense. 'Could you … It's so long ago … Could you refresh my memory about … the details?'

She heaved a sigh, but nodded assent. 'I can try. What I remember of it and what … I know.'

3

The barely three-year-old Mette Misvær disappeared from her home in Solstølvegen in Nordås on Saturday 17th September, in the short space of time between twelve o'clock and a quarter past.

'I was at home, busy with housework. Mette was sitting in a sandpit right outside the kitchen window. I kept peering out at regular intervals, but when she disappeared I was busy taking clothes out of the washing machine and putting them in the tumble dryer. As soon as I emerged from the laundry room I went to the window to check on Mette…'

When she didn't see her, at first she wasn't initially that concerned. The house they lived in formed part of a yard with four other houses, and it was not at all unusual for children to move around this protected area, where cars only came in on very special occasions.

'I thought that … perhaps some of the children from the other houses were outside playing and Mette had toddled over to join them …'

She leaned over towards the window, but still couldn't see Mette anywhere. Then she went from the kitchen to the front door and into the yard. She looked everywhere. 'No children anywhere, neither Mette nor anyone else.'

Then she went to the gate in the wooden fence on to Solstølvegen. The gate was closed. She opened it and walked out. Nothing. In the estate further to the west there were some adults walking around and pointing, and in the street below there were a couple of cars parked. There was nothing else to see.

Then she began to get seriously worried. She ran back into the yard, went to the first house on the left and rang the bell. The husband, Tor Fylling, came to the door. He was on his own. His wife and children had gone to town. He hadn't seen Mette. 'She must be at Else and Eivind's place,' he added. 'Try there.'

She nodded and hurried over to the neighbours' house. She rang the bell several times, but no one answered. 'It turned out later that the family had been away for the whole weekend, in their cabin on Holsnøy.'

She ran past the next house. They didn't have any children. Now there was only one house left, wall to wall with their own. 'I said to myself – why hadn't I gone there first? They had Janne, who was the same age as Mette.'

But when the mother opened the door she had Janne in her arms. She listened to Maja with alarm. 'Mette? No. Yes, I saw her half an hour ago, from the window, she was sitting outside and playing. But … can't you find her?'

Maja's neighbour, Randi Hagenberg, became more and more agitated with every question she asked. 'Have you looked in the garages?'

'No. I didn't think of that.'

'Let's look now then. I'll come with you!' She called to her husband: 'Nils, can you take Janne?'

Together, they dashed over to the garages, which faced Solstøvegen, east of the five houses. One garage door was open. It belonged to the family who had gone to town. They went inside and scoured the area, but Mette was nowhere to be seen. The other four garage doors were locked. They tried all four handles, but none of them budged.

Now Maja Misvær could feel panic seizing her. Without thinking she ran twenty to thirty metres down the road in one direction, shouting her daughter's name, stopped to listen, and when she heard nothing, turned round and ran in the opposite direction and repeated the action. 'All at once I couldn't breathe. My heart was pounding so hard I could feel my pulse up here, in my throat, and I could hear blood rushing through my body like a … like an echo in my eardrums.'

'We've got to phone the police,' Randi Hagenberg said.

'Yes,' Maja answered as tears flickered in front of her eyes, so suddenly that her vision was affected and she almost lost her balance. She took a few quick steps to the side and supported herself on the fence.

'But when I looked at the sandpit again ... it was then I realised. There was her teddy bear, abandoned in the sand, and, deep down, I knew ... she took it everywhere. She would never have left it behind!'

'No?'

'No...'

While they waited for the police they ran around the district, calling Mette's name. Many of the other neighbours came out and assisted with the search. Some went to talk to people on the estate, but no one had seen a little girl.

Someone had contacted Mette's father, Truls Misvær, who was at a football training session with the older of their two children, six-year-old Håkon. He drove back home as fast as he could. Soon he had joined the others in their increasingly larger circles around the hilly area, looking for the missing girl.

When the police arrived they immediately set up an organised search and radioed information to their colleagues. Not long afterwards the story was on the news: *Small girl missing from her home in Solstøvegen in Nordås.*

The police drew a blank. Tiny Mette Misvær was never found.

The investigation escalated over the first few days. From being a straightforward missing-person case it was quickly upgraded to a potential crime. With none of the enquiries bearing fruit and Mette still missing the day after, the system went into overdrive.

All the neighbours were summoned to interviews. None of them had observed anything at all, except for Randi Hagenberg, who was able to confirm that she had seen Mette sitting and playing in the sandpit immediately before she disappeared.

Adults from the estate were also brought in for questioning. A couple of them thought they had seen a car stop outside the gate. But it had been too far away for them to say anything definite about the make of car or any distinguishing characteristics. One of them thought it had been black, another dark grey. A four-door, dark-grey or black saloon was what the police had to go on when they alerted all the patrol cars and gave a description. Nothing came of this search either.

According to the press, everyone on the child sex offender register in Bergen, later in the whole country, had their movements on the day in question charted and recorded, but the results were as unproductive as everything else. The case remained unsolved.

Now that was almost twenty-five years ago. If Mette Misvær had been allowed to grow up she would be a woman of twenty-eight. The likelihood was she was lying in an unmarked grave somewhere, gone for ever.

After Maja had finished talking she sat staring despondently at her lap. She mumbled a word I didn't catch.

'What was that?' I asked carefully.

'Rose. She was my little rose. But I didn't pay enough attention and someone picked her.'

'And now you'd like to…?'

She raised her face and looked me in the eye. 'I'd like you to find her. I want you to find out what happened. Before it's too late. Before everyone who might know anything has also gone.'

4

After a short pause she said: 'I'd like to show you ... where she disappeared.'

'Do you still live there?'

She nodded. 'I always think ... that I have to be there for when she returns. So that she'll never have to go round looking for me.'

'But ... I rather think we should wait until tomorrow.'

'Have you got something else to do?'

'Yes, today I have.' I couldn't tell her the truth. Getting behind a car wheel was simply out of the question. The morning pick-me-up had been too potent. The taste of caraway was still on my tongue.

'But,' I added, 'I can still spend some of today getting my head round the case. Do you remember who you dealt with in the police back then?'

She sighed. 'It was ... we never really got on.'

'Really?'

'His name was ...' For the first time she showed something redolent of a smile, but it soon vanished. 'It was a curious name for such a large man.'

I had a suspicion. 'And the name was ... ?'

'Muus. Inspector Muus.'

Now it was my turn to sigh. 'You never really got on, you say?'

'No, he seemed so ... brusque, in my opinion. As though it were my fault Mette ... People should take better care of their children, he said once.' She looked into the distance with a sad expression on her face. 'No, I never did get on with him.'

'But there must have been others?'

'Yes, of course. There were many who were very sympathetic. A couple of women officers, amongst others. Cecilie Lyngmo, I think that was the name of one of them.'

'Yes, I knew both Muus and Cecilie. But they've both left the force now.'

'Yes...'

I had jotted down her address while she was talking. 'This neighbourhood ... Solstølvegen, that's in Nordås, isn't it?'

'Yes, with a view of Nordåsvatnet bay. At that time it was brand new and almost completely isolated. It was Terje Torbeinsvik's first big project.' When I didn't react to the name she added: 'The architect. I don't know if you remember. He was married to Vibeke Waaler, the actress.'

'Yes, I remember her. But she's in Oslo now, isn't she?'

'Yes. They got divorced. She's at the National Theatre.'

'And what do you mean by his "first big project"?'

'It's called Solstølen Co-op; there are only five houses, around a yard. It was designed as an environmental project; it was supposed to merge into the landscape and be capable of adapting to modern systems, mostly energy-saving ones, as they came on the market. Terje still lives up there and he's still developing new projects. The next one is aimed at harnessing ground heat – if that means anything to you. With the aid of deep boreholes.'

'Yes, I've read about it. It definitely sounds better than wind turbines.'

'Even then there was digging going on all around us. And now ... now we still have a wonderful location, but the view isn't quite what it was. New buildings have gone up between us and the water, and in the nature reserve where we searched for Mette there has also been some building.'

'Are there many people living in the co-op now who were there then?'

'Yes, most have been happy there despite what happened to Mette. Only one of the houses has changed hands. In several of the others there have been divorces. That's just the way it was then, in the seventies and eighties.'

I nodded quietly. I had been there myself.

'And the children have moved out, of course. Now there are only children in two of the houses.'

'Does that mean ...? What about you? You and your husband?'

'Yes, we … Two years after Mette went missing we split up. It was simply too much to bear. Håkon stayed with Truls. I would have been happy to look after him, but … all I thought about was Mette. It was as though I couldn't concentrate on any other children except her. Anyway, Håkon and Truls had so much in common. Football. Håkon even played for FC Brann for a few seasons.'

'I see.' I tried to recall his name in a football context, but couldn't.

'Afterwards I lived alone.' She said this in a way that suggested it hadn't been a loss, more the confirmation of a fact.

'So you haven't met anyone?'

'No.'

'And what's your relationship with … your ex-husband and his family? Håkon?'

She hesitated. 'Håkon came to see me regularly, of course, but … He's alone too, even though he's over thirty now. And he's moved away. I haven't spoken to Truls for several years. He…'

'Yes?'

'He could never forgive me. After all, I was supposed to be looking after her. It was as though he blamed me for all that happened.'

'I understand.'

'And he was right of course! It was my fault. If you had any idea how many years afterwards I went out searching for her…'

'You mean…'

'Yes, I couldn't sit still in the evening, I had to go out and look, even if it was absolutely pointless. As though she had only got lost and stayed away for two or three years. But I couldn't control it. My grief was so immense, my agitation so unmanageable that it's marked the rest of my life, every single day, every single night.'

I looked at her. There was something genuinely desperate about her features, something that reflected what she told me so much more clearly than the words she used: the dreadful experience the little mite's disappearance must have been … and for her never to re-appear.

I considered my options. 'Would you say there's any point me talking to the others who lived in the co-op when Mette went missing?'

She gave me a blank look. 'The police were so thorough. There was no reason to believe...' Suddenly she clutched at her throat and coughed, as though there was something stuck. 'I mean ... how could any of them ... we were such a tight-knit group.'

'Would it be OK if I went out to see you tomorrow?'

She nodded.

'In which case, would you mind making me a list of the people who lived there then? I mean ... as some of the families have broken up ... If I'm going to talk to them I'll try to get in touch with as many as possible.'

'Alright, I'll do my best. I mean ... yes, I'll do that. It's not that difficult.'

'OK.' I got up.

She didn't move. 'I was wondering if...'

'Yes?'

'How much will this cost?'

I pulled out a drawer from the desk and passed her a sheet of paper. 'This is a list of my charges. It might look a bit overwhelming, but once I've started, I work efficiently and ... there may be a discount.'

She perused the sheet and folded it without a further word. She was, like me, prepared for the worst. At least that was some comfort. She didn't have great expectations, either.

She stood up, and it struck me that I hadn't offered her anything to drink. I was a bad host these days.

'So you'll come tomorrow?'

I nodded. 'Around ten, is that convenient?'

She said yes and I accompanied her to the door. That was as far as my social graces stretched now.

I went back into my office, reached for the beaker on the shelf, opened the lowest desk drawer to the left, took out the bottle and filled the glass half-full. The aquavit was clear and shiny, like tears emanating from a deep well. There was more where that came from.

I toasted an imaginary adversary. Dankert Muus, of all people. The inspector who had hoped to see me again in hell now would have to see me alive. I didn't ring to warn him I was coming. That would have been too much of a risk.

5

With a pensionable age of around sixty it was not unusual for police officers who had completed their service in the force to take on other jobs, some of them on the margins of the same branch. Some were employed by insurance companies, some as investigators. Some worked as bailiffs in the law courts. Some worked for themselves and took on odd jobs, caretaker posts and the like. I knew one who had opened a marina, another who ran a hospice for drug addicts and alcoholics.

I had seen and heard nothing of Dankert Muus since he retired almost ten years ago. But he was in the telephone directory, with an address in Fredlundsveien, a reasonably peaceful location, as the 'fred' part of its name suggested, beneath the forest on the Mount Løvstakken side. The odd drug addict or drunk might turn up there too, but a deer was far more likely. Dankert Muus was probably still man enough to chase away anything that might stray onto his territory, whether it was on two or four legs.

On the bus up to Søndre Skogvei I had time enough to reflect that if I had an assignment now, the first in a long time, it would be advantageous to be able to drive my own car. If I was dependent on the local bus services I would have a lot of time to kill and I had never been that murderously disposed. But the very thought of meeting a new day without a dram from a bottle of aquavit sent heavy breakers crashing through me, waves from a vast, dark ocean where I had never found peace.

The house where Dankert Muus lived was a large, semi-detached property, half yellow, half green. Muus lived in the yellow part, with an entrance at the side, midway up a staircase. I rang the doorbell and waited.

The woman who opened was around seventy years old, white-haired, surprisingly petite and with a friendly expression on her face. 'Yes, what is it?' she said, looking at me expectantly.

'Fru Muus?'

'Yes.'

'My name's Veum. Varg Veum. It wouldn't be possible to have a few words with your husband, would it?'

'I asked you what this was about.'

'Well, it's … a cold case. I'm a private investigator.'

'Aha,' she said, pursing her lips as though this was not a profession whose existence she would necessarily accept. 'Well, Dankert's in the garden. You can walk round…' She pointed to the corner of the house at the end of the staircase. 'You'll find him there.'

I followed her instructions, completed the ascent of the stairs and rounded the corner of the house. I was confronted with a marvellous garden, impressive to behold even in March, not least for an amateur. I counted two apple trees, various soft-fruit bushes, a dominant rhododendron in the background, several beds of sprouting crocuses, snowdrops and some small, yellow flowers whose name I didn't know, as well as a freshly laid plot where the season hadn't quite got going yet. In the midst of this stood the biggest perennial I had ever seen, a Dankertus Muusius, with a much-used spade in his hand, staring at me as if I were a murderous Spanish slug that had strayed into Paradise without a visa from El Supremísimo.

'So this is where you bury your bodies, Muus.'

He stared at me in disbelief. 'Veum! What the hell are you doing here?'

'Inspecting the cemetery.'

'I really thought I'd seen the last of you.'

'So you haven't missed me?'

'Not for a second, Veum. Not one single second.'

I approached warily, keeping an eye on the spade in case he should strike.

He had aged in these ten years as well. His body didn't have the same brutal mass I remembered from when he was an inspector at

Bergen Police Station, and, even though I had succeeded in inflaming his temper once again, he didn't have the same fire as before. His hair had gone white, his skin was grey and he hadn't quite dealt with all the stubble when he had shaved that morning. His gaze was as dismissive as always and he caught me by surprise when he thrust out a huge paw to shake hands and said: 'I was sad to hear about your partner, Veum.'

I swallowed. 'So you heard about it then?'

'I still talk to some of the folk at the station. Jakob pops by once a month.'

'Hamre?'

He nodded. 'He's getting close to retirement as well now.' Then he added, not without a hopeful glint in his eye: 'But you must be too, aren't you?'

'No, no. People like me haven't got such an early retirement age as you, you know. And I have nothing to fall back on, yet. Less than nothing, actually.'

'Well…' He looked around. 'I love doing this. Gardening. I don't suppose you'd have believed that, would you?'

'No, you're right there. I've never seen you as the crocus type.'

'But in fact I have been for many years.'

'You can see how well we knew each other.'

'Yes.' He looked at me gravely. 'So what brings you here after all these years?'

'A case you worked on during your spell at the station.'

'Thought so.'

'I believe it was known as "The Mette Case".'

A shadow flitted across his face and his eyes darkened even further. 'I see.'

'You remember it, of course.'

He nodded. 'Yes indeed. But not in detail, it's so long ago. Has someone contacted you about it?'

'The mother.'

'Right.' He waved his hand in the air, struggling to find her name.

'Maja Misvær.'

'Yes, that's it. I remember her. She was absolutely hysterical, of course. Couldn't understand how we could draw a blank.'

'Not hard to see why.'

'No-oo.' He hesitated, even after so many years. 'But … you never forget cases like these, Veum. A small child and an unsolved crime. Sometimes I still wake up in the middle of the night and lie there thinking about precisely this case. And a couple of others. Not so strange, perhaps. The unsolved cases are always on your mind.'

'Could you give me the gist of the investigation? Even if you can't remember the details.'

He grimaced. 'I fail to see what a hobby-detective like you can do, and after so many years. But … better to leave no stone unturned.' He nodded towards the house. 'It's too cold to stand out here. Let's go in for a cup of coffee.'

Muus kicked the soil off his heavy boots and rammed the spade into the bed as a reminder that the day's work was not yet done. He removed his sturdy gardening gloves and stuffed them in the grey-brown parka he obviously wore outdoors over dark-blue waterproof trousers so that he could kneel down without getting soaked to the skin. Then he led the way to the house and a veranda door at the back.

We went on to the veranda, he pulled off his boots, motioned for me to do the same with my shoes, and then we padded into the kitchen in stockinged feet, where Fru Muus had telepathically already put on the coffee machine. Neither of them said a word to the other, but Muus articulated a few growls, which I interpreted as good-natured, and she nodded and smiled back. For a second or two I felt like an intruder in the Deaf and Dumb Association, but then Muus recovered his powers of speech and grunted: 'Take a seat, Veum, and I'll find us some cups.'

He fetched two large white mugs from a cupboard and put them on the table by the window. The kitchen was kitted out in standard Norwegian fashion. On a wall hung this year's Bergen calendar, with a picture of sunshine, as usual; to the right of the door leading into the apartment a bell rope with a flower pattern, probably embroidered by Fru Muus in her leisure hours while her husband worked overtime serving the general public. Through the half-open door I glimpsed the sitting room with its well-used beige, moss-green and red-speckled furniture: an armchair, half of a sofa and one end of a well-polished coffee table. I saw an oil painting on the wall opposite: a nature motif from a fjord landscape of the kind you found in most Norwegian homes with ageing occupants.

Muus poured coffee straight from the jug into the two mugs, pushed one over to my end of the table and then plumped down on the other chair. His wife withdrew discreetly into the inner rooms with no more than a faint chafing sound, like a distant cricket.

'Thank you very much,' I said, lifting the mug to my mouth and tentatively sipping the hot drink.

'So … what are you after, Veum?'

'You remember the case, I gather. You said you still wake up in the night thinking about it. Is there anything in particular that bothers you about it?'

His lips curled. 'No one likes an unsolved case. And this one was especially difficult. In reality there was nothing to find out. She just vanished.' He snapped his fingers. 'Just like that. Like a magic trick.'

'But naturally you initiated a full investigation?'

Muus rolled his eyes at being asked such a stupid question. 'What do you think? Of course we did. Shall I list the steps we took?'

'That would be good.'

'We checked the relationship between husband and wife, to see if there had been any disagreements. Nothing. The father's alibi was watertight – he was at football training with his son, the poor girl's brother.'

'They got divorced some years later.'

'Yes, we took note of that, but … in fact that's not so unusual in cases like this. It puts tremendous pressure on the family.'

'Yes, I know.'

'We checked him out, both in 1977 and a couple of years later, when we heard about the divorce. The boy stayed with the father when he remarried. That made us reconsider the mother's role in all of this, but we never got as far as directly suspecting her either.'

'Maja Misvær being behind the whole stunt?'

'Yes, but as I said, there were never any grounds for suspicion.'

I took another sip of coffee. 'And the neighbours?'

'We checked them out, one by one. Some were away when it happened – it was a weekend. Some were in town. Others were at home, but … What could the motive have been? And where was the girl? We searched every house in the co-op under the pretext that she might have toddled into a storage room, or indeed any room, or that there might have been an accident. That was what we said anyway, although deep down … you never know what lurks behind closed doors. That's my experience after a long career in the force, Veum.'

'Yes, mine too, for that matter. The accident theory…'

'Yes, we checked that out too, of course, properly. It's quite a way to Lake Nordåsvatnet, but we searched the beach and the water. Nothing. We organised a search party to comb the land around the co-op. There were a lot fewer buildings then than now and enough places for a child to … fall into a pond, get stuck in a bog, slip off a cliff. But all in vain. We didn't find a trace of her anywhere.'

'What about a car? A collision? Someone who picked her up and took her?'

He nodded. 'Yes, we considered that too. You might recall … there was a car that had been seen in the area at the time she went missing. We never got a decent description of it, but we concluded it was a dark-grey or black saloon, perhaps a Peugeot, but that was as far as we got. We put out a search, but no one responded and we never got any further with our own investigation either.'

'Do you mean to say that's the hottest tip you have?'

'Had, I think we say. Had, almost twenty-five years ago. However, I would definitely have liked to know more about the car. What make it was, who was driving and what they were doing at that time? These are the questions I ask myself most when I lie awake at night.'

'You checked all the neighbours' cars?'

'Yeah, yeah. None of them stuck out. Most of the neighbours weren't interested in cars. One of the men in one of the houses tinkered with an old Volvo, but it was light grey and at the time in question his wife was in town with it. Several of the other cars were absent that day because their owners were away.'

'You remember quite a lot about the case, I must say.'

'As I told you, it has never given me any peace.'

'Another standard question, Muus. Were there any registered sex offenders under the spotlight?'

He glared at me. 'All of them, actually. We door-stepped every single one of them at liberty in the Bergen district and we checked any prisoners on day release. Later we expanded the search to other police districts. Obviously, with such a large target group some didn't have alibis, but we never found anything on them, never got close to anything that could have been a clue.'

'How many are we talking about?'

'Of known child abusers – from flashers to rapists – we were probably talking about ten locally and between thirty and fifty nationwide. But that covered the country from Kirkenes to Cape Farewell.'

'Any names that stick in your mind?'

He scratched his head. Then he shook it. 'No. None I can put my finger on anyway. Some of them must be dead and buried. I hope so. This is the dregs we're talking about here, Veum. The lowest of the low. When they're in prison they go through hell, and they deserve to. Abusing small, defenceless children!'

I asked gently: 'Have you two got any children?'

He looked at me, granite-faced. 'No,' he said curtly and I understood at once it would be inadvisable to delve any further in that direction.

'But you suspect there was something like that at work?'

'Either that or, as you suggested, a collision with a car, and the driver took the body to get rid of it somewhere else. Not much to be proud of, either.'

'No.'

'Don't think we'll get much further than that, Veum.'

'Cecilie Lyngmo was working on the case, Maja Misvær said.'

Muus sent me a measured look. 'Yes? Probably was. The whole department was involved, at least at the beginning.'

'Would anyone remember any more?'

He shrugged. 'I sincerely doubt it. But by all means try. Most of them have retired now, like me. At least those who would have had anything to contribute.'

He pushed his mug aside and got up, a sign the conversation was over. Then he placed his fists on the kitchen table, leaned over and looked me in the eye. 'There's one thing you should know. If you solve this case, Veum, I'll forget everything that's gone on between us over the years. If you find out what happened to Mette Misvær that Saturday in September 1977 you have a friend for life in Dankert Muus.'

I thanked him, but on the way out I was not at all sure this was something I would anticipate with relish. From my side of the road, it sounded more like a threat.

6

Back in my office, after a brief search on the internet, I found Cecilie Lyngmo, who, after reaching pensionable age, had travelled 'home', as she put it, to a valley north of Flekkefjord.

When I rang her and introduced myself, she chuckled. 'Veum? How can I help you?'

'You remember me?'

'You made an indelible impression on me,' she replied, and not being able to see her I assumed there was an ironic expression on her face. 'Besides, we rarely heard from you at Bergen Police Station unless there was something you were after.'

'I was also taken there against my will on occasion.'

'Well…'

'I'm ringing about the Mette Case.'

The phone went quiet. 'I see … Have there been any developments?'

'None, except that it's approaching the statute of limitations and consequently her mother has contacted me.'

'I see … again. Have you spoken to anyone else?'

'I come hotfoot from Dankert Muus.'

Again she chuckled. 'The Muus that roared? How's he getting on?'

'Believe it or not, he's grown green fingers. He was digging in his garden on the side of Mount Løvstakken, but whether he was digging for gold or buried dogs, God only knows.'

'You had a chance to grill him, though?'

'Yes. In fact, he was amazingly communicative. But, as you know, it was a long time ago and the details are probably vague inasmuch as he hadn't got the case files to hand.'

'Was he going to get them for you?'

'There was no mention of that. I doubt I'll be given access to them. The reason I've called you is that I was given to understand by Maja Misvær, Mette's mum, that you and she got on well during the investigation.'

'Yes, that's possible. As a woman perhaps I was able to empathise more with how she felt.'

'Exactly. Could you give me your view of the case, now that so many years have passed?'

'Erm. Yes…' She hesitated. 'I can try.'

Cecilie Lyngmo had been forty-seven in 1977 and an inspector for Bergen Police with a special expertise in sexual offences. It was therefore not without reason that she was called in almost straightaway when Mette disappeared from her home that Saturday morning in September. During the first few days she participated in the general search, like everyone else in the department. As time passed and the focus turned to former sex offenders in the local area she was charged with interviewing them, often alongside alternating colleagues. Together with Dankert Muus she drew up the strategy for the developing investigation, and she was sent to several other police districts to interview potential suspects in those parts of the country. All to no avail; like the investigation in general.

In the end a feeling of despondency spread through the whole of the investigative team. It came as no surprise, either to her or her colleagues, when the case was shelved. Initially it remained 'active', as the police put it; later it was placed in the happily not inordinately high pile of unsolved crimes – the term 'incident' could not be applied as no one yet had the slightest idea what had happened to Mette except for the perpetrator or perpetrators.

Cecilie Lyngmo was childless, yet hadn't had any difficulty understanding the despair Mette's mother felt. She found it more and more embarrassing as time after time she had to say, on behalf of the force, that there was still nothing new to report. At length, naturally enough, contact became more sporadic. Now, as she enjoyed her retirement, going for long walks in the forest and beyond, birdwatching, fishing for cod and whiting from the little boat she had moored in Flekkesfjord harbour, and otherwise having as little as possible to do with her former occupation, she managed to put the Mette Case so far to the back of her mind that it was only seldom re-awakened, and then mostly when stories of similar cases appeared in the media. And then she reacted in the same way as Dankert Muus. She lay awake brooding until well into the night.

I tried to sum up what she had told me. 'In other words, you have no concrete theories on what might have happened, either?'

'Er … no. Actually I don't.'

'You hesitated.'

'Yes.'

'Why?'

'I'll give you two interesting titbits, Veum.' After another pause she continued: 'I don't suppose you remember someone called Jesper Janevik?'

'Never heard of him.'

'No. Well, he was a harmless sort, living on Askøy. He'd come under suspicion for indecent exposure and had been interviewed several times in that context. Later he was interviewed in connection with some unsolved attempted rapes. There was some link with him and the local area, and so, like many others, he was brought in for questioning during the investigation.'

'Yes?'

'Well … Muus was a bit too quick off the mark. He was arrested and held in custody for a day, but at our meeting it was decided to let him go. There wasn't an ounce of evidence.'

'Muus said nothing about this.'

'Understandably enough. The newspapers followed it up and Muus didn't exactly come out of it smelling of roses.'

'No, I can well imagine. Hm … anything else?'

'No, not really. I just had a gut feeling then that Janevik was holding something back, that he knew something he would never admit. For a while we had him in the spotlight, hoping he would give himself away.

We had undercover detectives after him, kept our ears to the ground, but ... well, we were banging our heads against the wall there, too. We quite simply had nothing to go on. I just mention this as one of the many gut feelings I still have, even today.'

'I'm taking note. But you said there were *two* titbits.'

'Well, the second's even vaguer, but ... there was something about that co-op, Veum. I had an odd sense there was something out of kilter. It could have been because of the case, of course. Several of the families had children, about the same age as Mette, and obviously they were anxious. Nevertheless ... there was something underneath it all. Do the same people still live there?'

'Some of them, yes. There have been the usual divorces though, from what I've been told. I'm going up there tomorrow as I don't have a proper overview yet.'

'Well ... don't quote me. But if there's anything else you need, you know where to find me.'

'Yes, if you haven't gone to the fjord, that is.'

'I never go so far that I can't find my way back.'

'Wish I could say the same.'

We finished the conversation and rang off.

There wasn't a great deal more I could do until I had been to the co-op. I ran my tongue over my lips. My mouth was as dry as a school sponge at the end of the summer holidays and in my desk drawer a remedy was calling. I pulled the drawer open and peered inside. My heart started beating abnormally at the sight of the familiar label with the little clipper loaded to the brim with barrels, all sails set for a foreign coast, where gold medals awaited. There were two people aboard, dressed in sou'westers, and for some reason I pictured Cecilie Lyngmo and myself going fishing, fully equipped with drinks in case we ended up stranded on an islet somewhere in the fjord.

I took out the bottle, undid the top and breathed in. The caraway aroma was unmistakeable. This was the water of life, *aqua vitae*, and my pulse accelerated until I gave in, stretched my hand out for the beaker on the desk and waited, filled the glass half-full with the shiny liquid, raised it to my mouth and took my first sip since breakfast on this remarkable Monday in March, when I was suddenly at work again.

I relished every drop while promising myself: *Tomorrow there will be nothing. Tomorrow you have to drive.*

To persuade myself, I had another glass. The decision dangled above me like a fish hook; indeed they both had me wriggling on it, Maja Misvær and Cecilie Lyngmo. But the person I sat thinking about most was tiny Mette, who had vanished into thin air almost twenty-five years before.

Was there any hope of salvaging anything so long afterwards? If so, there was one important decision to take. I screwed the top back on firmly, dropped the bottle into the drawer, finished off the very last drop and went down the stairs and out on to the pavement with a tingling sensation in my knees.

I walked to Bryggestuen and ordered the special of the day: fresh cod with Mandel potatoes. With the meal I had a non-alcoholic beer. Afterwards I went home. The die was cast. It was going to be a lengthy and troubled night.

7

For the first time in as long as I could remember there wasn't a bottle of aquavit to grab when the radio alarm went off at half past seven next morning. I'd had enough foresight to put an unopened bottle of lemon-flavoured mineral water on the bedside table. With trembling hand I unscrewed the top, put the bottle to my mouth and washed away the dry remnants of another sleepless night, the way a cloudburst wets the forest floor after a long drought.

With stiff muscles, I clambered out of bed. I went into the sitting room and did some stretching exercises and press-ups to get my circulation going, then went into the bathroom and freshened up. In the meantime, the water for my tea was boiling. On my return to the kitchen I cut myself a couple of slices of bread, put sheep sausage and cucumber on one and honey on the other, drank a glass of milk and a cup of tea and sat down in the best chair, unfolded the newspaper, which was delivered to the door each morning, and confirmed that the world hadn't come to an end overnight, despite tenacious endeavours. I felt unwell. My muscles ached as though I had a bad bout of flu.

Outside, there was chilly March weather with rain and localised hailstorms. The car, which hadn't been used during the last month, appeared to be relieved something was happening again. It behaved like a four-year-old Toyota Corolla should. It bounded off as I let go of the clutch and chortled with satisfaction as I drove to the top of Øvre Blekevei, turned left twice and then gingerly sneaked between the two long lines of parked cars either side of Henrik Wergelands gate. The white rows of houses had rear buildings that were reminiscent of the time most of the traffic in this part of town consisted of horses and carts and house-owners here had their own horses stabled in the backyard.

In Nordås I pulled into the kerb alongside the sign telling me this was the Solstølen Co-op. The area was bordered by a low wooden fence and a large box hedge. Five garages faced the street. To the left of them was the entrance to the co-op, a low gate, wide enough for a car to pass through if necessary.

I looked around. From the description Maja Misvær had given me I had imagined a more open location. Now neighbouring houses and vegetation had crept closer and from where I was standing it was hard to get a sense of the view down to the water.

I opened the gate and went into the yard. The five houses had been built in a kind of horseshoe shape. The tall two-storey facades, painted in strong contrasting colours, and the gently pitched roofs to the back betrayed their 1970s origins. The house forming the base of the horse-shoe was the biggest. It had been painted red, as was one of the others; two were yellow and one was white.

According to the description I had been given the previous day, Maja Misvær lived in the red house to the right, directly behind the garages. In front of the house was a little sandpit. In it were a bucket, spade and some other toys left scattered around as though the child had gone in for some food before coming out again to continue playing.

I went over and rang the doorbell. While waiting for her to answer I took another look around. There was no sign of life in any of the houses, nor would you have expected there to be on a Tuesday morning in March, with the Easter holidays still a long way off.

Maja Misvær opened the door with a jerk and looked out excitedly as though hoping Mette had finally reappeared. When she saw it was only me, she nodded resignedly and stepped aside to let me in. As I passed I noticed her stick her head out of the door and glance around quickly to check whether anyone had seen she had a visitor.

She closed the door behind her and led the way. 'First of all I'd like you to see…' We entered the kitchen, a practical design, with an inbuilt stove, fridge and washing machine. In front of the window was a kitchen table with four chairs around it. In the middle of the table there was a small, grey, decorative cloth with white cross-stitch. The other colours in the room were light green and white. There was a coffee machine on one worktop, ready with coffee and water, but not yet switched on.

'I just wanted to show you…' She went to the window, drew the light-coloured curtain to the side and pointed. 'She was playing there. Here – in the middle of the floor – was the ironing board, where I was. Then I popped into the laundry room…' She indicated where in the house with her hand. 'I put down the iron and pulled out the plug, to be on the safe side. But then, when I returned and looked out, I couldn't see her.'

She remained impassive and pensive, as though still wondering whether there was anything she could have done differently.

I nodded. 'The area wasn't as populated then, I'm told.'

'No. We were the only ones here. The neighbouring houses on both sides weren't built until the 1980s. And then there was the housing co-op up there…' She pointed to the south-west. 'That was being built then.'

'And people came to inspect the properties there?'

'Yes.'

'And across the road there were fields?'

'Yes. Now we have houses there too, but in those days there was just a path through the countryside up to what's known as Søråshøgda. In the really old days there were two farms here, apparently, Nordås and Sørås, but that's a very long time ago and I don't know any more. Terje can fill you in, if you're interested.'

'The architect?'

She nodded.

'Which one's his house?'

'The end one. It's red. It looks like the biggest one, but in one part there's a large communal function room, which we can all use…' She swallowed. 'For christenings, confirmations, family events, that sort of thing.'

'I see.'

She fidgeted nervously. 'But you asked me … Come into the sitting room. I've made some notes.' She caught sight of the coffee machine. 'Oh, yes! Would you like a cup of coffee? I've got some ready…'

'Yes, please.' My mouth was as dry as wood shavings. 'And a glass of water if you have one.'

'Yes, of course. Just … you go in and I'll … It's over there.' She pointed to a door at the end of the hallway. 'I'll be with you in a jiffy.'

I entered a large, light room with high windows looking over a part of the garden behind the houses. From here I could glimpse Nordåsvatnet between the houses and trees, a bit of one of the forest-clad, uninhabited islets south of Marmorøyen island and, like a motley-coloured steppe in the background, behind the water, the small towns of Bønes and Kråkenes up towards the southern side of Mount Løvstakken.

The sitting room was furnished in pine and light fabrics. There were bookcases, sideboards, cupboards, and pastel pictures on the walls. There was something impersonal yet cosy about the whole room, as if it had been taken from a furniture catalogue and was not somewhere a family lived. For the time being the family consisted of only one person and perhaps that was how she wanted it.

On one sideboard there was a large framed photograph of a small girl with blonde, slightly untidy hair, laughing at the photographer with her mouth open and her eyes sparkling. Squeezed to her chest she held a somewhat ragged teddy bear with a melancholic expression. Beside this, but much smaller, there was a photograph of a young boy in a maroon suit, probably a confirmation photograph, judging by the boy's age. He was blond with thick, arched eyebrows and a distant gaze. Like his sister's teddy, he had a distinctly mournful droop to his mouth.

Cups clinked as Maja came in behind me. She put the cups and plates down on the low coffee table and came over to join me. 'Yes, that's Mette … and that's Håkon.'

'Right.' You didn't need a university degree to realise that.

Again she was lost in her own world as she looked at the pictures, probably thinking there should have been a confirmation photo of Mette as well, and she had just forgotten to put it out.

'I'll probably need a photo of Mette like that one, or something similar, before I get going.'

'Yes, I've got lots of copies the police used. You can have them. I'll just...' She went to the kitchen. The aroma of fresh coffee was spreading and seconds later she was back with the jug. 'Now, erm ... do you take any...?'

'No, thank you. But a glass of water would...'

'Oh, yes, goodness me. I'd forgotten that.' She nervously poured coffee into the two cups, then took the jug back into the kitchen. I heard a cupboard door being opened, a tap running, and then she returned with a glass of water in her hand, almost at a run. 'Here we are! Do sit down.'

I held the glass, sat on one of the chairs and took a swig, which I washed around my mouth before swallowing it. My mouth was as dry as an atheist's at a revival meeting.

She perched on a chair, sipped some coffee, got up again and went to the sideboard. She opened a drawer, took out some papers, came back and sat down. 'Let me show you...' She turned one piece of paper round and pushed it in my direction so that we could both read it. 'I've made a kind of précis.'

I leaned forward and studied it. A very precise précis. She had divided the page into five sections, numbered from one to five, one for each house. Beside the list of the houses she had drawn two columns. She pointed and explained. 'The names I've written here are the people who lived here in 1977 when Mette ... disappeared. And those here...' She pointed to the column on the right. 'They're the people living here now. Or are still here. So their names appear twice.'

'Shall we go through them house by house?'

She nodded and pointed to the kitchen. 'In the first house, opposite us, that's where Helle and Tor Fylling lived then. They had two children.'

'She was in town with her kids when Mette went missing, wasn't she? He was at home.'

'Yes.'

'But they aren't married anymore, I see.'

'No, Tor moved out ... a few years later. After a couple of years she found a new husband. Lars Svendsen. But they don't have any children. The other two children are adults now, so only Helle and Lars live there.'

'Can I take this piece of paper with me afterwards?'

'Of course. So you don't need to make any notes, if that's what you were thinking?'

'The children there...'

'Yes, as you can see ... that's Asbjørg and Einar. Both of them were older than Håkon. They moved out ages ago, but drop in now and then.'

'This Tor then, he was at home on his own?'

'Yes, but I don't suspect ... He was as surprised as I was when I knocked on his door, asking about her. About Mette.'

'What did he do?'

'Do you mean what was his job?'

'Yes.'

'Well ... he had his own car business. Still does, I assume. Helle worked at an accountant's and she still does as well.'

'But they got divorced?'

'Yes, although ... maybe Lars was more her style. He's a consultant in some company or other to do with investments and so on.' She moved her finger. 'But there, in house number two, live Synnøve and Svein. They lived there then and still do. Two grown-up children as well: Eivind and Else.'

'And their surname is...?'

She put her finger on the surname. 'Stangeland.'

'And their jobs?'

'Svein works in a civilian capacity at Haakonsvern Naval Base. Synnøve's a teacher. They were at their cabin the weekend Mette disappeared, the whole family.'

I took notes. 'Then there's house number three. That's where Terje Torbeinsvik lives, I see.'

'Yes. The architect behind this whole project. Married to Vibeke Waaler, the actress, at that time. But they got divorced many years ago. Now he's married to a colleague. Britt. They have two small children.'

'How small?'

A painful expression crossed her face. 'Between six and ten, I would guess...'

'Great. I'll definitely talk to him. So that just leaves this house here.'

'Yes, Randi Hagenberg lived there, who helped me to look for Mette that day. But that relationship ended in divorce as well, and a new family's living there now. In fact, it's the second since ... then, so that house has been through the most changes.'

Randi Hagenberg, I wrote. 'And where are they now? The Hagenberg family, I mean.'

'Well, now they're not called ... She was using her maiden name even then. But I don't really know what's happened to her. And Nils ... he died.'

'Nils?'

'Nils Bringeland,' she said a little impatiently, as if I wasn't following.

'Bringeland ... ?'

'Yes. They had two children as well. Janne, who was the same age as Mette, and a boy called Joachim. He was a couple of years older than Håkon, but they were good pals anyway.' Her expression changed. 'Things didn't go so well for Joachim.'

'No?'

'He started on drugs very young. That might have been what caused the break-up. I know from my own ... yes. Today you'll find him among the regular clientele in Nygårdsparken.'

Another note re: the Hagenberg/Bringelands. 'And all of them were at home when Mette disappeared?'

'You mean ... ?'

'The architect and his wife; Bringeland.'

'Yes, Terje was at home. Vibeke was at the theatre. They were rehearsing a new play. And Nils was at home. I remember Randi shouting to him. I don't know where Joachim was. I don't remember.'

'Well, his parents probably will. But you said Nils was dead, didn't you?'

Again she looked at me as though I wasn't following. 'I told you! It was one of the reasons for me coming to you. It was vital to try again before everyone who could remember anything was gone.'

'And by that you meant Nils Bringeland?'

'You must remember that. He was the man who was shot in the street during the robbery in Bryggen before Christmas last year.'

'I thought I'd heard the name before.'

'Really?'

I sat looking at her. But she had no more to give me, and I couldn't see how the murder of a casual passer-by during a robbery three months ago could have anything to do with a disappearance twenty-five years earlier.

'One last detail, Maja. Your husband … Does he still live in Bergen?'

Her eyes flickered. 'No, he … they moved a few years ago. Him and his new wife, Gudrun. To Oslo.'

'So he re-married?'

'Yes, he did, quite early on.'

'Right. Too early, you mean?'

She shrugged. 'It was his decision and she's nice enough, Gudrun is. I've only met her a few times. At Håkon's confirmation and I think there was one birthday.'

'I suppose you have his address?'

'No, but…'

'I can find it myself. It's easy.'

Her eyes filled with tears. Her lips trembled unchecked as she exclaimed: 'Can you imagine what happens to you when you go through something like this? When you lose a child?'

'Yes, I really can…'

'You blame yourself! What could I have done? Was it my fault this happened? What did I do wrong?'

'Yes.'

'I should have paid more attention, of course I should. I shouldn't have let her out of my sight for a second.'

'That's impossible.'

'Yes, it is! But that's how you think. I can tell you that, Veum. Not a day has passed since that Saturday in 1977 when I haven't thought about it. What did we do wrong? What could we have done differently?'

At the back of my mind I noted that she had changed the pronoun from *I* to *we* as she repeated her appeal, but I wasn't going to go there. It was probably no more than a way of speaking, an unconscious need to have someone to share the blame with.

She sat gazing into the air as though I was no longer present. When finally I coughed gently she looked up at once, wiped her tears away with the back of her hand and got to her feet with a perplexed expression, barely aware of where she was.

I took her précis with me as I left. If nothing else, it gave me more than enough to do in the coming days. And I had to start somewhere. I felt like a cat chasing a mouse in a refrigeration plant where all the doors had been hermetically sealed years ago. Without a hope, in other words.

8

I stood in the yard looking around. I tried to summarise what she had told me.

Nils Bringeland and Randi Hagenberg next door. New family there now.

Opposite Maja, the Fylling family then. Fru Fylling has a new husband now.

Next door to them, the Stangeland family then. Stangeland parents now.

And, like a transverse connecting roof between the two terraced houses on each side: Terje Torbeinsvik – then with Vibeke Waaler, now with Britt and two kids.

Relatively simple so long as I didn't include those who no longer lived there: divorced partners, children who had grown up, other possible acquaintances of the various families.

I stared at Torbeinsvik's house. If anyone could tell me anything in general about the others it had to be him.

I met his gaze through one of the first-floor windows. He was standing at the back of the room as though he didn't want to be seen, but the reflection was not so strong that I couldn't see him. I pointed at him with one hand and then back at myself as a sign that I would like to speak to him. He didn't react, but he left the room.

I crossed the yard and waited in front of his door. When no one opened up I rang the bell. After a while I heard vague noises inside. Then the door opened and Terje Torbeinsvik stood before me.

In many ways he resembled a stereotypical architect from the 1970s, from the smock-like shirt, the leather waistcoat and the worn jeans, to the slightly over-large beard, shaggy hair and the classic

I've-been-sitting-at-the-drawing-board gut, rounded like a well-fed farmed salmon. Originally his hair had been fair, but now there were flecks of grey and his beard was almost white with some dark tufts under his lower lip. His mouth was full and not without sensuality, his gaze sharp and alert beneath the bushy eyebrows, and when he finally said something it was in a dark, resonant voice that would have become a precentor at any funeral. 'Yes, how can I help you?'

'My name's Veum. Varg Veum. And you're Terje Torbeinsvik, I believe?'

'That's me, yes.'

'You probably saw where I came from.'

'I did happen to see you coming out of Maja's house, yes.' He said this with an undertone, as though I had done something illegal, or at least unseemly.

'Yes. So you can imagine what this is about.'

'No, I'm afraid I can't.'

'No? OK. I must have forgotten to say. I'm a private investigator.'

'I see.' That was all he said, but my understanding was that now he knew what this was about.

'May I come in for a moment?'

He eyed me doubtfully, as though unsure what purpose this would serve. Then he shrugged. 'By all means. You're stopping me from working my first shift of the day, but…'

'You work from home?'

'Two days a week.'

'You didn't seem that busy just before.'

'Really? And on what do you base that assumption?'

'Well…' It was my turn to shrug. 'Nothing in particular. Just a feeling I had.'

He sniffed in contempt without any further elucidation. 'We can go in here.'

From the long, rectangular hallway he showed me in through a side door to what turned out to be his office. It was simply furnished with a large drawing board, shelves of professional literature, but mostly files, and some contour-less pencil sketches on the walls – several variants of the view of Nordåsvatnet – and a couple of new children's pictures pinned to empty spaces between the shelves and the framed pictures.

He indicated a wicker chair beside the drawing board and took a seat himself on the high-backed swivel chair. When he swung round he was outlined against the window looking on to the yard. The daylight hit me in the face. This made me feel uncomfortable, as though I had been summoned to an interview somewhere and I didn't have a clear conscience.

To counteract this I went on the offensive. 'This co-op is your project, I believe.'

'Yes, you could say that.'

'Maja said you knew everything about this area.'

'Mm, yes … If not everything, most things. I presume you don't mean the genesis. We live in Nordås, which was the neighbouring farm to Sørås. Originally there was only one farm here and its name, as you can perhaps imagine, was Ås.' He half-turned to the window and glanced outside. 'You can still see the hill.'

'Yes.'

'In the Middle Ages Nonneseter Convent owned the farm, and when all the convents were transferred to Vincens Lunge in 1528, Ås went with them. The farm known as Nordås belonged to famous Bergensians, such as the Krohn and Reimers families, until the nineteenth century, when it was partitioned into smaller farms. That was when Fana was still an agricultural village. They were turned into housing estates in the 1970s, and that's when we – by which I mean me and my company – came into the picture, early that decade. We were in a position to choose the best plots…' He motioned towards the other side of the house. 'With, amongst other things, a splendid view of Nordåsvatnet. And then we got stuck in.'

'Maja said it was a sort of idealistic project.'

'Well…' He hesitated. 'This was the 1970s, as I said. We were all young and idealistic. Not exactly flower-power types, but some of us had slightly alternative views on housing and lifestyles. We tried to develop a community here. We made a communal function room in this house, where we could meet when we were free, in the evening or afternoon, at the weekend, have a beer or a glass of wine, bring along an instrument and jam together, organise recital programmes, amusements for the children according to how they felt, in short, to try to create a community we might otherwise have missed in society at that time. Occasionally we had communal meals, bring-along parties, where we sat round a long table and shared food. A kind of modern, Nordic variant of the Mediterranean extended family.'

'Semi-hippie colony, semi-mafia.'

He smiled acidly. 'More a Norse *skytningsstove*, if you know what that is.'

'A *schøttstue*.'

'Yes, if you prefer the German version.'

'Well, a canteen at any rate. And how did you recruit the inhabitants?'

He stared evasively into the middle distance. 'Erm, that depended. Some of us knew one another from before. Which was the case with me and Tor Fylling, who lived over there.' He nodded to the house Maja called house number one. 'We were old school pals. As indeed was Nils Bringeland.'

'I see.'

'Then they knew other people. In brief … We never did any advertising or the like. By and large Nils and I attended to the meetings with interested parties to try and have the most harmonious group of people possible. Then we met all the candidates, as it were, and drew up some common guidelines before we even started building.'

'That early?'

'Yes.'

'But this would mean you all knew one another well?'

'Yes, that's true. Better than many others in a similar situation.'

'But the project can't have been a hundred percent successful after all.'

'Really?' He arched his eyebrows.

'Yes, if you consider the number of divorces in the co-op. Slightly above average, even for our times, wouldn't you say?'

He gave me a scornful glare. 'Monogamy's antiquated, Veum. I thought you knew. We only reflect modern society. Nothing very remarkable about that.'

'Mhm.' I shrugged to signal that I understood what he was saying, but I didn't necessarily agree. 'Serial monogamy is fashionable at any rate, isn't it?'

'Yes indeed. But I don't suppose you wanted to speak to me to discuss this.'

'No. As you clearly realise, this is about the Mette Case.'

He sighed. 'Yes, that was a sad business. In many ways what happened cast a shadow over the whole of our project. What was supposed to have been a modern idyll became ... something else. We were all drawn into the case for good or ill. It was impossible not to be involved. We knew Mette of course. Many of the families had children. We became suspicious. If an unfamiliar car or a walker appeared in the locality you were on your toes immediately. And when it gradually emerged that the case would never be cleared up ... well ...' He shook his head vigorously. 'That destroyed a lot for us. It was never quite the same again.'

'Yes, would you say ... the high divorce rate, could it have had anything to do with it?'

'You're the one calling it abnormally high, but ... No, I don't think so. Or maybe yes, in some of the families.'

'Are you thinking of someone in particular?'

He hesitated, as though deliberating. 'No. Not really.'

'Not really?'

'The answer's no, Veum, if you need to have it spelled out.'

'And you ... do you have any theory as to what could have happened to Mette?'

'Me? Why should I?'

'You were at home that day.'

'Yes, and so what? Vibeke, to whom I was married at the time, was an actress. She was at the theatre rehearsing that morning. A leading role, probably. She was one of the best in town at the time.'

'Yes, I remember her.'

He gave me a mocking look. 'You're not the only one.'

'But you were at home,' I repeated.

'Yes, I was probably here in my office working. There was a lot of work in those years, early in the morning and late at night, and a Saturday morning was an oasis of peace – for those of us who didn't have children.'

I nodded towards the window. 'So you could see Mette playing.'

He met my gaze with an expression that suggested he was talking to a complete moron. 'Yes, I could, Veum. And don't you think I told the police that – countless times? My drawing board has always stood where it is now, because of the light. If you use your head and your eyes you will see that the way I sit – and draw – I am facing a completely different direction, and if I had turned round I'd have seen the house opposite the Misvær family's.'

'Yes. You would have seen, for example, Tor Fylling going out.'

'Correct, Veum. I would. But I didn't. I didn't see Mette playing and I didn't see Tor going out. Everyone can tell you what I saw. To be precise: this. I saw Maja ringing the doorbell at Tor's and asking him something. Afterwards she broke into a run. She never came here though. But I went out after a while to see what all the fuss was about, and then I joined the search party, like everyone else.'

'Well … I'm not sure I've got any more questions to ask you, this time round. How did you react to the news of Nils Bringeland being killed in the winter?'

'How did I react? What do you think? With shock, of course. Shot down like that, in broad daylight. You never think anything like that can happen, at least not to someone you know.'

'Did you maintain contact after he left here?'

'Not really. My circumstances have changed, as you perhaps know. New wife, small children. Not much time to keep up with old school friends.'

'The same applied to Tor Fylling?'

'The same applies to everyone. Was there anything else?'

'No.'

'I think then I should accompany you to the door so that I can return to my work.'

'Thank you.'

'Nothing to thank me for,' he said, and almost swept me out of the office towards the front door.

Once outside, I was reminded of what Cecilie Lyngmo had said when I phoned her. There was something about that co-op, she had said, she'd had a feeling that something was out of kilter there. Now I had that self-same feeling. They were holding something back from me, both Maja Misvær and Terje Torbeinsvik, some information that might not have had anything to do with Mette, yet still made me hesitant. As was my wont, I decided I wasn't going to give in until I found out what it was.

With my back to Terje Torbeinsvik's house, and with Maja's house on my left, I contemplated my surroundings. I looked at the gate, tried to picture little Mette playing in the sandpit on the left, twenty-five years ago. What would have made her leave the sandpit? Another child? An animal? Someone standing by the gate and showing her something exciting? Someone she knew and wasn't afraid of … or someone else? And whoever it was, how could he – or she – be so sure they wouldn't be seen? Why had no one seen anything? How was it possible for the small girl just to disappear – into thin air – and so completely that not even the massive police investigation in 1977 and all the years afterwards had led to her being found?

So many questions and, thus far, no answers. Once again I felt the assignment was beyond me. What could I find out that the police had not already unearthed?

I left through the gate, the same way Mette had gone that time, to all appearances. Again my mouth felt dry. I ran my tongue over my lips, as if the aftertaste of yesterday's aquavit was still there, but in vain. All I tasted was my most bitter defeat. The taste of sorrow and loss, and the eternal craving in your stomach that only aquavit could assuage, for a brief moment or two. With trembling hands I unlocked the car, got in behind the wheel, inserted the key in the ignition and started up.

I had to begin somewhere. It might as well be at the police station.

9

Nothing was as it had once been. You used to be able to walk straight into the police station in Allehelgens gate, take the lift up and find the officers you were looking for, with little resistance, apart from the sceptical glares from people who knew who you were and those who didn't. Those who knew me were often more sceptical.

Now you had to report to reception, where the man or woman behind the counter would phone up to determine whether the person you wished to see was in the building. In this case it was a him, but Helleve had to come down by lift and fetch me himself – or send someone else.

This time it was Solheim who appeared. Despite the fact that he was getting on for forty, Inspector Bjarne Solheim's hair was still charmingly untidy, even if it was cut short enough around his ears and down his neck. His boyish smile was quick on most occasions, and it wasn't far away today either. 'Helleve asked me to take care of you,' he explained. 'As you're taking the case.'

We caught the lift up to the third floor, and Solheim held the department door open for me before leading me down the corridor to one of the offices with a window looking out onto Nygaten. It had started to rain and through the wet panes we glimpsed the line of houses opposite and the slanting rooftops of the old wooden houses in Marken.

Inspector Atle Helleve stood in the doorway of the adjacent office. He stroked his well-tended, grey-speckled beard and regarded me with curiosity. 'Can you tell us anything about the robbery in Bryggen, Veum?'

'Tell might be putting it a little strongly. But I do have a couple of questions.'

He smiled wryly. 'And why am I not surprised? However, Bjarne has this case. Talk to him.'

'Actually my assignment is for the Mette Case.'

'The Mette Case. Isn't it time-barred?'

'Not yet. It was 1977. Do you remember it?'

'Just hearsay. It was way before my time.'

'Yes.'

'And you're going to crack it twenty-five years later?' The sarcastic tone was palpable.

I shrugged. 'Well, I'm going to have a look at it anyway.'

'And what on earth has it got to do with the Bryggen robbery?'

'Nothing, except that the man shot in Bryggen was one of Mette's neighbours.'

'Aha.' He didn't seem very impressed. 'Well ... you'll have to see what time Bjarne has for you.' He was on his way back into his office when he half-turned. 'Veum...'

'Yes?'

'If you stumble on anything we can use, you will tell us, won't you?'

'Naturally.'

'How are things going otherwise?'

'Muddling through. Some days are better than others.'

'Alright ... see you.'

We nodded to each other and I followed Solheim into his office.

He shoved some files to the side of his desk, sat down behind it and indicated the vacant chair nearby. On his computer next to the desk some dancing circles revealed a screensaver. If you sat looking at them for too long you went dizzy.

'You mentioned that the guy who was shot had something to do with an old case?'

'Yes. That is...' I briefly explained what I knew of the Mette Case, the co-op in Solstøvegen and how Nils Bringeland's name had come up. 'I was wondering ... My plan is to do the rounds and try and contact the majority of the people who were living out there when Mette went missing. I can't speak to Bringeland, so the question is: how far have you got with the murder ... and the whole case?'

'You were thinking...'

'Yes ... I assume his shooting was an accident?'

'There's no reason to believe anything else. He has ... he had an office at the end of Bryggen and was on his way there when, according to an eye-witness, he collided with one of the robbers, a few words were exchanged, and Bringeland was shot before the robber ran off after the others.'

'A few words were exchanged?'

'Yes, that's what the eye-witness said. But obviously ... he was sitting in a car in Bryggen, so the details...' He waggled his head from side to side to emphasise how shaky the statement was.

'Did he hear any of the words?'

'No, unfortunately not.'

'As far as I remember, there were some customers in the shop.'

'That's right. A mother and a daughter. We spoke to the daughter. The mother seemed a bit out of it.'

'Did they hear anything?'

'Of what was said outside? No.'

'How much did the robbers get away with actually?'

He smiled wryly. 'I'm not authorised to say, but ... it was a pretty good hourly pay rate, considering the length of time and their getaway.'

'Yes, how long did it take?'

'Five to six minutes all in all, we estimate.'

'But the owner was covered by insurance?'

'He's given us a list of the items and their prices. I can't pass it on, though.'

'I understand. Well ... it's not so important. They got away in a boat, did they?'

'Yes, but it's never been identified. It was seen as it rounded the Nordnes point and that's the last definite sighting we have.'

'There are not that many places it could hide, are there?'

'No. It's probably moored on either the Nordnes side or Laksevåg, or it might have been sunk before they continued by car. All of this is speculation though. There's nothing based on actual sightings.'

'Strange.'

'You can say that again.'

'It would take time to sink a boat.'

'Well, all you do is pull the plug, so it wouldn't take that long. Besides, we weren't exactly on the spot immediately afterwards. It took several days to check all the places they could have landed.'

'Mm ... often robbers come from an organised crime background. Was there anything about their MO that was reminiscent of other robberies?'

'Thing is, Veum, generally speaking, in our neck of the woods we've been spared the great wave of robberies, simply because, geographically, it's hard to make your getaway. There aren't enough escape routes – on land or water. We've had our share of burglaries, safe-breaking and so on, often carried out by gangs doing the rounds, but robberies of this type are more the domain of Østland, or along the Swedish border, or in a radius of ten to twenty kilometres around Oslo. That's where the main groupings tend to be. There are additional gangs coming from abroad, Sweden or Eastern Europe predominantly. And from more distant countries, such as China. However, as I said, this came as an immense surprise to us, and locally there are no obvious crime hotspots that we can target. So we're at an early stage in our enquiries and this is new ground.'

'They were wearing shell suits, I understand.'

He smirked. 'Yes, and what's that supposed to tell us? They were a gang of pensioners out to replenish their bank accounts?'

'No, but amateurs maybe?'

'Hardly, Veum. Not when this was carried out so professionally, with guns and so on. No, there was a precise plan behind this.'

'What about bikers?'

He wasn't convinced. 'Well ... there are not many of them around here either, and it's the drugs rings we suspect will be heading our way. The drugs trade more than robberies of this kind. However, Veum ... I still don't understand what this has to do with your case.'

'No, nor me. I wanted to find out about Nils Bringeland. To see whether there could be any reason why he, of all people, was killed during the robbery. But ... clearly there wasn't.'

'Not as far as I can see. Unless you had anything else on your...' He turned to the computer as though the circles were enticing him back with their bewitching movements.

'No, I'd better ... drop by later, if anything springs to mind.'

'You do that, Veum.' He got up. 'I'll show you the way out.'

'I can find my way.'

'I'm sure you can, but...'

'I know. The new regulations.'

'Nothing is as it was, Veum.'

'No, I was thinking the same myself. And it's never going to be, either.'

He accompanied me all the way down and stood waiting until I was out on the paved terrace outside the building, as if to ensure I didn't commit some offence he could not fail to mention to his superiors, whoever they might be. Jakob E. Hamre would be one, I assumed. Another of those officers who used to heave a deep sigh at the mere sight of me. I headed for Bryggen and Nils Bringeland's office in Bredsgården.

10

Bredsgården was the longest street in the part of Bryggen that was left after the fire of 4th July 1955.

I could remember that summer evening myself; I was twelve years old, standing in Klosterhaugen with my parents and looking down across Vågen to the burning houses, the terrible cloud of sparks and smoke that drifted and drifted and finally lay like a bluish-grey haze above large tracts of Bergen. Not far from us stood a girl from a parallel class with her mother, looking in the same direction. I was head-over-heels in love with her, but she never knew it. Many years later I met her at a party, and late in the evening, after several glasses of wine, she confided to me with a sardonic smile: If only you knew how in love with you I was then ... What could you say to that? Nothing, only return the same sardonic smile.

Throughout history many have wanted to demolish the timber buildings in Bryggen; plans were presented again after the great explosion of April 1944 and then after the fire of 1955. But the plans were never realised. Now Bryggen was on UNESCO's World Heritage list, heavy traffic was routed via tunnels through Fløyen, and walking along the quayside one rainy day in March, a month or two before the great tourist invasion of the town, was like walking past a memorial to the glories of yore, a row of façades painted in classical colours: red, yellow and white.

The company Nils Bringeland had run was up two floors, off the enclosed veranda and with an office facing the street. There was still an unmistakeable smell of dried fish in the woodwork, an odour not even the hundreds of years of Bergen rain that had fallen since the last dried fish had been transported from the area had managed to expunge. The sign beside the door told me this was where Bringeland Papir & Kontor resided. I knocked, waited a few seconds, then opened the door and stepped inside.

The room confirmed the description: It was an office, and there was a lot of paper. Along all the walls there were shelves of goods testifying to the fact that this was indeed a paper business: boxes of envelopes in various sizes, packets of photocopy paper in various colours and of various qualities, and a wide selection of other office equipment. Not enough to sell directly, most probably they were examples of the range they had to offer potential bulk buyers.

Behind a desk dominated by a computer sat a woman. The screen was placed in such a way that she could see on to the street. The two windows were covered by two half-drawn blinds, which completely shut out the sunlight when it was too intrusive, seldom the case in Bergen. Now, in reaction to my entrance, she swivelled her chair round to the door.

She was fifty or thereabouts, had short, greying hair, a slightly sad expression and was elegantly dressed in a black skirt and white blouse; a delicate blue-and-red cardigan from Oleana hung from the back of her chair in case it got cold.

Her voice was clear and well modulated. 'How can I help you?'

'My name's Veum. Varg Veum. Private investigator. I was wondering if you were a colleague of Nils Bringeland?'

She half-rose from her chair. 'What do you mean – private investigator?'

'Erm, I'm here about an old case.'

'Not the murder, then?'

'No. That is … no.'

'Well…' She pointed to a vacant chair. 'I doubt I can help you with anything, but … I'll try of course. What old case is this?'

'The Mette Case. Does that mean anything to you?'

'No, not immediately.'

'A small girl who disappeared from her house in Nordås about twenty-five years ago.'

'I see. I'm not sure … I was young then and probably had other things in my head.'

'Nils Bringeland was one of her neighbours.'

'Oh … from when he lived there.'

'Did you know him back then?'

'Yes, I … but not that far back. I've been employed here for almost twenty years. But you don't mean to say that Nils had anything to do with that case, do you?'

'No, no. Not at all. I'm just feeling my way. He and his then wife got divorced. I don't know when.'

'Well, I can …' She coughed. 'There's something I should make clear to you right now, so that there won't be any misunderstandings.'

'Oh, yes?'

She pursed her lips, as though this was not going to be pleasant, then continued: 'My name is Sølvi Hegge. It was me … I was … I lived with Nils for fifteen years afterwards.'

'Ah, I see! Sorry for bothering you with this then.'

She pursed her lips again. 'It's … fine. I'm over the initial shock now.'

'How—?'

She interrupted me. 'It was a shock. I'd been expecting him back in the office from meeting a customer in the town centre so that we could drive home together. We lived between Morvik and Mjølkeråen in Åsane, so if we travelled together we could get home faster and start cooking.'

I nodded.

'He didn't come … After a while I became restless. I tried to phone him on his mobile, but couldn't get through, and then … It must have been about five, suddenly there was a policeman at the door asking – a bit like you just now – if this was where Nils Bringeland worked. I said yes, you can see it is, and pointed to the sign outside. He nodded and coughed and finally came out with: There's been an accident. We'd like to contact his closest family. That's me, I said. And then he told me the whole story. He'd been passing by the jeweller's in Bryggen and had been shot in the melee. How serious is it? I asked, and then he told me that he was …' Her voice cracked. 'Dead.'

She sat staring into space. From Bryggen we heard the sound of a passing bus. 'It was incomprehensible. Dead. One minute happy and on his way back from a hopefully successful meeting. The next, dead. No warning. No sick bed, no symptoms we could draw conclusions from. Just because he happened to be in the wrong place at the wrong time.' She shifted her gaze back to me. 'You have to admit it has no meaning.'

'Of course. I can well understand how you feel.' Better than she imagined, in fact. 'And I come here bothering you with ... quite different matters.'

'Yes.' She looked at me, almost aggrieved.

'I can talk to other people.'

She raised a hand in defence. 'No, I'll answer whatever questions you have, but as I said ... I don't think I can help you.'

'No. But ... You said Nils Bringeland and you had lived together for fifteen years?'

She nodded.

'And you've been employed here for around twenty?'

'Yes.' She quickly added: 'There's no denying it. We met here. I was taken on in 1982, and we got to know each other well, of course. It was just us here, plus customers and delivery men now and again. But mostly just us. So, occasionally, when things were quiet, we sat chatting, naturally enough. We went out and had a meal together sometimes, when it was convenient. We knew each other pretty well before ... well, starting a relationship, which ended in us moving in together in 1987.'

'And that was when his previous relationship finished, of course.'

She glared at me. 'Of course. Although ... I have to be honest and admit ... we started the relationship before Randi and he had finished, but the relationship between them had been ice-cold for years and he had never stopped to think why. He was extremely loyal.'

'To Randi?'

'Yes. He never went into any detail about what had gone wrong. Didn't want to talk about it. He just said ... something had happened and nothing was ever the same again.'

'Something had happened?'

'Yes.'

'And there were no details?'

'None.'

'Hm.' I reflected on that for a while. 'Did he have any contact with Randi … later?'

'Yes, of course. They had two children, Joachim and Janne. And they had to be looked after, between them. Joachim was eighteen when Nils and I moved in together, Janne was thirteen. In principle, they lived with Randi, but there were problems with Joachim, and Janne wasn't getting along too well, either.'

'Perhaps they'd been affected by what happened to the girl, Mette?'

'Well … now you say that. I had no idea … it was never discussed.'

'What was the problem with Joachim?'

'Already then he was mixing with … dubious types. Today you'll find him in Nygårdsparken, with the veterans.'

'Drugs, I take it?'

'Up to his ears! A human wreck, if you ask me. Nils was absolutely desperate, but what could he do? The guy was an adult, he had no influence over him, and you know how much help you get from the state. As good as nothing. In this country you have the state's blessing to go to hell in a handcart, just behave nicely in the park and don't go robbing old ladies or turn to prostitution.'

'Well … there are some state institutions.'

'But not enough!'

'I cannot disagree. And the daughter?'

'Janne lives in England. She went there as an au pair, met a guy and never came back. You'll have to ask Randi about her.'

'OK … she doesn't live in Nordås any more, is that right?'

'No, she moved to Bergen after Nils left. I had a little contact with her regarding the funeral in December.' She nodded to the window. 'She lives over there, in Nordnes. In a sixties block.'

'What does she do?'

'She's a sales assistant in one of the shops in Kløverhuset. Ladies' clothing for teens of all ages.'

'Were they at the funeral? All of them?'

'Oh, yes. Joachim and Janne and her English husband. In fact, he was bad-tempered and stroppy and not unlike a football player after he's been given a red card. None of them spoke afterwards. Nor did Randi. Not a single one of them.'

I couldn't help myself, but I had developed a bit of a soft spot for Sølvi Hegge. I liked the way she expressed herself, her commitment, frankness and the sober way she tackled her grief. And her smile was sardonic and a little despondent; it was the way my old school friend from Nordnes had smiled, when we met so many years later.

'Did you and Nils have children?'

She sighed, and her eyes glazed over. 'Helene. She's ten. Of course, she doesn't understand anything. It's impossible to explain … why such things happen, as you know. You can become an atheist for much less.'

'Yes.'

I would have liked to stay there longer, but there was nothing to suggest she had anything to tell me about Mette, and she hadn't offered me a cup of coffee, surprisingly enough for a morning visit to a Norwegian office.

'Well, perhaps…' I got to my feet. 'If you happen to think of anything that might have some significance for the case, then…' I passed her my card and she stood up to take it. She was ten centimetres shorter than me and a waft of something reminded me of funerals: king lily and chrysanthemum.

Her eyes were steely grey as she looked up at me. 'Why has the case come up now, after so many years?'

'Another mother wondering what actually happened.'

She nodded slowly. 'It's not always that easy to explain.'

'Not for any of us.'

With those words we parted, for ever, to all appearances. But you can never be sure of anything. Perhaps we would meet again, at a party in some years' time, and sit smiling philosophically at each other.

11

The houses in Bryggen are divided into two parts as a result of the decision at the end of the nineteenth century to demolish all the timber houses and replace them with new brick apartment buildings, after a design inspired by the old trading houses in the German Hanseatic town of Lübeck. The jewellery shop was in the first of these brick buildings, with a sign saying *Wilhelm Schmidt & Sons*. On my way back from the meeting with Sølvi Hegge, driven by a sudden impulse, I opened the shop door and went in.

The female assistant, a dark-haired, well-groomed woman in her forties, looked up sharply when I entered. She watched me stiffly as I approached the counter, as though fearing that at any minute I would pull out a gun and start yelling orders at her. It was only when I spoke to her that she appeared to relax, but she still wore a tense expression for as long as I was in the shop.

'Hello, my name's Veum and I … A case I'm investigating has a connection with what took place here in December.'

'A connection? I don't understand.'

'To do with the man who was shot outside here, that is.'

'Oh, him!' She put her hand to her mouth in terror, as though she had almost forgotten him.

'He exchanged some words with one of the robbers.'

'Yes, he did.'

'You were…'

'But none of us heard what he said!' She raised her voice. 'I've explained that to the police countless times.'

From the room at the rear I heard the sound of an office chair being pushed back. Seconds later, in the doorway appeared a man who I recognised from the newspapers as Bernhard Schmidt. He was a little plump and in his early sixties with thinning hair and a barely visible pencil moustache. 'What's the matter, Kjersti?'

She turned to him. 'There's a man here … He says he's investigating … the robbery.'

'No,' I said quickly. 'Not the robbery. Another case.'

Schmidt looked at me, curious. 'What was your name, did you say?'

'Veum. Varg Veum.'

'Are you from the police?'

'No, I'm a private investigator.'

'And you're investigating … another case?'

'Yes.'

'Please come in here.'

I nodded to the assistant called Kjersti as I passed. Schmidt closed the door behind us and before I'd taken a seat he said: 'Are you employed by an insurance company?'

I failed to answer at once and instead left the question hanging in the air as partial confirmation.

'If so, I would ask you to contact my solicitor, Kristoffer Kleve. There's no reason to query the list we sent in. It's a hundred percent in accordance with our inventory, purchasing invoices and whatever else you might like to scrutinise.'

'The thing is …'

'Being forced to open the safe has nothing to do with it. I just kept … personal items there.'

'What I'm trying to tell you is …'

'Items of sentimental value primarily, mementos of those who ran the business before me – my father and grandfather.' He nervously stroked his pencil moustache, which was greying, like the rest of his frugal hair growth.

'This is not the case I'm investigating, Herr Schmidt!'

He sat looking at me. 'Not this case? What the hell are you doing here then?'

'I explained that to Kjersti outside. My investigation is connected with the man who was shot here.'

'I see!' He glared at me impatiently. 'He was a casual passer-by, wasn't he? Is there any reason to believe anything else?'

'No, no. However, every time someone insists there isn't, I have a feeling that, well, maybe...'

'So let me repeat my question: what the hell are you doing here?'

'I was wondering if any of you heard what was said between the shooting victim and the robbers.'

'Nothing. We didn't hear a sound, apart from the shot.' He held his head. 'Sometimes it feels as if I can still hear it.'

'Yes, I...'

'If only you could imagine how long an experience like this stays with you! One of the assistants has already handed in her cards and I'm not sure how long Kjersti will last. Had she had any alternative, I'm convinced she would have gone on the spot. If the perpetrators of such crimes had any idea of the trauma they inflict on others ... well.' He gesticulated with his hands. 'I doubt it would make any difference to that type of person, but ... mm yes.' He stood up. 'As I said, there's nothing we can help you with, Veum, wasn't it?'

'Yes.' I got to my feet. 'Aren't you interested to know what the other case is?'

'Which case?'

'The one I'm actually investigating.'

He held his head as if to signal that he had rarely experienced so much foolishness in one day. 'No, I'm not! I'm not in the slightest bit interested. I have more than enough problems of my own.'

'I understand. Which insurance company are you with?'

'That's none of your bloody business, Veum. Have you got me?' For an instant his eyes flashed; something new and dangerous, which hadn't been there before; like a threat – concealed but present nonetheless.

With that thought at the back of my mind I left the shop with a valedictory nod to Kjersti, who once again had entrenched herself behind the counter with her wary gaze directed at the door, a pose which, from what I could see, she would adopt for as long as she was still in employment there.

12

Kløverhuset had once been one of Bergen's best department stores. From my childhood I remembered the incredible Christmas window displays, in Strandgaten and Strandkaien, and at the front, facing Strandkaien, black-and-white films of Woody Woodpecker and Abbott & Costello were shown for children and adults during Advent until the late 1960s. We stood in the rain and wind, staring up at the flickering images from an antiquated projector placed on a lorry in the midst of us. It was hardly a coincidence that it was here the town's 'real' Father Christmas, the Kløver Father Christmas, had had his prime. After he had called it a day I had myself filled in for one Advent some years back. But once was enough. As in most areas of my life, I achieved only limited success, even as a Father Christmas.

Kløverhuset had been divided up and today it was a modern shopping centre with ever-changing owners: men's clothes, women's clothes, discount jeans, perfume boutiques and shops selling gifts.

When I located the shop where Sølvi Hegge had said Randi Hagenberg was working there was only one assistant in it. Alone behind the counter, she was leaning against the wall, and every second appeared to be death by boredom. She was barely able to keep her eyelids open enough to focus on me when I entered. She was elegantly dressed, in a tight-fitting green dress with a brown belt on the last hole to emphasise how slim she was, with discreet but effective make-up and flame-red hair in a modern, carefree cut. But her face looked lean and tired, her nose protruded like a beak, too thin and pointed and perhaps also too big.

'Randi Hagenberg?' I said.

This seemed to rouse her. Her gaze was a notch more focussed. 'Yes? What do you want?'

I told her who I was and why I was there, and she shook her head in bewilderment. 'Mette? After so many years! Why on earth...?'

'The case will soon be shelved for ever and her mother has asked me to have another look.'

She shrugged and looked a little resigned. 'Really? For my own sake, I've tried to think about it as little as possible. It was awful. A tragedy.'

'You were there when she disappeared.'

She examined my face with suspicion. 'Yes ... and?'

'Maja told me.'

'Yes, it's true. I was at home that day. She came to the door distraught and asked me if I'd seen Mette – you see, we had a little girl of the same age and they used to play together, sometimes in our house, sometimes in theirs. But ... I hadn't. That is ... I had seen her playing in the sandpit a bit earlier, but not right before Maja turned up, not then.'

She looked at me as though expecting more questions. When none was forthcoming she continued: 'Straightaway I said she could be with other children, in their houses ... but no, Maja had been round already. I stood there with Janne in my arms and I could feel myself getting terribly worked up. This is what parents of small children fear most, one of their children suddenly going missing. I called Nils and asked him to take Janne...'

'Your husband was at home?'

'Yes?' She stared at me in surprise. 'It was a Saturday.'

'And your son?'

'Joachim? No, he was out somewhere with some friends. Probably playing football or something. That's what they usually did.'

I nodded. 'And then...?'

'Yes, well ... then Maja and I ... ran out through the gate to the garages.'

'Do you remember if the gate was open?'

'She made a vague movement with her head. 'No, I don't ... I think it was slightly ajar. That was why we thought she must have gone out.'

'And it wasn't lockable?'

'No.' She looked at me quizzically. 'Can I go on?'

'By all means.'

'Then we ran to the garages, went in one that was open and had a look around, but nothing. No Mette. The other garage doors were locked. We crossed the road – at that time it was open countryside – and searched there. Maja ran down the road in both directions. There was a building site further up, and we went there too, I think, unless that came later. It must have been me who said we should call the police. I accompanied Maja back and we rang from her phone. While we were waiting for them to come … ah, that was when we went to the building site. Many of our neighbours went with us … At least I can remember Tor Fylling … and Nils, of course. He rang Truls, Maja's husband, and told him about Mette. He was at football training with Håkon, their son. Nils rang the clubhouse and managed to track him down.'

She gazed into the air, with a gloomy expression. 'The rest was chaos. The whole co-op was turned upside down for weeks afterwards. We searched high and low, and we were all questioned by the police. Most of us were summoned to the police station to tell them what we knew – again. So that they had it on tape, I think.'

'What you knew?'

'Yes. What we knew about, well, what I've just told you. The events of that day, where we were and so on.'

'Did that apply to the children as well?'

'Children? Most were too small.'

'And Joachim? I suppose they wrote down where he was too, did they?'

'Tell me … what are you trying to suggest? Joachim was eight then and I've told you where he was. Out with friends playing football.'

'Or something, you said.'

'Did I?' A kind of sneer flitted across her lips. 'You'd better ask the police then, if you don't trust me. They must have it all documented.'

'What do you think happened?'

She shrugged. 'What are we supposed to believe? She was never found in the countryside around us … so someone must have taken her, I suppose.'

'You don't remember anything special about that day? Something that made it stand out from other days?'

'Such as what? There was a telephone that kept ringing and ringing, that was all.'

'A telephone?'

'Yes, in one of the houses across the yard. It rang and rang and no one answered it. And then after a while it started again. This happened again and again. It must have been at Svein and Synnøve's. They weren't at home of course. But Tor Fylling and Terje Torbeinsvik were.'

I nodded without making any comment. After a short pause I carried on: 'What was your relationship with Maja Misvær?'

'My relationship with Maja? Pretty normal, I think. We'd been neighbours since we moved in, in the early 1970s. Now and then there were some communal functions, but otherwise we didn't have so much to do with each other. Most of us had small children. Some of us knew one another from before, but Maja and Truls came via Tor.'

'Oh, yes? I understood your husband ...'

'My ex-husband! Ex-partner!'

'OK. I understood Nils Bringeland, Terje Torbeinsvik and Tor Fylling were school friends.'

'Yes, they were. And Tor and Helle had been neighbours of Truls and Maja where they lived before, so that was how they came to the co-op. The last family, Svein and Synnøve Stangeland ... the link there was Svein. Nils knew him through work. Svein was at the Haakonsvern base and Nils had a contract to deliver forms and so on there. They often joked that they should start their own firm: Bringeland & Stangeland.'

'Your children ... how are they getting on?'

'How ... what do you mean? Has anyone said anything?'

'The thing is ... To do my job I have to try and contact everyone who lived there at the time Mette disappeared, so that's why I was wondering.'

'But I've told you ... Janne was three then and Joachim eight!'

'But they're grown up now.'

'Yes.' She hesitated. 'Janne lives in England. She got married there.

Joachim ... well, he's just moved. I'm not entirely sure ... I haven't got his new address yet.'

'But he lives in Bergen?'

'Oh, yes.'

'Which part of town?'

'I think it's ... yes, it's definitely Møhlenpris. Or maybe it was Nygårdsgaten. It's a bit confusing. He moves a lot.'

'Oh?' I wanted her to tell me herself, but she fell quiet. 'His name's Bringeland, is it?'

'Yes, he ... Nils and I were never married. We just lived together. But both children have his surname. We thought Hagenberg Bringeland was a bit too much, and as far as nursery and school and all that were concerned we reckoned it was better for them to have the same surname. Which one we chose made little difference.'

'I've heard rumours that Joachim's on drugs.'

Her eyes went vacant. 'I see. Yes ... he is, at various times. There's no hiding it. But ... I don't want to talk about it. It has nothing to do with this case anyway.'

Two women came into the shop and made a beeline for one of the clothes stands. Randi Hagenberg looked at me with relief in her face as she pointed to the women. 'I'll just have to tend to these customers.'

I nodded. 'I can wait.'

'Oh...' She struggled to conceal her displeasure.

I stood flicking aimlessly through a rail of women's clothes as she went over to the two customers. But who could I surprise with a present from Kløverhuset?

Behind my skull a latent headache was beginning to build. I had what felt like knotted muscles in my temples, taut and thick. The saliva in my mouth was sticky and slimy, my throat as dry as a bone. The thought of a glass of aquavit created such a craving in my stomach that I almost left the place at once and headed home before the demon turned temperance preacher.

But I stood my ground. The two women found it hard to come to a decision, but in the end they agreed on a black silk blouse, which was nicely gift-wrapped and paid for with a card. When they left they brazenly stared in my direction, and from the balcony I heard one of them say something and the other laugh, a low, gravelly chuckle of the indecorous kind.

Randi Hagenberg reluctantly came towards me.

'I have only one more question.'

'Right.'

'Your husband apparently suggested … Your ex-husband or partner, I mean. Since you did split up…'

'Yes?' she said impatiently.

'That the reason you split up was something that happened and it was never the same again between you.'

She flushed to the roots of her hair and when she did answer it was more like a gulp: 'And who the hell told you that? And what the heck has it got to do with Mette?'

'It…'

'Answer me that, Mr Private Detective.'

'Not…'

'No, you can't, you see, and now this conversation is over. Is that clear?' She scowled at me. 'Clear off! Otherwise I'll call the security guard.'

'I didn't mean to…'

She immediately turned her back on me, stomped to the counter, lifted the telephone receiver and stood there with it in her hand. 'I mean it! I'm calling…'

I raised both hands in defence. 'That won't be necessary. Call if you like – I'm on my bike. Thank you for your … help. We probably won't see each other again.'

'I hope not! If you set foot in here again, I'll call security. Have you got that?'

'Message received loud and clear. That's fine. I've already gone.'

Actions spoke louder than words and I left Randi Hagenberg where she was, telephone in hand and an angry expression on her face, wondering to myself what button I had pressed this time, and what had made her react with such ferocity.

It was becoming more and more of a problem that Nils Bringeland was dead. But it was still possible to track down Joachim, whichever address he was staying at.

13

Even after Karin's death I had still maintained my links, which went back many years, with the National Register. Several of her colleagues, whom I had met through her on various occasions, had promised me that if the worst came to the worst and there was something I needed help with – in total confidentiality, naturally – all I had to do was give them a buzz. And the worst did actually come to the worst, before anyone could have anticipated it. How long their charity would last was impossible to say, but so far I'd had no reason to complain. Not about that, at any rate.

The last registered address for Joachim Bringeland was a hostel in Jonas Reins gate, which I doubted the highly respected parish priest and Independence Party man the street was named after would have viewed with much more than the very scantest forbearance. The stench from the staircase in the dilapidated old house with a chimney must have been worse than the odour from Gehenna, the pile of rubbish outside Jerusalem which, according to bible researchers, had been the inspiration for the traditional description of hell. As I stepped inside the front door a well-nourished rat darted into the hall, stopped and kept a wary eye on me in the semi-gloom in case I should lay my hands on the overturned dustbin just inside the door.

A few floors above me I heard loud music, and from somewhere else in the house the sound of two people involved in a fierce slanging match, although it was impossible to make out what the quarrel was about. The theme was unlikely to have been theological.

The light in the hall was dim, but someone had hung a handwritten note on a door to the left, announcing in big, black, felt-pen letters: OFFICE. RECEPTION. On the wall beside the office door hung what

I assumed were the house rules, but the print was so poor it was impossible to read much more than the heading. Before knocking I took the liberty of picking up the dustbin, to the angry hisses of the resident quadruped at the back of the room.

I already knew the situation, so it came as no surprise. If you were homeless in Bergen and received help from the local council you could end up in anything from a tourist hotel to a workman's shed, and the range of hostels was phenomenal, from the relatively well run to the scandalous, which appeared in the newspapers at regular intervals, not infrequently in connection with violent crime. This was clearly one of the latter category.

A hoarse voice welcomed me to the hostel, but the eyes I met categorically denied the proposition. Behind a tatty desk, so flimsy it would have had difficulty passing muster at the Salvation Army charity shop, sat a big, burly man, looking like a fatted pig two weeks before Christmas and as endearing as an aching abscess on your backside. A shaver hadn't come near his face for the last week and a haircut was unnecessary for the as-good-as-hairless pate. He was wearing a yellowish shirt, which might originally have been white, and a black leather jacket that could not have been blacker. Gehenna PLC had an administrator to match the establishment, lucky them. Nowadays this was the best the backstreets had to offer.

'Yes?' the voice said.

'I'd like to visit someone called Joachim Bringeland. He's staying here, I've been informed.'

'Jokken? Yes, he drops in now and then.'

'Drops in?'

'Yes, he's got a room here. That's right. He generally uses it to doss in. He's not there now though.'

'How do you know?'

'I know my con artists, let me put it like that.'

'I see. Has he lived here long?'

He scrutinised me from under heavy eyelids. 'Who's asking?'

'Varg Veum.'

'You're not from the papers, are you?'

'No. I'm investigating a case.'

'You don't look like a cop.'

'Thank you. I'm a private investigator.'

'Right. Well, diddle ma dangle. Now I've seen the lot.'

'Joachim Bringeland,' I said with emphasis, to get us back on track. 'This is a low-threshold establishment. Did you notice?'

'That's more syllables than I thought you could manage.'

'It means the door is high and the gate is wide.'

I nodded silently without saying what I had on the tip of my tongue: It had to be. Otherwise he wouldn't have got in.

'Jokken's been on drugs since his teens. Now he's past thirty. There's little more than skin and bone left of him. He rattles his way up to the park every day. First into town to get some dibs – don't ask me how! Then into the park to haggle for the dose of the day. He might have a cup of tea later on. At night he comes back here. If he's still in the black he might have a packet soup with him, which he heats on the hotplate in his room. We have to check every night that he and the others have remembered to switch them off. We do the rounds at about ten to be on the safe side and sometimes later if we're nervous.'

'I see you take your job seriously.'

'We do indeed, Mr Private Detective! Without people like us, Jokken and the rest would be sleeping rough, and you can imagine how that'd be – in winter anyway.'

I nodded my agreement. A roof over your head was better than nothing, even if the house beneath was rat-infested. 'Tell me Mr Manager ... I didn't catch your name.'

'You can call me Tiny. Everyone else does.'

'OK. Is that what your birth certificate says?'

'None of your bloody business.'

'Why don't you try and keep the place out there clean?' I nodded towards the hallway. 'It stinks of rotting rats.'

'Yes, well, I'll tell you why, pal. First, we've been ordered by the authorities to keep our rubbish indoors, but whenever one of the lodgers comes home you can bet your life they kick a dustbin over and send it flying. Half of them don't reach their rooms without shitting themselves. The other half spew up like pigs at some point in the night, so what's the point? We had some women from Africa to clean up for a while, and that was pretty good, but they had to be paid, right, and we had a budget to keep, so eventually we decided to do it ourselves.'

'With the obvious results.'

'Look, we do the cleaning once a week. You've just come on a bad day, OK?'

'I see. So if I want to find Joachim Bringeland you'd recommend I go for a walk in the park?'

He smirked. 'Go for it! They like your sort up there. Just leave your wallet at home. And afterwards it's best if you don't say you've been there. Catch my drift?'

I nodded, turned to the door and left.

'Bye, snoop!' came a mutter behind me.

I couldn't be bothered to answer, just nodded, then slammed the door so hard that the rat, which was now standing on top of the dustbin in an attempt to get the lid off, recoiled, landed on the floor and slid along the wall back into the hall. Upstairs the music had stopped and no one was quarrelling any more. This seemed like a bad omen. But I didn't go up to check. It was outside my remit for the moment.

14

If I was going to search for Joachim Bringeland in Nygårdsparken the right place to begin was what was known as Flagghaugen – Flag Hill. It had been given this name after the Battle of Nygård on 18th May 1869, when the boys from two of the town's biggest marching bands met right here. It was on this hill that the Nygård boys defended their flag while the Nordnes lads had to carry their, later legendary, 'blood flag' back to Nordnes, stained red with blood. Typically, no one ever agreed on who won the battle.

What everyone did agree on was that Nygårdsparken had changed character from the time it was established as a recreational area to improve people's health. A walk in the park in those days had been like wandering through a wonderland, a mixture of a British park and a Chinese garden, where white swans swam serenely around the lake and the only sounds you could hear were the chirruping of birds in the trees, the quacking of a duck in a pond, the tinkle of the evening tram over in Møhlenpris and the faint petticoat swish of the young lady who accompanied you before you paused beneath a tree and kissed. A walk through Nygårdsparken nowadays was a far riskier enterprise, at least if you ventured up to the area around Flag Hill, which Bergen's drugs milieu had turned into its headquarters since the late 1970s. Ten years later the local council, with the help of the police, had decided to clear the park. The result was that the drugs community spread to the town centre; but when syringes were left outside the entrances to the Bergensian ladies' favourite cafés their mille-feuilles went down the wrong way and they immediately demanded that the guilty parties were sent packing whence they had come. With that the outcasts returned to the Garden of Eden on Nygård Hill, where the snake had taken its place on the royal throne and Adam and Eve had long been forgiven their indiscipline. Since then things had only got worse.

With my past in social welfare and present in crime investigation it was rare I went there without meeting someone I knew. The same happened this time too. A couple of them nodded and said hello. Many demonstratively looked in another direction.

On the hill I caught sight of Little Lasse in one of the huddles. He was easy to spot, one metre eighty-five tall, long hair like a louse-ridden lion's mane down to his shoulders. His enduring survival made him a winner in these circles, though hardly in any others. On catching sight of me he looked away. He never liked me visiting him here, and when I beckoned to him he left his group only with the utmost reluctance and cut across to meet me. He was followed by a handful of suspicious stares. The owners were probably wondering what he had to do with me.

'What the hell are you doing here, Veum?'

'Coincidence meeting you here, Lasse. I'm looking for someone called Joachim Bringeland. Down at the hostel he went under the name of Jokken. Do you know him?'

He licked his lips. 'Terribly dry for the time of year, isn't it.'

I got the hint, took out my wallet and peeled off a blue banknote for him. 'Will that do?'

He shook his head as if clearly rejecting an advance, but with a swift dart of his hand a conjuror would have envied, he pocketed the note before I even had time to register it was gone.

'Do you saw women in half as well, Lasse?'

'Only if they ask.' He stretched out his hand in the shape of a soap dish. 'From the bottom up.'

'I was looking for Jokken Bringeland...'

He craned around and squinted at one of the rhododendron bushes. 'I think that's him sitting on the bench. He and Mottled Marte have split a dose.'

'Mottled?'

'White hair with black blotches. Fits, doesn't it.'

'Thank you.'

'And Veum … Don't come here again. You're bad for my reputation.'

'Most of them know who I am. I'm on their side, for Christ's sake.'

He grimaced. 'Up here you're a cop all the bloody same.' With a brusque movement he turned and went back to the huddle where he was before. He was returning to his own, but they didn't receive him warmly. He's been infected by a Mr Clean&Sober, he has. But then they knew nothing of my alcohol consumption over the last three years. From that perspective, we were in the same boat, the whole lot of us.

I strolled in the direction he had pointed, rounded the rhododendron and surprised the somewhat moth-eaten couple on the bench: she had just inserted the syringe and only the whites of her eyes were visible; he was nervously fiddling with the same syringe, her blood had tinged the tip red. When I appeared he fumbled with the syringe and hid it beneath his threadbare, greyish-brown parka. His eyes sought mine, from an angle and wavering, like a whipped cur, ready for another beating.

'Joachim Bringeland?'

He nodded mutely. 'Yes?'

The description Tiny had given me was accurate. Joachim consisted of nothing but skin and bone, protruding eyes, spikey unwashed hair and a sparse blond beard around a mouth of bad teeth. He couldn't have weighed much more than the latter end of forty kilos. The woman beside him was not much better, leaning against him, her legs spread in filthy jeans, her mouth agape, her eyes looking inwards and her face as expressive as a plaster mask. They looked like two castaways on a raft somewhere in the ocean, far from land and beyond all hope.

'My name's Veum. Your mother told me where to find you.'

His flickering eyes tried to focus. 'My mother? How?'

'I'm working on an old case and trying to talk to everyone who might know something about it.' When he didn't react I added: 'The Mette Case.'

This time I had a reaction. A sudden convulsion went through him, as though I had hit him. His upper body swayed and he gripped Mottled Marte even harder, as if for help and comfort. 'Me-Me-Mette?'

'You remember it, I can see.'

'Who the hell has started digging that up?'

'The mother. I'm sure you remember her.'

He nodded weakly. 'Håkon's mother.'

'And Mette's.'

'Yes…' He sat staring in front of him, then added: 'But that's one helluva long time ago.'

'Soon be twenty-five years.'

'We were only kids.'

'Yes.'

Apparently he didn't wish to say any more, so I continued: 'Do you remember anything from then?'

'Hardly. I was six or seven years old.'

'Eight, I was told.'

'OK. Eight, then.' His voice quivered and he spoke in such a low voice I had to lean forward to catch the gist. 'But I don't remember anything. Nothing except the fuss.'

'The fuss?'

'Yes, all the searching. The questions. Everyone was summoned to the police station, even my mum and dad. Yes, and a woman came to talk to us kids as well, but we knew nothing of course. What could we know?'

'No? You never saw any suspicious persons lurking around?'

'Suspicious … The only person was that pedo who used to visit Eivind and Else and them.'

'Eivind and Else…' I took out my notebook and flicked through. 'The Stangelands, do you mean?'

'But everyone knew about that. He was even put inside for a while.'

'Are you talking about Jesper Janevik?'

'Don't remember what his name was, but probably.'

'He was only held in custody for a night.'

'Alright. So that wasn't anything, then.'

'But he used to visit the Stangeland family?'

'Yes, he did.'

'Mm, did he ever try anything?'

'How do you mean?'

'He had convictions for indecent exposure, or something like that.'

'He didn't expose himself to me, anyway.'

'And … Eivind and Else didn't ever say anything about him?'

'He was their uncle for Christ's sake. Or some kind of relation.'

I flicked through my notebook. 'Do you remember where you were on the day Mette disappeared?'

'Eh! That's more than twenty years ago. Do you remember where you were?'

'Where I was, nothing that serious happened. Or I'd have remembered.' When he didn't react to that I went on: 'The police must have asked you.'

'Yes, it's possible, but honestly I don't remember. I was probably at home. It was a Saturday after all.'

'Håkon was at football training.'

'Yes, but he was smaller than me and I only played football in the street. I never liked it.'

'Really?'

'No.'

'So what did you like, Joachim?'

He chewed his lip. 'What I liked? Well, I … Music maybe. Sitting at home and finding radio stations where they played cool songs. Making the walls reverberate. Mum and Dad would go nuts at times, but I still didn't stop. That was my music, you know. My songs. Later I found out the names of the groups I liked. ZZ Top, AC/DC, that sort of thing.'

'So the day Mette disappeared you were in your room with the sound system on full blast and your head in hard-rock heaven?'

He grinned wanly. 'Maybe.'

'And what was it that brought you here?' I spread my arms to take in the park around us.

He shrugged and looked down. 'Nothing in particular. It just happened.'

'It just happened?'

'Yes.'

'And you've never tried to do something about it?'

For a second or two he met my eye. 'No. Never.' Then his gaze went inwards and was lost.

I stood looking at him. Not much hope there. The lights were on, but no one was at home. And the hand inside his jacket was shaking as though he suffered from serious convulsions. I knew what he was after. I knew he wanted me to go. So I fulfilled his wishes, cut down through the park to the road and walked to the gate. Each visit here left me as depressed as the last. But the craving to slake my thirst had not abated. I had to find something to do.

I looked at my watch. It was almost six o'clock. Dusk was advancing on the town. Perhaps there was time for another trip to Solstølen, now that most people would be home from work. And what could be better than a visit from a dogged PI coming to remind them not only of the bad old days but, for some, the worst days of all?

15

In the pitch darkness, with lights illuminating the houses, Solstølen looked even cosier than earlier in the day. All the kitchen windows shone; in some of them I could see people moving around. From the house where Randi Hagenberg and Nils Bringeland had lived came the sound of children crying; from the Torbeinsvik family's house something redolent of music.

There was a workaday, reassuring quality about the whole situation that filled me with an acute longing for the times thirty years ago when Beate, Thomas and I had constituted a little family. Beate had played with Thomas in the sitting room while I knocked up a simple meal in the kitchen: Thomas, still not capable of forming words correctly, let out whoops of enthusiasm, Beate laughed, the steam from the pans settled on the window pane like dew, the radio was on low in the background … moments like these would never return. Thomas and Mari lived in Oslo and were expecting their first child in a few months, Beate was living the merry widow's life in Stavanger, and I was wandering restlessly through life's back streets, where it was always dark and those who were out seldom had good intentions.

Once again I saw the sandpit where Mette had been playing on that fateful Saturday in September 1977. When Thomas had been six and lived with Beate and her new husband in Sandviken. I had been making my living as a PI for two years already, without impressive results to show for it. I had stumbled on my first corpse, and Dankert Muus had long had me on his hate list. And Mette – what had happened to her?

So far no one had found the answer and from where I was standing, looking around the yard, I was not at all sure the answer was to be found here. But it was worth a try. I didn't have much else to do.

The house where a new family had moved in was of no interest. I had already talked to the architect. That left two houses. I chose the one on the far left. A simple door-sign told me this was where Synnøve and Svein Stangeland lived. They had been living there when Mette disappeared, they had children of approximately the same age and they were the only couple that hadn't split up. Furthermore, they had a relative who had been on the police's radar in 1977. The latter point was not uninteresting.

I pressed the doorbell. It wasn't long before the door opened and a somewhat chunky little man stood in the doorway. He had thin, dark hair, which was combed forward into a fringe and lay flat on his scalp, pale skin and a suggestion of a rash on his chin, neck and at the corners of his mouth. He stared at me inhospitably. 'Yes?'

'Svein Stangeland?'

'Yes.'

'The name's Veum. I'm a private investigator.'

He arched his eyebrows. 'Oh, yes?'

'Maja Misvær has asked me to examine the details surrounding the disappearance of her daughter, Mette.'

A twitch seemed to go through him. Then he came out onto the step, pulling the door to behind him and said gruffly: 'Yes?'

I nodded towards the door. 'Could we have a little chat?'

'We have nothing to say. We were at the cabin the day it happened and we were unable to help. Not then and not later.'

'But you had children yourselves. You must have been alarmed by what you heard?'

'Of course we were alarmed. Everyone was. But I just told you we have nothing to say about the matter.'

'Yes. I heard you. You were a close acquaintance of Nils Bringeland's, I understand.'

'Yes. What has that got to do with anything?'

'You must have heard he was killed during the jewellery robbery in Bryggen last December?'

'Naturally. Let me just repeat … what has this got to do with anything?'

'Well, in a way it's the cause. Maja Misvær's afraid more people will pass on before they've said what they know.'

'Aha. Did she think Nils knew something?'

'Not from what she's said to me. But that's why I'm doing the rounds now. To find out if anything might have been overlooked at the time.'

'And you're such a smartarse you're going to find what the police, with all their resources, couldn't?' There was a glint of mockery in his eyes. Then he turned to the door. 'Well, as I said, I've nothing to tell you.'

'You had a relative under police investigation at the time.'

He stopped in mid-turn, seemed to close his eyes, as if to count to ten, slowly opened them and turned round fully. 'Not again! The police left no stone unturned then and they had nothing on him. He was innocent. He's been a victim of gossip and slander all his life.'

'Is he your relative? Jesper Janevik?'

'No, he's my wife's. Her cousin. But we never see him anymore.'

'Why not?'

'It's obvious. All that went on then. He was placed in custody as well!'

Suddenly the door opened and a woman with short-cropped blonde hair and narrow glasses stuck out her head and looked at us anxiously. 'What is it, Svein?'

'Nothing. It's just a Jehovah's Witness. Go back in.' He yanked the door to and she didn't try to open it again.

'Jehovah's Witnesses work in pairs,' I mumbled.

He looked around angrily and snapped back: 'All this chit-chat behind our backs!'

'Chit-chat? About Jesper Janevik?'

'Yes! As though everything were our fault, because he'd come to see us a couple of times.'

'But he was released. He was never charged.'

'No, because he never had anything to do with the case.'

'You're sure?'

'One hundred percent.'

'That sure?'

'Yes.'

'But you stayed here?'

'We hadn't done anything wrong! Why should we move? You can…' He paused. Once again he scanned the yard as though searching for something to catch his gaze.

'Yes?'

'You ask the others about their damned New Year party games! Ask them about that … Veum, was that your name? And see what answers you get.'

'Party games?'

'Yes! Synne and I know nothing about them either. We went home!' Without another word he turned to the door, opened it, stepped inside, swivelled, sent me a look that might have knocked me over if I hadn't been prepared, and then slammed the door.

I stared at the closed door. *New Year party games*?

With one more question to ask I walked next door and rang the bell at Helle Fylling and Lars Svendsen's house. Perhaps, at least, they could give me an answer.

16

Here, at any rate, I was invited inside. The man of the house opened the door here too, a surprisingly elegant man for an accountant. His golden-yellow hair was high and thick, went back in waves and curled gently over his ears. He had broad, well-tended eyebrows and glasses with a light-brown frame, a colour that matched his hair to perfection. He was wearing a dark suit, as though on his way to a meeting, but he had no worries about inviting me in when I had explained my assignment, and there was nothing to suggest he was in a hurry to get away. Perhaps he just dressed like that: at home and to go out.

'You'll have to talk to my wife,' he said as he led me through the hall to the sitting room. 'I … erm … arrived on the scene later.'

'Yes, so I understand. Your relationship with the Mette Case is…' I stopped in the hall to hold him back before we went in.

He just looked at me blankly. 'Yes, well, I don't know anything about it, of course. My wife has told me, naturally. But at that time I just followed it in the press, like most other people, I assume. It was a case that occupied people's minds. Is there a new approach since you've re-opened it?'

'Yes, now it's just me. I'm a private investigator, as I told you.'

'Yes, yes, but … if you discover anything will you pass it on to the police?'

'Yes, yes, that goes without saying.'

He nodded with satisfaction, opened the leaded-glass door to the sitting room and led me in. 'Helle … there's a gentleman here with a few questions for you.'

Helle Fylling stood up beside a low table, on which there were two cups of coffee and two cognac glasses, which sparkled enticingly. Yet again I had an unpleasant dry sensation on my palate, as though it were fine sandpaper, new and rigid and ready for use.

She was a small-limbed woman with well-kept hair like her present husband's, auburn in colour with a studied cowlick across her forehead. She was wearing a plain grey dress, tight to her slim body, as if to emphasise that she was not carrying a gram too much, more the opposite if you like your women full-bosomed.

She sent me a quizzical look. 'A few questions? I don't understand.'

I introduced myself and said: 'This is about the Mette Case.'

'Oh, that...' For some reason I had a feeling she was relieved. She came round the table to shake hands. 'Helle Fylling. Pleased to meet you.'

I nodded and mumbled: 'Pleased to meet you too.'

'Can I offer you anything?'

I stared longingly at the cognac glasses. 'Just a cup of coffee, thank you.' After a tiny pause I added: 'I'm driving.'

She nodded and smiled. Her husband said: 'I can get it. It's you he wants to talk to.'

'Thank you, Lars.'

She showed me to a chair and I sat down. I glanced around me. The big windows faced out on to the little planted garden between Solstølen and the houses to the west. A tall hedge marked the boundary between the properties. The furniture in the room was as elegant as the attire of the two people living there, period style in dark, polished wood. On the walls were large paintings, all with easily recognisable motifs, but in a more impressionistic style than classic landscapes. In one an apparently naked young man rode a horse along a beach, but the man and the horse were stylised in such a way that no one could be offended by the picture. Another was divided horizontally between a lush flower meadow and an intensely blue summer sky, where a solitary bumble bee hung in the air above one of the flowers, eagerly anticipating honey or other goodies.

Lars Svendsen came in with a cup and a saucer, placed them down carefully and poured coffee from a shiny silver Thermos that was already on the table. Afterwards he sat down, raised his cup to his mouth and took a little sip while watching us from the side-lines in a kind of umpire position.

Helle Fylling looked at me expectantly. 'How can I help? I wasn't at home when it all happened.'

'No? Where were you?'

'It was a Saturday. I was in town with the kids. I think we went to the cinema and later a burger place.'

'And you didn't hear anything … from your husband?'

'No, not until we got back home. He thought the children would only be alarmed, and they were still hoping to find her, weren't they? Mette, I mean.'

'How old were your children then?'

'It was 1977, wasn't it?' I nodded and she continued: 'Asbjørg was ten and Einar eight.'

'Older than Mette, in other words.'

'Yes, they never played together. Asbjørg had to look after her when she was smaller and had to be pushed around in a buggy, but when she was … three, it must have been … that was over.'

'And Håkon? Her brother.'

'Yes, he and Einar kicked a ball about now and then. But there were two years between them, so that was a bit of a difference. But I remember Håkon was good for his age, actually. I think he ended up playing for FC Brann, unless I'm much mistaken.'

'No, you're right. So … have you any idea what might have happened to Mette?'

She looked at me a little helplessly. 'No, what can I say? It was a terrible business. We were very frightened afterwards. I doubt there was a child playing outside without adults around. A few couples here had children. Randi and Nils, Svein and Synnøve, and … there was Håkon too. Only Terje and Vibeke didn't have any. I'm not sure if you know who I'm talking about.'

'Yes, I've got a sort of overview now. Many of you knew one another already, I've been told. Sort of round about.'

'Yes.'

'You knew Maja and Truls Misvær, didn't you?'

'Yes, we'd been neighbours before. In Landås. And then Tor – my ex-husband – knew Terje and Nils from before. They were old school friends. When we were offered this place, we thought of Maja and Truls, who lived in the same building in Mannsverk, and then they were asked to join the co-op as well.'

'Would you say you were close friends?'

'Yes, I suppose I would. I suppose we all were up here. We had get-togethers over in the architect's house. In the function room, as we call it.'

'And everyone joined in?'

She hesitated. 'Yes … when there were communal arrangements. There were private parties too. Christening celebrations, big birthdays, parties with … other friends. From outside, I mean.'

She glanced at Lars Svendsen, as though that was where he came into the picture. He just smiled gently, leaned forward for his cognac glass, raised it to his mouth and sipped the contents.

I leafed through my notes. 'At that time someone was held in custody, then released after police discussions.'

'Yes, that … I remember it.'

'He'd been visiting your closest neighbours, Svein and Synnøve Stangeland.'

She waited and watched.

'You can't remember … you never heard of any incidents in that regard?'

She shook her head. 'No. Not at all. Before this happened, we didn't even know who he was. I mean, we all had visitors at one time or another, and this man … What was his name again?'

'Jesper Janevik.'

'Yes, I should have remembered. He … Well, I could barely recall seeing him, and we asked the kids afterwards, carefully, but they hadn't seen anything … strange, as we put it. Anything unseemly would have been beyond them.'

I flicked through a few more pages, only for appearance's sake. I knew what I was going to ask. I looked up, my head tilted, and said: 'One of the neighbours mentioned something about ... "New Year games" ...?'

Her jaw fell. Two small, bright-red patches appeared high on her cheeks, as though someone had pressed them with their thumbs, hard. Gradually her slender neck turned scarlet.

For the first time, Lars Svendsen contributed to the conversation. With a little smile, he said: 'Are we talking ski-jumping here?'

Helle Fylling's face was noticeably stiffer when she answered: 'New Year games? I don't know about anything ... like that. Who told you about this?'

'Erm ... some of the others.'

'Then I suggest you go back and ask them what they're talking about.'

'My understanding was they hadn't taken part.'

'Right.' I could see from her eyes she immediately knew who. 'Well, at any rate, I don't know what they meant.'

'And it couldn't have anything to do with Mette's disappearance?'

'What importance can it have? New Year party games ... After all, she disappeared in ... September, wasn't it? No, this is just rubbish, a waste of time.'

I nodded and made a note in my book: *Just rubbish?*

'Your previous husband, Tor Fylling, he ran a car repair workshop, I understand?'

'Yes, he still does. In Sotra. He doesn't live far from it, either.'

'Has he also got a new ... partner?'

'Lars and I are married.'

'But your ex?'

She shrugged. 'To be quite frank ... women come and go. That was how he was. If he has someone, it's hardly likely to be for ever.'

'I see. What about your children?'

'Asbjørg will soon be thirty-five. Her husband's in the Norwegian Agency for Development Co-operation, so they're in Africa at the moment. Tanzania. But Einar lives in Sotra. He and his wife work for Tor, actually, both of them. Einar's followed in his father's footsteps and works in the garage, while Marita's in the office doing the accounts and so on.'

'But you have contact?'

'Yes, yes. They visit us. It's harder with Asbjørg. It'll soon be two years since they left and the contract's still got a year to run. They only come home in the holidays.'

'Well,' I said, opening my hands. 'Then I won't disturb you any longer. But…'

She looked at me nervously. 'Yes?'

'I may be back.'

'If there's anything I can help you with, to do with Mette, then by all means…'

I noticed that she stressed it had to be relevant to Mette, and I didn't feel the invitation was especially sincere. Perhaps she was one of those people who always feared the worst when strangers came to the door, whether they were Jehovah's Witnesses or a lousy PI from Strandkaien 2.

Lars Svendsen accompanied me to the door and bade me a measured farewell, as though he had been contaminated by his wife. And that wasn't so surprising. These things tend to go in families.

Before leaving, I asked him: 'You don't place any importance on these New Year games either?'

'No, as I said … the New Year means ski-jumping. Nothing else.'

'With an Austrian on the podium?'

'That kind of thing.'

'Well … If anything should occur to either of you, here's my card.' I passed it to him, and he stuffed it into his pocket without a second glance. So far, so bad. There was obviously nothing else to be gleaned here. Not today.

17

I crossed the yard and rang the bell at Maja Misvær's. She opened the door at once. When she saw who it was she exclaimed: 'Oh! Have you got anywhere?'

'Not yet, I'm afraid. But I realised … I'd forgotten to take the photo you promised me.'

'Yes, what a nuisance. It struck me after you'd gone. Come in!'

I followed her through the hall into the sitting room, where the television was on, but the volume was so low it was hard to hear what was being said on the screen. On the coffee table was an open newspaper next to a cup of coffee.

She pointed to the cup. 'Would you like a coffee?'

'Yes, please, but only if you've got some on the go.'

She nodded and went into the kitchen. Immediately afterwards she returned with the jug from the machine. The coffee looked black and bitter, like a poisoned chalice from the beyond served by a brimstone preacher on the first Sunday of a fast.

She poured me a cup, was off again and returned with a copy of the photo of Mette that was on the sideboard. 'So that we don't forget this time,' she said, pushing it across the table to me.

I took it, held it up and looked at it. A sweet little girl with a big smile, a gap between her front teeth, wild hair and eyes full of life. In her arms she was holding a battered teddy. Two or three years old, without a thought for the life that lay ahead of her – or perhaps didn't. It was hard to understand why anyone would want to harm such a small creature, let alone actually do it. I recognised the feeling I'd had when I was in child welfare. Mistreating a child, killing a child – for me they were still the most heinous of all crimes, actions that were difficult, not to say impossible, to forgive, a script so dark in a book so sombre that no one would want to open it. I felt a shudder go through me, like frost. And I knew what it was. I had experienced it before. The frost was the incomprehensible, the coldness of a foreshortened life.

She watched me in silence. Finally, she said: 'You … can see her?'

I raised my eyes and met hers. 'Yes, I've worked in child welfare in my time and have experienced the fates of many children. But…' I raised the photo. 'There's nothing to suggest any mistreatment here. Mette looks like a perfectly normal, happy little child.'

'She was!'

'All the more baffling, isn't it.'

She nodded. 'Yes! It is.'

'But…' Again I raised the photo. 'This cuddly toy…'

'Yes, her teddy.'

'You said something, the first time you told me what happened, you said she would never have left it behind voluntarily.'

She nodded and swallowed.

'Does that mean … you still have it?'

'No, I … Not anymore.'

I watched her, waited for her to continue.

'It … I left it outside, so that she would see it … I mean, so that it would be the first thing she saw when she came back. But … she didn't come back and one day it was gone.'

'It was gone?'

'Yes, but … I thought … perhaps the crows had taken it.'

'The crows?'

'Yes.' Again she swallowed, as though it was difficult for her to speak. 'One morning I was woken up by the sound of crows outside. Then I went to the window and looked out … there were lots of them in and around the sandpit and one of them was pecking at the teddy. I opened the window to shoo them away and they flew off.'

'But…'

'The following day it was gone. The teddy.'

'And you think it was the crows that took it?'

'Who else could it have been?'

'Mm.'

We sat in silence for some minutes. Then I spoke up again. 'Well ... At any rate, I've started my investigation. It might be a good idea if I interview some of the people here without their partners, so I have a couple of questions for you.'

'Oh, yes?' She looked at me, a little confused. 'Who in particular?'

'Synnøve Stangeland. She was a teacher, wasn't she? Do you know which school she's at?'

'It's a secondary school. I think it's Gimle.'

I made a note. 'And Helle Fylling, where is she employed?'

'An accountant's office in the centre somewhere, but I've no idea what it's called, I'm afraid. Why ... What are you wondering?'

I shrugged. 'Well, as I said to you earlier today ... I'll try and speak to everyone who was living here then. See if I can find something no one has considered before.' I tried a new angle with the photo. 'You know all about Jesper Janevik, don't you?'

She blanched. 'The man who was arrested, yes. But the police said it was a blind alley. Have you discovered anything else?'

'No, no. But I'm going to pay him a call. What I wanted to ask you was ... Do you remember him being here at all? Earlier, I mean.'

'Before ... Mette?'

'Yes.'

'No. It came like a bolt from the blue when we heard there was a ... one of his sort had been here. At once there was a bit of a commotion. I think Svein and Synnøve felt they'd been hung out to dry, as though everything was their fault. Truls...'

'Yes? Your husband...'

'He went over there the second he heard and I don't think he minced his words. He apologised to them later when it was clear there was nothing to it, but ... the relationship with Svein and Synnøve was never the same. It's odd they stayed.'

'Yes.'

Again we sat in silence. I tasted the coffee. It was as expected – more bitter than broken New Year resolutions. That gave me the link.

'One of the neighbours mentioned something about "New Year games". I watched her. She looked taken aback. 'Can you tell me what he meant by that, Maja?'

'New Year games? What … who mentioned it?'

'It was Stangeland.'

Her mouth twitched. 'I see. That's got nothing to do with Mette.'

'No? That's what Helle Fylling said, too. But neither of them will fill me in on the details.'

'… It was a … party game.'

I leaned forward. 'Right. And what sort of game?'

She shook her head. 'It's got nothing to do with this, Veum. It's not worth talking about. I'd rather not … say anything.'

I sat looking at her, expectant. In the end she glared at me. 'Yes? Anything else?'

'I'd like to talk to your ex-husband too. You said he'd moved to Oslo, but you didn't say what he does.'

'Truls is an electrical engineer. Nowadays he's working for a large company. They've got a branch in Bergen, but the headquarters is in Oslo, and when he was promoted, naturally, he moved there. He's a director, but not the overall boss.'

'Well, there's no shortage of directors in that business. What's the name of the company?'

'Magnor Data. The headquarters is in Aker Brygge.'

'As is only right and seemly. Do you think he'll talk to me?'

'I can't imagine why not. He'll be just as interested in finding out about Mette as I am.'

'Then I'll go to Oslo in the next few days.'

'That's fine. Just put it on the bill. I've got money.'

I nodded. 'Is there anything else you can tell me, anything at all?'

Her mouth tightened. 'No.'

I got up, and she followed suit. I walked towards the front door. It could have been a well-rehearsed cabaret number, but there was no response from the auditorium and after she had quietly closed the door behind me, no one got up and applauded.

There was still light and life behind the windows of all the houses in Solstølen Co-op, but they all had their own pasts to ponder and no one had come up with anything important. The person who had divulged most so far was Randi Hagenberg and she had threatened to call security if I went back. But now I had more questions to ask her and so there was only one solution: wait until her working day was over.

18

The staff entrance to Kløverhuset faced Strandkaien. I had waited in the bitter evening wind on the opposite side of the street for more than three quarters of an hour before she finally appeared with two other women, presumably from other shops in the mall. They stood chatting before going off in separate directions, two towards Torget, Randi towards Nordnes.

I crossed the street, accelerated my pace and caught her up half a block later, walking towards Murhjørnet. 'Sorry! Randi...'

She stopped suddenly, turned round and glared at me with furious eyes. 'Didn't I tell you? The next time I'd call the...' She cast around. 'I'll shout for help if you try anything.'

I held my hands up in the air. 'I have no intention of trying anything on anyone. There's just one thing I have to ask you. It's about these bloody New Year party games.'

Once again I had a very clear reaction, and this was the fiercest so far. Randi Hagenberg looked as if I had slapped her. 'What! So you've heard about that too! Who told you? Not Terje, I assume.'

'Terje Torbeinsvik?'

She curled her lips as if she had a piece of rotten meat in her mouth. 'Yes, the master architect!'

'No...'

'Can't you understand that I don't want to talk about this?'

I had heard people say such things to me before and the conversation ended with the opposite, so I sagely kept my mouth shut.

'Do you understand?'

'I know it can be difficult.'

She looked to the left and the right. 'Is there somewhere we can go?'

The Sahara had opened a new branch in my mouth. 'There's a bar close by.' I nodded towards Strandkaien.

She nodded briefly. 'Let's go there.'

There were big changes going on in the building where I had my office. The hotel which for many years had been on the top two floors in this and the next building had now taken over the whole of the adjacent building, moved reception down to street level and the bar to the first floor. In addition, plans were ready for making the whole of Strand-kaien 2 into a hotel. I had been sent a formal letter about it by the owner, informing me that the hotel manager would contact me. So far I hadn't heard anything, but I had been to my bank box and taken out the rental agreement that promised me a stipulated right to the office in the build-ing for as long as I lived, made a photocopy and returned with it to my office to await developments. Three years ago I had lost my girlfriend. If I were also to lose my office now it would feel as if my life was collapsing around me.

The bar might have been moved down three floors, but the staff were the same and the bartender with the red braces kindly ushered us to a discreet table in an unoccupied corner and took our orders.

'A beer and a Simers,' I said with desert sand on my tongue.

'A glass of white wine, semi-dry,' she said, rolling her eyes as though she had been tricked into something she would have preferred to avoid.

The bartender nodded and smiled, and disappeared like a genie from a lamp. Not long afterwards he was back with our glasses, placed them carefully on the table, winked jovially at me and withdrew quietly, as though giving space for a wish to be fulfilled.

I took a long draught from the beer glass and it felt as if I had found an oasis in the desert. Then I lifted the aquavit glass and drank deeply. For a second or two I had to close my eyes. I was sailing into a harbour I had left much too long ago, and on the quay stood people I hadn't seen for years, who received me with cheering so quiet that I could hear my pulse throbbing in my ears.

Randi Hagenberg sipped from her glass of wine, shot me an ironic glance and said: 'Shall we get to the nitty-gritty?'

I quickly put down my glass. 'Yes.'

Then her lips tightened. 'But I won't say a word unless you tell me who told you about this.' As I didn't answer she defined 'this'. 'The New Year party games.'

'Well … it was … Svein Stangeland.'

A little grimace revealed what she thought about that. 'Right. I see. Yes, they went home.'

'Yes, he said something like that.'

A silence fell between us. I took another swig of beer, but left the aquavit this time. 'Would you tell me what this was all about?'

She stared into the air. Then she shrugged. 'Well, *I* didn't do anything wrong.'

'No?'

It was New Year's Eve 1976 and midnight had passed. It had been bitingly cold for Bergen, the thermometer had sunk to well below zero. All the adults were gathered in the function room in the architect's house for the annual New Year party. The youngsters were asleep and the eldest children had been sent to bed, now the fireworks were over. Tor was the most practical and he had organised the display in the yard. Not much had been fired skywards and several of the families hadn't enjoyed it, but Tor had been unstoppable. *'The young ones have to have a bit of fun too!'* he had said, looking around with a big grin on his face.

Vibeke had finished her stint at the theatre and got back at half past eleven, dressed in some dramatic creation, red and black with a split at the side that went right up to her hip bone. She rubbed her hands theatrically as though she still had King Duncan's blood on them, and when Terje asked why she was so late she said with an intentionally ambiguous smile: 'We had a glass of champers … afterwards…'

Champagne corks were popping in the function room as well. The food was eaten, they had danced, and spirits were high when Terje tapped his glass at around half past twelve. He kept tapping but it was only when Vibeke started clapping her hands beside him that he had the group's attention.

Randi had looked around. Clothes maketh the man, the proverb went, but it was usually the opposite, people chose an outfit that reflected their character. Terje stood on the low podium with a big, red bow-tie he had tied by hand, a white shirt with a kind of golden lily pattern and a dark-green velvet suit. He had pulled Vibeke up with him. She towered above them with her red hair, long white neck and dramatic costume. At the side of the room stood Svein and Synnøve, Svein in a dark suit and silver tie, Synnøve in an attractive brown dress, both of them wearing slightly reserved expressions. Tor was dressed in a way which Terje had earlier in the evening somewhat heartlessly called 'Striler boy with ambitions': Striler were people who lived outside Bergen – he wore a dark suit with stripes, cream shirt and a checked silk scarf tied casually around his neck. He was so loud that Helle regularly had to tell him to quieten down. Helle herself was tastefully attired in a black, waisted trouser suit with a black-and-white spotted blouse under her jacket. Truls had put on a dinner jacket and was decidedly the most elegant of the men, and Maja didn't look half-bad either, in a tight-fitting black blouse and a multi-coloured skirt which flew when she swung round, dancing. Randi herself and Nils were dressed in black, him in a black suit with a blue tie, her in 'a little black number', so short that she showed a maximum of what she knew was her best feature, her attractive legs. When she had danced with Tor earlier in the evening, he had patted her on the bottom and said the same: 'The best legs in the room, Randi...'

'We've decided it's time for a party game,' Terje said from the podium once he finally had everyone's attention.

'We?' said Vibeke, looking at him askance.

'Listen to him! Listen to him!' Tor shouted.

'We're calling this the New Year games,' Terje continued.

Everyone was attentive now. This was something new. It was true they had tried something similar a couple of years ago, a miming game where you had to guess the titles of famous songs, films, books or plays, but Vibeke and Terje had been so much better than anyone else that the others were soon sick of it and the experiment had never been repeated.

'Not the same as the last one, I hope!' Tor heckled.

'No,' Terje said, with a smirk. 'This is something new. Something … quite different.' For a second he stood scanning the audience with a look Randi found difficult to interpret, but which gave her a strange disquiet in her stomach, as though she guessed what was about to come…

'It came as a shock to us all, of course,' she said, before grasping her wine glass and taking a good swig this time. She swallowed and continued: 'Or a surprise. Even Vibeke was visibly taken aback, although she tried to conceal it. But the people who reacted strongest were Svein and Synnøve. That is, it was probably more Svein. Synnøve rarely had anything to say.'

Svein reacted at once. 'What? Are you out of your mind, man? Who do you think we are?'

Terje didn't move, he watched him with a little wry smile.

Svein turned to everyone. 'And the rest of you? Are you going to join in this madness? All of you?'

She followed his gaze round. Something happened to the party after he had made his suggestion. One of the couples – Nils and herself – had somehow moved closer together. The others had moved slightly apart, as though everyone found themselves in isolation, unique and abandoned at the same time.

Svein grabbed Synnøve's hand, turned and said aloud: 'We're going home, anyway! Come on, Synne!' In the doorway he stopped and looked back. In a loud voice he announced: 'And a Happy New Year to you all!' The sarcasm was tangible. When the door closed behind them, people looked at one another, and a nervous, tremulous laughter spread through those present. Even Tor was obviously caught off guard.

'Well, are you ready?' Terje shouted from the podium. 'Shall we start drawing lots?'

Randi paused as the barman came in and took my empty glasses. We waited until he had brought back two fresh ones before continuing the conversation.

'So what were the New Year games?' I said.

She nodded without speaking.

'You had to draw lots to find out ... who you would spend New Year's night with,' I prompted.

She took a deep breath. 'Yes. He stood there ... and there wasn't a man in the room who didn't want ... the main prize.'

'You mean ... Vibeke Waaler?'

'Yes, I do mean her!'

By now Vibeke had got over her initial surprise as well. She had been standing on the podium with one hand on her hip, a split up her dress and the tip of her tongue in the corner of her mouth. She scanned the room and the three men stood there like trained dogs staring up at the podium: Truls with his nostrils quivering, Tor with his jaw hanging down, Randi's own Nils with an expectant smile on his face. On the stage Terje, smiling his dubious smile, eyed one woman after the other, all of them except the wife who was standing next to him.

'But ... we could end up with ... our own partner, could we?' Randi said.

'No. In that case you would have to draw a new lot.' There were two bowls with five slips of paper in each, one in each colour. But when Svein and Synnøve left he took a slip from each of the bowls, the same colour, so now there were only four left.

'Everyone ready for the draw?' Terje shouted from the podium. 'Anyone else want to go home?'

Again hurried glances went from husband to wife and back, but no one budged; everyone was prepared to ... well, they were all ready.'

'Afterwards I often thought ... What made us act as we did? But I think ... it must have been the champagne. We were all ... how shall I put it ... a bit merry and frivolous. And I suppose it must have been the excitement of the suggestion. The titillation of it. I mean ... we'd all been married for a few years. Or been living together. Everyone except Terje and Vibeke had children. Perhaps ... I'm not complaining. Nils and I were happy together, in all ways, I think. But ... maybe that wasn't true for everyone. And ... that was a special time, from a historical perspective. Women had become freer, more independent. Perhaps we would finally experience some of the freedom men had had for generations. I suppose we all had our family histories … which we'd heard about, I mean…'

She examined my face, as though I had one to contribute as well.

'Certainly,' I said, gesticulating agreement. 'You don't need to apologise to me. I've been single and divorced for most of my life, so I have my own skeletons in the cupboard. Both while I was married and unmarried, so to speak.'

She nodded. 'See. There's no reason for anyone to get on their high horse.'

'No, can you see any?'

'Any what?'

'Horses?'

'Well – no…' For the first time she gave me the trace of a smile, as though we had at last found some common ground in humour.

'Let's raise our glasses for a toast first!' Terje roared from above. 'One for all and all for one!' And then he added a little slogan for the event: 'Variety is the spice of life, isn't that what they say?'

Then the drawing of lots began.

19

Rarely had a glass of beer and an aquavit tasted as good as on this Tuesday evening. The malty flavour of the beer and the strong infiltration of caraway in Simers Taffel lay like a reflection of an autumnal landscape in my mouth, red and yellow leaves mirrored in a dark watery surface, so dark that you could hardly imagine the depths it concealed.

I looked at Randi Hagenberg in the same tight green dress as earlier in the day, with the brown belt around her waist and the slim body that looked younger than the slender, careworn face, where not even judicious make-up could camouflage the fact that it had seen its best years. She had long passed fifty, perhaps even more, winters. But at that time, twenty-five years ago, she must have been something of a trophy too.

'So … how did the draw go?'

At once there was silence in the room. The last cassette had finished and no one had bothered with another.

'Let's start with the gentlemen,' Terje said. 'Nils! Would you like to come up here?'

Nils, at sixes and sevens, looked around him. 'Me? But … I didn't quite understand … How's this supposed to work?'

'Just come up here and we'll sort it out.'

'OK …' He looked in her direction, almost apologetically, but she just nodded for him to go on up, she encouraged him.

Vibeke was holding up the yellow bowl in an elegant pose that emphasised the shape of her breasts, and Nils fumbled like a confirmation candidate as he reached for the bowl, put his fingers in and drew the first slip of paper. It was red. He stood holding it in the air, embarrassed. 'Red,' he said, as though he were telling them something they couldn't see.

'Now the first lady.' Terje looked around. 'Perhaps you'd like to accompany Nils, Randi?'

As she went up to the stage she felt for the first time that evening that her skirt was too short. She discreetly pulled at the hems, not that it helped much, and to her it was as though she could feel the gazes of the three men below brushing her calves, knees, thighs and – in their imaginations – even higher.

She met Vibeke's eyes. They were both redheads, but Randi's colour was genuine. Vibeke's hair was dyed for her role; normally she was blonde. The look she received was provocative, almost feverish, as though she wished she…

Randi turned to Terje, who was holding the red bowl in the air. He looked at her with the same smile he had worn all evening, and with a shudder she imagined what it would be like to be kissed by him, with that beard of his … then she stretched up and drew a slip of paper. 'Blue!'

'No re-draw necessary then. But so far we don't have a couple either. Tor! It's your turn…'

Tor came to life. He winked at Randi before stepping up to the podium with quick, manly strides, walking directly towards Vibeke, putting one arm around her waist and, with his other hand, stretching up to the bowl she was holding aloft. When he held out the slip of paper you could read the disappointment on his face. 'Pink!'

'We'll do as we did before. Now it's your wife's turn. Helle…'

Helle came forward, slight more tentatively in her posture than her husband had been. She drew a slip: 'Red.'

Four eyes met. Nils looked at Helle. Helle looked at Tor, and then at Nils. Nils shifted his gaze from Tor and finally to Helle.

Terje clapped his hands and Vibeke joined in. 'The first couple has been formed! Helle and Nils…'

Nils still looked embarrassed. 'Well, shall we … erm … go, do you think?'

'Yes, unless you want to follow the rest of the draw, then…'

'Yes, we'd…'

'… Like to,' Helle added.

'Good! Then I suggest you go next, Truls.'

Truls went up and drew: 'Green.'

'The tension's mounting!' Terje shouted. 'Maja!'

Maja glided across the floor and up on to the stage with an almost supernatural, fairy-like movement. Terje held the red bowl above her head.

'Not so high, if you don't mind.'

He lowered the bowl a fraction; she stretched up and took a slip of paper. Without a word, she held it up.

'Pink!' Terje called out. 'Tor and Maja! Another couple.'

Their eyes met, and they smiled, a little bewildered, both of them, as if this wasn't an option they had considered.

Terje continued regardless: 'There are not many lots left.' He looked from Vibeke to Truls and said: 'Actually the rest is obvious, but we'll have to carry on so that everyone can see that everything's above board.'

They chose. Vibeke drew green and he held up the last slip of paper: 'Blue!'

I tried to follow as well as I could. I took out my notebook and wrote as I talked. 'In other words … correct me if I'm wrong. Truls Misvær won the main prize, as you put it: Vibeke Waaler.'

She nodded.

'Your husband got Helle Fylling. So it was Tor Fylling and … Maja. And you ended up with Terje Torbeinsvik.'

She bristled with annoyance. Either she regretted having told me so much or there was something awful she was trying to shake off. 'But what does this have to do with the Mette Case? I really don't understand!'

'Nor me … yet. So … what happened?'

'What happened? What do you mean?'

'Well, I was thinking about … You must have had some kind of system for … the game. There were small children in most of the houses, weren't there?'

'Ah, I see…' Again her eyes wandered. 'Yes, he'd devised some rules. We had about five hours, from about one till six. So it was off to the marital bed. And we went back to the women's houses. That was because Terje thought that if any of the children woke up it would be more reassuring for them – and probably most normal, as he said in his usual sarcastic way – for the mother to look after them.'

'Five hours of New Year's fun and games, in other words.'

'You don't need to rub salt into the wound. It was nothing to get excited about, I can tell you.'

'No? But you said before … that you didn't do anything wrong, anyway.'

She looked past me with a film of frost over her eyes. 'No, *I* didn't…'

'But others … did?'

She suddenly leaned forward and snarled at me so I recoiled against the back of the chair. 'I was raped!'

'You were…?'

'By Terje Torbeinsvik, yes. When it came to the crunch I didn't damn well want … he wasn't particularly attractive with all that beard and hair, and when he started groping me … my stomach turned. I said…

'No, Terje! I don't want to! Stop it!'

'You don't want to? You've got no choice! I won you.'

'You won me?!'

'You didn't object before! You could have gone on your way, as Svein and Synnøve did! Come on. I won't hurt you! I'll do it better than you've ever…'

'I'm telling you, no. No, no, no…'

But he had put his hand over her mouth – 'You'll wake your kids!' – and lifted up her skirt and pulled down her knickers and…

At once she had tears in her eyes. 'It was terrible. The worst thing I've ever experienced! And he didn't stop after the first time. Twice more he forced himself on me. And I just gave up. I lay there, passive, taking it, crossing my fingers and praying Joachim and Janne wouldn't wake up and come in…'

'But … you could have reported him.'

'Oh, yes. Three cheers for little me. Of course I could have reported him, Veum. And you know how rape victims are treated. I'd agreed to it, hadn't I? He'd won me, as he put it! No, I just had to grit my teeth and keep my mouth shut. And that's what I'd done … until now.'

'But … your husband. You must have told him?'

'Nils! Are you crazy? He came home at six as happy and bewildered as he'd been all New Year's Eve. I don't think he understood any of what happened.'

'But … you split up?'

'Yes. After a few years. That night destroyed so much. Now perhaps you understand a bit better why things went as they did up there. Why we're all divorced, except for Svein and Synnøve – who went home. They did the right thing. That's what we all should have done. And now he's dead.'

'Nils, yes.'

'And this has nothing to do with Mette?'

'No, there's no reason to believe it has. But … did Nils say how he and Helle Fylling got on?'

Again she rolled her eyes. 'Oh, yes. He came home happy and content with the world's best conscience, he said.'

'Really?'

'They had just chatted, he said. Helle and him. He'd never had such a good chat with her before, so, as far as he was concerned, we could happily repeat this game.'

'But you didn't?'

'No, you can bet your life we didn't. It was never mentioned again – and from that day on until you heard about it from Svein Stangeland I don't think one of us ever brought up the subject. We just put it behind us and that's where it should have stayed, Veum. Do you understand?' Again she sent me an accusatory look. 'And now I'm off.'

I stood up. 'Let me get you a…'

'And I don't need to be taken home, either. Thanks, but no thanks!' She grabbed her coat, which she had hung over the back of her chair, took her bag and opened it, found a hundred-kroner note and flung it onto the table in front of us. 'This should cover the wine.'

'Yes, but let me…'

'Goodnight, Veum! And let me repeat what I said last time. Next time I'll call security. Have you got that?'

I nodded and plumped back heavily in my chair.

It wasn't long before the bartender reappeared. 'Another round?' he said sympathetically, as though assuming I had been given the elbow; it was a fairly accurate assessment of the situation, although there hadn't been such strong feelings at play, from her side or mine.

'Please,' I said feebly, and lowered my head to meet the storm, as I was wont to do.

Late the same night I stumbled back up to Telthussmauet. I had been given a lot to chew on. In my mind's eye I tried to visualise them as they crossed the dark yard at Solstølen Co-op, as the New Year's rockets were still crackling in the winter sky that frosty night twenty-five years ago. Tor Fylling had gone home with Maja Misvær, while her husband, Truls, perhaps only had to take the indoor route to Vibeke Waaler's bedroom and whatever happened there. Nils Bringeland joined Helle Fylling, with whom he had chatted for the rest of the night, according to what he had said. And Terje Torbeinsvik … Yes, he became a rapist overnight with Randi Hagenberg as his involuntary victim, if I was to take her at her word. And why shouldn't I?

On this night there were no stars and no fireworks being set off. Like the lonesome wolf I was, I sought my lair up the mountainside, with a good view of the town but practically no insight into what I was supposed to be finding out: what happened to Mette Misvær on that September day in 1977? Did it have anything to do with the New Year game eight or nine months earlier?

I staggered up the stairs to my flat. There I unscrewed the top of a new bottle of aquavit, put it to my mouth and drank deeply, as though it was life I was imbibing – or death. Because you could hardly get closer. The liquid burned like phosphorus in my throat, flames from hell. Next morning I found myself lying on the floor by my bed, clueless as to how I had got there and without a clear thought in my head.

20

It was the dream that had woken me. I had my head between Karin's legs and was luxuriating in her velvet charms when suddenly she began to resist, and when I looked up it was Randi Hagenberg lying there, writhing madly as she slapped my face and pushed me away. I got up and stumbled towards the half-open door, where I bumped into Sølvi Hegge, who, elegant and stylishly dressed, stood disdainfully surveying my naked body, my member jutting out like a gnarled twig. She leaned forward, as if to kiss me, when a powerful blow struck me on the head and propelled me out of the dream. I lay huddled on the floor, bathed in cold sweat and with rotating lava in my abdominal region.

I crawled to the bathroom and leaned over the toilet bowl. The eruption started with cramp-like pains that washed up from deep in my body to my scalp. I spewed like a marathon runner after passing the tape, my last remaining strength gone.

After I had finally finished I poured cold water over my head, let the water run, drank straight from my hands and rinsed my mouth as best I could. Then I staggered into my bedroom, got into bed this time and collapsed in a restless semi-doze from which I didn't wake until late in the day. Even after opening my eyes I found it difficult to get out of bed.

I could feel the symptoms again. When I flew home, after Karin had been buried, I drank steadily, on average between two and three bottles a week. This put strains on both my finances and my health: the former causing me to take on jobs I normally wouldn't touch with a barge pole; the latter such that I only managed occasionally to complete the seasoned running pattern I had – three times a week. The result was that my bank balance was catastrophic and my physical shape the worst I had been in since the early 1960s. My moral state was even worse.

The infidelity cases I had taken on for well-heeled clients, but deceived spouses nonetheless, had left me with an even more bitter taste in my mouth than the one I woke up with most mornings. And some of the women I had slept with over the past two years I had pasted into my book of oblivion for all eternity, hoping I would never meet them again. Several of them had been paid for the services they rendered, with varying degrees of TLC. When I looked at myself in the mirror on such mornings, I turned away sharply, and the days I arrived at the office, unshaven and unkempt for the same reason, were not inconsiderable. It didn't make any difference anyway. Clients in office hours were few and far between.

I had tried to break out of this pattern many times, but abstinence laid its clammy fingers around my throat, lifted me up and shook me until I was gasping for more alcohol and grabbed blindly at a bottle of aquavit. My mouth was dry, cold sweat ran down my body and I was dizzy in the street. A couple of times I experienced what I defined afterwards as panic attacks. I couldn't breathe. It was as though my legs wouldn't move beneath me, my heart throbbed, my pulse mercilessly pumped blood through my veins at a much higher rate than normal, and I wondered where this would end. For an instant I was convinced I was going to die there and then. So I closed my eyes, took deep, regular breaths, talked calmly to myself and slowly got myself moving again. On several occasions I noticed the same angst at the exact same locations where I had experienced the panic attack the first time, so gradually I began to give these places a wide berth, as though it was the geography that had induced this intense distress.

For long periods I was feverish and uneasy, and when I finally got home and hit the hay it was impossible to sleep. Often I wandered restlessly through the town at night, blessed by the darkness but pursued by demons. They whirled around my head, whispering her name mockingly in my ears: Karin, Kar-in, Kar-iin ... I went to the tip of Nordnes peninsula, clambered down to what we, in our childhood years, called Balangen, the remains of the old ballast quay, stood on the slippery rocks, listened to the waves splashing around my feet and thought how wonderful it would be: just to let go, dive in and start swimming ... into the darkness, across the border, to see if we would meet there after all, on the other side. But I didn't. There was still something holding me back. Thomas, Mari and...

One day eighteen months before I had flown down to Stavanger to visit my ex-wife Beate. I'd had my hair cut, shaved and stayed sober for several days. Nevertheless, she scrutinised me sceptically when we met at a café by the market square, with a view of Alexander Kielland and the cathedral.

'You look terrible, Varg,' she said. 'A mess.' But not as in the messes we'd had at least twice before, after the divorce: once in Bergen and once in Løten. With unfinished business and another illusion shattered I travelled back to Bergen. 'I've got someone else now, Varg. A true friend,' she had told me. 'And what's his name?' 'Her name's Regine,' she had said with the smirk I had known so well a long time ago.

Then it was back to the bottle. One open and a second in prospect, until empties clinked wherever I turned, whether at home or in the office. I was the emperor of the empties, and I had hundreds of vassals, empty, silent and glassy-eyed.

But now for the first time in three years I had a case that occupied my mind. There were some thin threads I felt I was slowly beginning to unravel. Tiny Mette Misvær, who disappeared from her home twenty-five years ago. Her parents' and others' lively – or not quite so lively – New Year fun and games. A robbery with fatal consequences for someone who was in all probability a casual passer-by. A possible sex criminal. An unknown killer.

What had been said between Nils Bringeland and the robbers? Was there anyone who could tell me? The two women from Askøy who had been customers at the jeweller's? And what did the other neighbours in Solstølen have to say to about the fun and games? What had happened behind the other closed doors, which, nine months later, had repercussions for tiny Mette?

I got back on my feet, determined to defeat my weaker self. In the kitchen I opened a cupboard, felt in the right-hand corner at the back, where I kept an unopened bottle in reserve. Just having the neck of the bottle between my fingers was enough to make me gasp for air and the sweat to come pouring down again.

I closed my eyes, took a deep breath and opened them again. Then I put the bottle down on the worktop and left it there. I boiled some water, brewed myself a cup of tea, thinner than a New Year's resolution after three months, buttered some crispbreads and manned up for a simple meal, all with the shiny bottle in the corner of my eye, absolutely determined to ignore it. When I sat down at the worktop I stared into the whites of its eyes, chewing the crunchy crispbreads and washing them down with tea and pretending I was living the life of Riley while actually at rock bottom.

I won the first skirmish. The bottle stood on the worktop untouched, and I left it where it was, like a kind of *memento mori* for the days to come. I went back into the sitting room, opened my laptop and started hunting for addresses on the net.

Tor Fylling had two addresses close to each other in Fjell, on the larger of the two Sotra islands: one was the garage he ran, Fylling Bil Dekk & Karrosseri.

Vibeke Waaler lived in Oslo, in Professor Dahls gate.

Truls Misvær had an address in Nesodden, the peninsula accessible by ferry from Oslo.

Håkon Misvær lived in Ålesund, in Ivar Aasens gate.

The woman whose name was mentioned in the newspapers after the Bryggen robbery, Liv Grethe Heggvoll, was resident on Askøy, with an Ask postal code.

I couldn't find an address for Jesper Janevik, nor any other information about him. But he was a cousin of Synnøve Stangeland, who taught at Gimle School, if Maja Misvær's memory was reliable. And there she wouldn't have her husband hovering over her. I moved her name to the top of the list and decided to start with her.

There was another possibility. Late that afternoon I rang Karin's colleague at the National Registration Office. She didn't object to my enquiry. 'This is easier than ever now, with the new computer system,' she said. I heard her pressing a few keys and soon afterwards she had a result. 'The only address we have for him, for Janevik, is on Askøy. Postal code Ask. As far as I can see, he's lived there all his life.'

I thanked her warmly for her help and jotted down: *Ask*, with a thick line underneath. Another invisible thread, a coincidence no one had expected to stumble over.

I didn't get much more done that day. In the evening I donned a track suit, walked up to Fjellveien and ran from there to the bottom of Isdalen and back again. Nothing more than water passed my lips before I went to bed and the next morning I was in pretty decent shape. At least I was in shape to drive, and the first stop was Gimle School, where I assumed they started early in the morning, as bright-eyed and bushy-tailed as I felt on this chilly Thursday in March with hail in the gutters and no obvious signs of spring.

21

Gimle School stood in what seemed to be the Catholic part of Bergen, as all the streets were named after saints. The classic 1960s building with three floors and a flat roof was in St Olavs vei. I found my way to the staff room, where I was informed that Synnøve Stangeland was already teaching, but if I didn't mind waiting, I was welcome to do so. I replied that I would prefer to go for a walk and return in the next break.

Hence I had an additional half-hour to speculate about the choice of street names. In the closest vicinity I found St Halvards vei, St Torfinns vei and St Sunnivas vei. In Norse mythology Gimle was the name of the golden-roofed hall where righteous men would spend eternity in the company of Odin. Thus, the area was a bizarre mix of Norse faith in gods and Catholic worship of saints. A committee with an immense sense of irony must have been behind this project.

South of the school was a sports arena, Haukelandshallen, and Brann Football Stadium with its training facilities. There, naturally enough, the symbolism changed, streets were named after sports and such heroic polar explorers as Amundsen and Nansen and their ships, Fram and Gjøa. I wasn't going to either the South or the North Pole though, but back to Gimle, where I would spend a break with Synnøve Stangeland in the school playground with a view of Mount Ulriken, on which you could see the last snow around the TV mast at the top, like a cake decoration.

She had insisted we should talk outside. She had looked at me with sceptical eyes behind her narrow glasses when I referred to the brief meeting with her husband two days ago. 'Yes, that's right. You were a …'

'Jehovah's Witness, your husband said. But I'm afraid that's not true.

I'm a private investigator and I'm taking a closer look at the Mette Case, which you might remember.'

She asked me to wait while she fetched her coat. On our way down the steps she said: 'Of course I remember it! But why did he say you were...?'

I shrugged. 'You'd best ask him that.'

'But ... I have nothing to tell you – as Svein's already said.'

'But you didn't hear what he said.'

'No, I didn't. So?'

'Well, I was only thinking ... you might have something to add.'

'And what might that be? It was a terrible tragedy. I still think about it regularly. How painful it must be to lose a child, and in this case ... Not even knowing what happened to her, where she ... is. Even worse.'

'You were at home that day, weren't you?'

'No, we...' For a moment she looked away. 'We were ... at the cabin.'

I tried to catch her eye, but she was evasive. Around us, youngsters watched with curiosity written on their faces. Who was I? they wondered. Why was I talking to Fru Stangeland?

'Or weren't you?'

'Yes, we ... we all went there, but Svein ... had something to do in town, so he went back.'

I felt a muscle tauten in my neck. 'Oh, yes? But you didn't tell the police this?'

'Yes, we did ... I think.' Still she couldn't look me in the eye.

'What was it your husband had to do?'

'Well ... you'd best ask him that.'

For a second or two I thought of the telephone Randi Hagenberg had heard ringing – from the other side of the yard. But if it had been in their house, he hadn't been there either...

'Did you try to ring him that day? At home, I mean.'

Now I had eye contact, at last. But I read irritation there, as though I had given her what she had been expecting: a reason to react.

'Mm ... there was someone who heard a phone ringing and ringing that day – which no one answered.'

'Then it must have been in another house.'

'Yes. Probably.'

I waited, in case she wanted to add something. She pulled her coat tighter around her, as though she were cold. Under it she was wearing a loose, flowery tunic that hung over her dark-blue jeans and covered most of what she must have had beneath, so as not to overstimulate the imaginations of the hormonal male adolescents she taught. Not far from us some children were playing with a dark, skin-coloured basketball while a huddle of pale-faced kids admired their shooting skills. I wouldn't deny that I envied them a little too. My own shooting skills were far from impressive at the moment.

As she didn't say any more I continued carefully: 'A cousin of yours, Jesper Janevik, was in the frame for a while…'

Her neck flared up and her eyes glinted as she answered: 'And he was released! But … it destroyed our relationship for ever. I've hardly seen him since that time except for at … a couple of funerals. My parents' funerals. His parents died before. So at least they were spared it.'

'It?'

'Yes, there had been a few incidents … long ago.'

'And you're sure he didn't have anything to do with this?'

'Jesper wouldn't hurt a fly. The way he took care of his sister and his daughter, when she was alone, tells you everything. The cases he came under the spotlight for were … rumours and exaggeration. I know myself how kids of that age can fantasise about something that is completely innocent at the outset. And he was drawn into the Mette Case because he'd visited us a few times! No wonder he didn't want to set foot in our house afterwards!'

'But … couldn't you visit him?'

'It just felt unnatural. He didn't want anything to do with us. In a way, he blamed us.'

'For being drawn in?'

'Because we invited him up, yes. Otherwise, obviously, nothing would have happened. I mean … otherwise he wouldn't have come … under suspicion.'

'He lives on Askøy, I understand.'

'He lives in Janevik, which he has done ever since he was born.'

'In his childhood home?'

'Yes, in his childhood home.' She looked at her watch. 'I've got a lesson in a couple of minutes. Was there anything else?'

I thought quickly. 'No, not today. But maybe an—'

She interrupted me. 'I've got nothing more to say!'

'Not even "good luck"?'

'Good luck?'

'Yes, because, after so many years, you want the case cleared up too, don't you?'

'Yes, yes, of course.' But as she concluded the conversation her eyes betrayed her innermost thoughts: she didn't think I was up to it. With that she turned on her heel and walked with determined step back to her classes.

I strolled back to my car. There was a strong argument for me heading west for the next part of the investigation. First to Sotra and Fylling Bil Dekk & Karosseri, then to Askøy. Perhaps a trip to Haakonsvern and Svein Stangeland too.

As I pulled away from the kerb I noticed a dark-grey Audi A3 do the same a few cars behind. The Audi followed me up Ibsens gate and down towards Danmarks plass, and when I crossed over Sotra Bridge a quarter of an hour later, it was still in my wake, with a couple of vehicles between us. When I turned north from Ågotnes, it was still there. But when I braked to drive into Fylling Bil Dekk & Karosseri, it carried on and was soon out of view. The reflection from the car windows made it impossible to see who was inside or how many of them there were, but it made me wonder anyway: what I was doing wasn't *that* interesting – or was it? And if so, for whom?

22

There was a sense of paint-peeling decline about the garage hiding beneath the sign *Fylling Bil Dek & Karosseri*. Typically, the second 'k' in *Dekk* – tyres – was missing.

Around the two-storey building, in which the first-floor windows had curtains and flowers on the window sills, stood ten or so old cars with price tags behind the windscreens, and they weren't very high either. Sherlock Holmes-style, I deduced that someone was living on the floor above the garage and that the establishment also offered sec-ond-hand cars at a price that was unlikely to appeal to anyone except this year's school-leavers. Such low prices presaged trouble from the very first drive.

I parked my Corolla beside a rusty 1980s VW, which, to judge from its appearance, should have been cremated long ago, after a brief cer-emony. As I stepped out I checked the price: ten thousand kroner.

A garage door opened. A man in his fifties with a well-rounded taxi-driver's paunch, curly hair, greying around the ears, and a professional smile on full lips appeared beside me. 'Interested?'

'I've got a car.'

'Yes, I can see,' he mumbled with a side-glance at the Corolla. 'But perhaps you need one for madame?'

'And you think she'd like driving around in this?' I said, motioning towards the jalopy in front of us.

'Well, there are all sorts of women,' he said, with a chummy wink.

'Tor Fylling?'

His eyes instantly became more circumspect. 'Yes … and you are?'

'Varg Veum, private investigator.'

I let it sink in before continuing. I noticed his eyes quickly check the less-than-impressive array of cars. Were there some he hadn't registered perhaps?

'You're not from the tax authorities, are you?'

'No, nor from the Ministry of Transport. I'm investigating the circumstances surrounding Mette Misvær's disappearance in 1977.'

His eyes opened wide. 'Right! After so many years?'

'Yes. Her mother … You know her, don't you?'

His eyelids flickered a couple of times, as if to remove any sudden dust he had there. 'Maja.'

'Yes.'

I couldn't help thinking that these two had ended up together during what they called the New Year games of 1976. A somewhat odd couple, if you asked me, however … they had already known each other, they were neighbours in Mannsverk. What had they done that New Year's Eve? Sat chatting, like Nils Bringeland and Helle Fylling, or gone for it without ceremony, as Terje Torbeinsvik had done with Randi Hagenberg? Would any of them answer if I asked straight out?

'I'm not sure I can help, but … come in. We can't stand here getting cold.'

He led me into the garage through a door that could hardly have been washed for the last twenty years. Inside, there was a strong smell of oil and turpentine. From down in the service pit under a car at the front came the banging of metal on metal. In a glass cage at the back of the garage a woman sat looking at us: brown hair with strong, heavy-ish facial features, not that dissimilar to a female gorilla in a zoo. Crackly pop music from a not particularly discriminating radio station blared through the open door.

'Marita! Have you got two cups of coffee?' Tor Fylling shouted.

The woman nodded, got up from her seat and stood with her back to us for a few moments. The banging under the car in the middle of the floor stopped and a man in his early thirties, wearing oil-stained overalls and carrying a spanner, crawled up. His hair was darker than Fylling's, but otherwise he looked identical. 'What's up?'

'Nothing to do with you, Einar. Just someone who wants a chat with me.'

Einar Fylling looked suspiciously from his father to me and cast a glance at the glass box, where Marita had finished with the coffee machine and was on her way out with two mugs of steaming black coffee. The logo on the mug advertised a well-known car make.

Fylling nodded to her. 'Marita, my daughter-in-law. She takes care of the paperwork here.'

She nodded.

'And this is Varg Veum. He's a private investigator, he says. Working on a cold case. Nothing to do with us.'

Again I had a feeling that, early in the financial year, he was glad this wasn't a surprise morning visit from the tax authorities. I guessed their book-keeping was as rusty as the cars on the forecourt and with even more hidden blemishes.

I glanced at the young man. 'And this is your son, then?'

'This is Einar, yes.'

Einar nodded briefly, as if to confirm identification.

The father raised his voice. 'And he's busy!' He motioned to the car and Einar followed his gaze.

'I was just wondering if you needed any help,' he muttered, before slowly manoeuvring his way back into the pit.

'With what?' his father mumbled. 'The business doesn't run itself any longer and we have to hold on to the customers we have. But I'm glad Einar and Marita work here. I mean … they're the ones who will take over one day. They even live in the flat above, so they're all set up.'

Einar went back under the car with an unhappy expression on his face, and Marita didn't look that enthusiastic at the thought either. After handing over the mugs of coffee she withdrew to her glass box. The banging from the pit resumed.

Tor Fylling ushered me to a couple of chairs by a battered work table under a rear window. In the middle of the table was a tin ashtray with *Cinzano* written on it and so full of cigarette ends that it was like the cornucopia from hell, the Cancer Foundation's horror movie.

'As I said, I have no idea how I can help you. It was a terrible business, but it's quite a few years ago now. If Mette had been allowed to grow up she'd have been the age of … well…' He nodded towards the glass box. 'Marita, for example.'

'You were at home when it happened, weren't you?'

'Yes, I can remember it as if it were yesterday, literally. Maja came to the door and asked if I'd seen Mette. But I hadn't. Not then at any rate, and so she carried on looking. Later it became a huge operation and I joined in the search for her, but, as you know, without success.'

'Yes. Neither your wife nor your child was at home that day?'

'No, they were in town and couldn't help either.'

'Why weren't you with them?'

'Well, I … I had something to do in the house, there was a pipe that needed fixing, and anyway … shopping in town has always bored me, even when the kids were small.' He smiled wanly, as though he was really a little embarrassed about this.

'You knew Truls and Maja Misvær from…?'

'Yes, we were neighbours in Landås, and as far as I remember Mette was born right after they moved in there. I think Maja was well gone when they were moving. I helped Truls to sort things out. He wasn't much of a handyman.'

I nodded. 'How well did you know Maja?'

He frowned and looked at me in surprise. 'How well did I know … What do you mean?'

'Erm … I was thinking about the New Year games in 1976.'

He flushed a dark red. 'You're thinking about … Who the hell told you that? It can't have been Maja.'

'No, she didn't say anything. But several of the others did.'

'About Maja and me?'

'Well … What would they say about you two?'

'Nothing! I mean … nothing but … Tell me, did they really tell you about what went on that night? What an idea!'

'You're referring to what you called the New Year games?'

'We didn't call it that … Terje called it that! It was his idea.'

'And the result was…?'

'You must have heard that too? We each went off arm-in-arm with a new woman, happy and content. Except for one of the couples, that is. They went home before … lots were drawn.'

'Yes, I heard that.'

'I got Maja.'

'And how was that?'

He banged his mug down on the table so hard the ashtray jumped. 'None of your fuckin' business, Veum! That's a private matter. And anyway … what the hell's this got to do with Mette?'

'No? Could it have had something to do with her, do you think?'

'I haven't got a clue! But … it was obvious who … I told some of the lads at the time. Shall we go out to Askøy and knock the living shit out of him until he tells us what he did with her?'

'So you were sure it was him?'

'Who else could it have been? He had previous.'

'Did he?'

'That's what the word was.'

'I see. But you didn't do anything?'

'No, we … came to our senses. After all, it's the police's job to deal with all that sort of thing, and if it'd been him they'd have nailed him. No one knows what happened now.'

'Well, someone, or some people, know.'

He eyed me thoughtfully. 'Yes, you're probably right. Someone knows.'

'You and your wife got divorced some years afterwards…'

'Yes, and so what? Is that also s'posed to have something to do with…?'

'Perhaps with the New Year games anyway. You weren't the only couple to split up.'

'No, but let me tell you something, Veum. Helle and me had been on the slippery slope long before New Year – in fact, that was probably why neither of us went home when the suggestion came up. I mean … we no longer had anything to lose, emotionally like.'

I nodded without making any further comment. 'Mm … may I ask if you've seen Maja – or any of the others for that matter – since?'

He sent me a surprised look. 'Well, I lived there for a year after ... a year and a half. But then I moved out, and since then I haven't set foot there, apart from ... well, there was Einar's confirmation; that must have been in 1984. It was held in the communal ... the Function Room we called it.'

'Not once since then?'

'No. I've got more than enough to do here to keep the wheels turning, literally.' He scanned the wretched state of the workshop. Marita was sitting in the glass box with a mug of coffee to her lips as well now. The work didn't seem to be piling up there either.

As I left it struck me that, incredibly enough, there were perhaps businesses going even worse than my own. Most people had a car. But most people had worries too and they weren't beating down my door. Perhaps most people managed well enough on their own, as far as cars and worries were concerned.

As I came out to the forecourt a clapped-out, old Volvo drove to the garage. The car parked and a little squirt of a man jumped out; under his nose he had an unsymmetrical moustache resembling an oil stain. He was in his work gear and glanced at me with minimal interest as he ran into the building.

I got into my car, started up and turned right onto the main road. At Ågotnes I did a U-turn and faced the town again. I had seen what I wanted to see. The dark Audi was parked by the kerb thirty or forty metres down from Fylling Bil Dekk & Karosseri. I considered my options for a few seconds, then I pulled in behind it.

I sat behind the wheel looking at the Audi. Through the darkened glass I could see the silhouettes of two people at the front. They turned and looked back.

I opened the car door and got out. In my hand I had my notebook and I made it obvious I was writing down their registration number. Then both doors opened. Two guys came out, a kind of second-millennium version of Laurel and Hardy, but neither of them made me laugh.

The bigger one was the beefcake type, pumped up on anabolic steroids from his mother's milk, from what I could tell. He was wearing a black beanie over an apparently shaven skull; the look he shot me was heavy and unambiguous. He wore a kind of shiny red track suit, which was tight and revealed his bulging muscles, from his biceps down to his thighs.

The smaller of the two looked even more dangerous, it was the eyes that did it. I had seen eyes like his before, restless and irascible and always on the move. It was as though his whole body quivered with sublimated aggression, and I knew because of his size he was bound to have a knife or two up his sleeve to compensate for his muscular deficiencies. He was dressed for the occasion too, jeans and a light jacket, which allowed him maximum freedom of movement if he had to draw a knife. His face was pinched, his hair dark and slicked back, and his ears protruded conspicuously.

Laurel spoke up. 'And what the fuck d'you think you're doing?'

I looked at him. 'Me? I've always collected car registration numbers. Ever since I was a boy.'

His eyes narrowed, and he came a few steps closer. His friend on the other side of the car did the same, as if controlled by invisible threads.

'And what the fuck you gonna do with it?'

'Didn't you hear? I collect them.'

Two steps forward. I kept an eye on his hands. His right hand was in his pocket, the other one he held at his side, like a gunslinger in a Western before the last duel in Tombstone.

'Or maybe I should ask … why the fuck are you following me?'

He didn't answer. Hardy opened his mouth to say something – or he was drawing breath before launching himself into action.

'I've been watching you, all the way from St Olavs vei, and it's no coincidence you're parked here. Or have you two got something going?'

Hardy went a deep red, Laurel a corresponding white. I could see the muscles in his jaw bunching. 'Veum…'

'So you know my name as well. Is it so strange I've taken your number?'

'Now you just listen here … We know who you are, we know where you live, we know where your office is.'

'I keep office hours. Why don't you visit me there if you have something on your minds I can help you with?'

He continued undeterred: 'We know who you are, where you live, we know where you…'

'I got all that the first time round! Tell me what you want.'

He held out his left hand. 'I want you to give me the number.'

I pointed to his car. 'Have you forgotten it? It's there.'

'Thor…'

At first I didn't understand what he meant. Then I realised it was an order. Hardy, whom he called Thor, lumbered towards me. Laurel did the same, in a mirror-image arc, and, out of nowhere, there was his knife. Clenched in his right hand, ready for use.

I took a step to the side, threw myself through the open car door, put the engine in reverse and slammed the accelerator to the floor. The car skidded backwards, just in time to prevent them reaching me. On the tarmac I spun round and almost ended up in the ditch on the opposite side. Then I straightened the car, changed gear, kept to the far side of the opposite carriageway and put my foot down.

Alongside them I braked sharply, rolled down the window and stuck my head out. 'You know where to find me. Let me know when you're coming and I'll lay on a sports drink!'

Thor stared, his eyes heavy and humourless. Laurel brandished the knife in the air and drew a finger across his throat, as though planning instant suicide. However, it was me he was looking at and I liked his eyes even less than before.

They didn't try to cross the road, but I had an unpleasant feeling that our paths would cross again on a later occasion. They didn't follow me either. I kept looking back in the mirror, all the way over Sotra Bridge to the mainland and then over Askøy Bridge out to the next island. No dark Audi to be seen anywhere. Perhaps they had found something else to do. Or else they had deferred the showdown. I was unlikely to have scared them off.

23

With the aid of the map I had lying on the back seat and a helpful lady at a till in the nearest supermarket I managed to find my way to the little house where Liv Grethe Heggvoll lived. It was set back from the main road, hidden behind a tall hedge, with a view of the fjord to the south of Holsnøy island, of the village of Frekhaug in the municipality of Meland, and of Salhus and Morvik in Åsane, with Nordhordsland Bridge like a gigantic belt between it all. It didn't feel like being out in the country any more, as it would have done twenty years ago, when you still had to catch a ferry to get to Askøy.

Around the house were flowerbeds, a few fruit trees and a tool shed with a padlocked door. I walked down the garden path, searched in vain for a door bell and ended up knocking as hard as I could.

The woman who opened the door was about thirty years old, had short, reddish hair, big blue eyes and, as far as I could see, needed no help from cosmetics to look young and fresh. She was wearing brown cord trousers and a plain, dark-blue jumper. 'Yes?' she said, looking at me enquiringly.

'Liv Grethe Heggvoll?'

'That's me, yes.'

I introduced myself, told her my profession and explained that I was actually working on another case and that the Bryggen robbery had thrown up a connection.

'And?'

'I was wondering whether you'd be willing to answer a few questions.'

'Well … I can't imagine I have any more to say than what I've already told the police, but … You'd better come in.'

She opened the door, which led into a pleasant blue hallway. Before we went any further she stopped and looked down at my shoes. I took the hint and did as you often do out of town: removed my shoes. On stockinged feet I quietly followed her into what was obviously her sitting room.

The room had a view of the sea and was simply furnished. The wooden walls were bedecked with landscape paintings and several woven tapestries in mellow colours. In a high-backed rocking chair sat a woman of roughly my age with some knitting in her hands. Her hair was grey with streaks of white and collected at the back in a tight bun, which lent her a severe, almost Puritan, appearance. But she was dressed as casually as the person I assumed was her daughter, in brown trousers and a grey-and-white jumper with a traditional pattern. I guessed, from what she was holding, she had knitted both hers and her daughter's. When I went in, she looked up, scowled at me, confirmed she didn't know me and went back to her knitting, without even so much as a hello.

Liv Grethe Heggvoll smiled sadly and whispered: 'My mother's in a world of her own.' In a louder voice she said: 'A cup of coffee?'

'Please.' The coffee was a short cut to everything that was good in this country. Without a cup or ten Norway would grind to a halt. That was probably also why most of us regularly held our stomachs: we could always feel a craving coming on.

While Liv Grethe was in the kitchen I gazed through the window. 'Nice view you've got,' I said to her mother.

'Mmm,' the woman said to her knitting. She had lean facial features, but noticeably black bags under her eyes. Her neck was wrinkled and dry, and in many ways she looked older than she probably was.

On the shelf of a wooden corner-stand there was a framed black-and-white photo of an elderly couple in front of a dark car, from what I could judge, a Fiat from the latter half of the 1960s. The man was much taller than the woman and stood, his arms around her shoulders, with a proud air of ownership as they both leaned against the car. Whether it was the woman or the car he was proud of was impossible to say.

Then Liv Grethe was back with a small tray on which stood three cups and a jug of coffee. 'You'd like a cup too, wouldn't you, Mummy?'

'Yes, please,' the mother said quietly, looking at her daughter and smiling softly, as though actually thinking about something quite different.

'She had a nervous breakdown when I was a child,' the daughter said in a muted voice, but not so low that her mother couldn't hear. 'She's never been herself since.'

I nodded to the photo I had been looking at. 'Who's that?'

'Oh, that…' She smiled the same sad smile. 'That's Grandad and Grandma, the last picture that was taken of him, I think it was 1969. The car was new and Grandad was immensely proud of it. But Grandma didn't have a driving licence, so after he died it just stood in the garage until they sold it, at some time in the eighties. I can barely remember it. But it's a nice photo, don't you think?'

I nodded, and we sat down at the low table where she had placed the cups. The coffee was a bit thin for my palate, but bearing in mind the next eight cups I would drink, statistically speaking, that was probably no bad thing.

'So … what was it you wanted to know?'

'About the robbery. Could you tell me what happened?'

'Well … what should I say? It was a terrifying experience. I've never been through anything like it. We … Mummy and I went to town to buy a watch for Uncle Jesper – one of my uncles – for his fiftieth birthday. We hadn't even had a chance to look at any – the assistant was about to unlock a cabinet to take some out – when the door burst open and three people charged in, dressed in … like shell suits, I suppose. And with those … balaclavas over their faces and … guns. They ordered Mummy and me back against the wall, with the assistants, and then two of them started emptying drawers and cupboards. One of the assistants had to unlock them. The manager came out of the back room, but one of the robbers ordered him back in and went with him. Through the door we could hear him being forced to open … erm … we read in the papers it was a safe. I can't remember how long this all took. It felt like an eternity, but I suppose it was only a few minutes. Mummy turned to me and whimpered and I was paralysed with fear, terrified … how can I put it?'

'Yes, it obviously wasn't a pleasant experience.'

'No, I'll vouch for that!'

'But then, when they'd finished...'

'Yes, they finished, said something or other, don't move or do anything, and then they ran out and of course that was when the worst part happened. The shot outside. It went through us like an electric shock. For a moment we thought they were shooting at us, but then I realised they weren't and...'

'Yes?'

'Mm, it's all a bit fuzzy. We stood still. Mummy was clinging to me. One assistant went to the door and screamed: *They've shot someone! He's on the ground bleeding!* She hesitated a bit, then opened the door and went out for help. Lots of people came, and not long after that we heard sirens, and then the police came.'

'Tell me ... looking back, do you remember what happened before the shot? Was anything said?'

She sat gazing into the distance. 'I've given that a lot of thought, and I told the police what I could remember too, of course. But I ... In a way it's as if the shot has cast a shroud over everything, as if everything started there ... but something was said before the shot. I'm sure of that.'

I leaned forward. 'You mean ... between the robber and the victim?'

'Yes, I suppose so. At least from the outside.'

'You didn't hear what, though?'

'No, I don't think so. At any rate, I can't remember anything. It's all a blank.'

I nodded. After a while I said: 'In the papers you're quoted as saying you thought one of the robbers was a woman.'

She smiled, resigned. 'Yes, that was something I said spontaneously to the manager when he came out to us, and then he told the police. I don't know what made me say it, but I suppose it must have been the way she was moving. Somehow, with a little more care, not as unrestrained as the other two. And she didn't say anything. If it was a woman, that is.'

'But they spoke in English?'

'Yes. It wasn't their native language, though. I could hear that. It must have been to hide who they really were … Eastern Europeans, Norwegians, what do I know? I'm not very linguistically minded.'

'No? What do you do, actually?'

'At the moment I'm on sick leave because of a slipped disc. Usually I work in admin at Askøy local council. Office work.'

'I see.' I paused. 'You mentioned … this uncle you were buying a watch for…'

'Yes, that came to nothing. We ended up buying a lawnmower instead.'

I smiled. 'Right. You called him Uncle Jesper?'

'Yes.'

'Not Jesper Janevik by any chance?'

Instantly a wariness that hadn't been there before flitted across her face. 'Yes. And?'

I sat flicking through my notebook. 'His name has cropped up earlier. I mean … in the case I'm working on. The man who was shot in Bryggen is involved as well.'

'Really?' Now she looked more confused.

'That's why I came here, to see … if there might be more behind the shooting than meets the eye.'

'I still don't understand what it has to do with us. Or with Uncle Jesper.'

'He's your mother's brother, is he?'

'Yes, he is, and as far as the accusations that were made about him are concerned, I can assure you they're absolutely unfounded.' Her face was red. 'Uncle Jesper has been like a father to me. When my mother was left to … well, this is none of your business, but since … I'll tell you.'

I nodded.

'I was born in Drammen, but when I was only a few months old, my father left us – for another woman – and since then we've never had anything to do with him. Mummy packed her things, took me, caught the train and travelled home. Here she had a total breakdown. At that time my grandmother was alive – she didn't die until a couple of years later. I don't remember her. But she and Uncle Jesper took care of us. And afterwards, when Grandma died and Mummy was recovering, he was the one who supported us. Helped us with everything of a practical nature. Helped me with my homework when Mummy … couldn't. If I went swimming…' She gestured towards the sea: '… he always came out and kept an eye on me. Sat on a rock watching. In short … I wouldn't be sitting here if it hadn't been for him. And these girls who hurled their accusations…'

'Which girls?'

'Some here on the island. They said he'd exposed himself. It never got to court, and later he kept himself to himself, at the children's home, he had a job in town, but had trouble hanging on to that too, and now he's on the dole, but he's still like a father to me. We see him, if not every day, then several times a week, and we always have Sunday lunch together, the three of us.'

'Just you three?'

'Yes.' She added: 'And if you're wondering if I've got a boyfriend, I had one, but it didn't go very well, so right now I'm … alone.'

I shrugged. 'I am too, for that matter, so … as regards that … well.'

She tossed her head and for a moment or two looked almost provocative. 'Anything else you'd like to know?'

'You talked about a sexual offence, but did you know … of course you were small when it happened … but did you know he was questioned by the police to do with another case? In 1977, to be precise.'

'1977? I never heard anything.'

'No one told you about it?'

'No.'

'Well, people have clearly been very considerate.'

'Can you stop beating about the bush?'

'It's called the Mette Case. A little girl went missing, from Nordås, one September day in 1977. Your uncle had visited a cousin close by – Synnøve Stangeland – several times.'

'Right. We never see anything of them.'

'No, she said that too.'

'So how did it turn out? Nothing serious, obviously.'

'No, the police let him go, and since then he's never been in any trouble.'

'No, of course not!' She bared her palms. 'There you go.'

'But he lives nearby, I understand?'

There was something measured about her look now. 'He lives in his childhood home, yes. Down in Janevika. Where he and his mother grew up.'

'Does he welcome visitors?'

She shrugged. 'No one ever asks. But if you were thinking of bringing up this topic I think it's better you don't bother.'

'Out of consideration for whom?'

'For him, naturally. He's had enough on his plate, I think.' She got up with a little grimace and held her back before continuing: 'I think you should go, Herr… Veum, wasn't it?'

'Yes.' I looked at her mother, who had been sipping at her coffee during the whole conversation, not reacting to anything, not even when her life was being discussed. Now she had put down her cup and was knitting again, in a way that suggested she was on automatic pilot. 'Thank you for talking to me,' I said, actually to both of them, but only Liv Grethe accompanied me to the door and she didn't invite me back.

I was used to that. I was an unbidden guest almost everywhere I went, and I was never asked to sign the visitors' book. But I found my way down to Janevika without any further help.

24

The house stood on a slope down to a stony beach. It was a white construction, probably from the 1930s, perhaps even older. A narrow road led down to an empty garage to the west. Through the open door I glimpsed various garden tools: spades, rakes, hoes, lawnmowers and something resembling a shredder. The area around the house was in astonishingly good order and I noticed several flowerbeds decoratively framed with boulders from the beach below. Along the north-eastern façade of the house there was a large bed where last year's rose bushes still hadn't lost their leaves and gleamed yellow and green.

I went up the steps to the door in the middle of one long side of the house. There wasn't a bell here either and I resorted to the same method as at Liv Grethe Heggvoll and her mother's: I knocked hard on the door.

From inside I heard nothing until the door burst open and a tall, thin man was standing in the doorway. He was wearing dark-blue jeans, a red-and-black checked shirt hanging loose outside his trousers with a white vest visible at the neck. His dark hair was specked with silver, and short everywhere, down to the scalp. The way he chewed his lower lip gave you the impression his mouth was slightly askew. His eyes were dark and tense, as though he wasn't expecting any good to come of this visit.

'Jesper Janevik?'

He nodded. 'I know who you are. My ... Liv Grethe rang to say you were on your way.'

'Well ... May I come in?'

He didn't move. I looked down. He had only thick socks on his feet, which perhaps explained the lack of sound before he opened the door.

'I don't think we have anything to talk about.'

'Yes, we do, quite definitely. I've been commissioned to...'

'I know what this is about. But I've got nothing to say about that case. I had nothing to do with it and ... it's much too long ago.'

'Not long enough for some. For her mother above all.'

Again he chewed his lip, as though he were taking an exam, I was the examiner and I had just asked a difficult question. 'But why should I bother about that? I was dragged into this case as an innocent bystander. I've got nothing to say, I tell you.'

'Yes, I hear what...' I looked around. It wasn't raining, but the sky was grey and white, and there was a touch of late winter in the air. 'Are you sure you don't want to let me in?'

'Yes. Absolutely.'

'Then we'd better have the conversation on the steps.'

'I don't want that either.' He started to close the door.

I jammed my foot in the door. 'This is childish, Janevik. I assume you don't want the police on your back again?'

His eyes narrowed. 'With what justification, might I ask?'

'You have to admit that not even being willing to answer questions twenty-five years on is suspicious.'

He stared at me. He was standing in his house and was also close on ten centimetres taller than me. Towering over me. Yet there was something delicate and fragile about him which quelled any fears I might have had regarding a full-on physical confrontation.

I lubricated my voice with social-worker oil. 'Listen, Janevik. I completely understand that you have every right to feel aggrieved about your treatment in 1977. But you have to put yourself in the girl's mother's shoes too. You yourself ... Liv Grethe told me how you supported her and her mother, your sister, when they came back here after the divorce.'

He straightened up. 'That was family. You take care of your family. I helped my father too when he fell ill, and Mum ... in her last days. It goes without saying that I would support Maria and Liv Grethe.'

'Then I'm sure you can understand how painful it must be to lose a child.'

He nodded. 'Of course I can. But I didn't ... All I did was visit my cousin Synnøve and her family at ... their place. Often, when the children were outside playing, we sat on the doorstep watching them. Some of the other children came over, ate waffles Synnøve gave them and chatted with us. There was never any ... That was all there was to it.'

'You've never been back?'

'No, I've avoided the place like the ... I've hardly been in Bergen since the early 1980s, unless there's been a pressing reason.'

'So what was the justification for involving you at that time?'

'It was the police. They went through what they like to call "their records" and there they found my name, along with many others naturally, but some of the people at the co-op had got wind of my name, and had perhaps heard something, what do I know? Anyway, it came as a shock when I found the police at my door, and as if that wasn't enough ... I was taken to the police station and held in custody!' He had a long, thin neck with a pronounced Adam's apple, which was going up and down now as he swallowed hard. 'I was kept there for twenty-four hours until I was released after their remand hearing. My solicitor said I could claim compensation, but I said no. I didn't want any more fuss. I'd had more than enough!'

'But why were you there in the first place? I mean – in the police records.'

He pressed his mouth into a straight line. I could see his jaw muscles churning the answer, and his voice was barely audible when he spoke again. 'Because some giggly girls on the island spread rumours about me!'

'Rumours based on what?'

He was torn between the desire to tell me to go to hell and the need to justify himself. Again he squeezed out the words. 'Let – me – tell – you.'

It had been a Saturday in October, in the late 1960s. He was seventeen and there had been a dance in Bergheim, near the famous coastal town of Florvåg. He and some pals had taken beer with them, which they necked down at the back of the hall, and later – when he got off the bus home – he needed a pee like never before. It felt as if his bladder was exploding and he staggered off the bus – he was also a bit unsteady on his legs – then unbuttoned his fly and pointed, just in time, the jet was like a fountain at the side of the road.

While he stood there with his tackle in hand he heard girls sniggering behind him, and he vaguely remembered the three girls sitting at the back of the bus. They must have been at the dance too, but he had never felt at ease with girls and definitely not when there were lots of them. He couldn't dance, and as for standing there moving to the music … no, he'd rather hang out with pals by the wall and generally he kept his mouth shut, being by nature the silent, introverted type.

There the girls stood, like a three-headed troll, sniggering and shouting: 'Let's have a look! Oh, what a clever boy! You can piss all the way into town, you can, Jesper Janevik!'

He stood there like a sculpture in Frogner Park, unable to stop himself, pee streaming out of him from an inexhaustible source, displayed in all his glory. 'What a big boy! Show us some more, Jesper! Let's have a look at 'im!'

And at that moment a car arrived, picked him out in the headlights, brakes screaming as it skidded to a halt, and a policeman from the local station stepped out. 'What's going on here?!'

The three-headed troll turned to the officer, a tall, good-looking guy with curly, blond hair and a charming smile for anything in a skirt, and they burst out, more or less in unison: 'It's Jesper Janevik! He was flashing us!'

The officer glared at Jesper, who had finished at long last and was fumbling with his fly. 'Is that right, girls? What do you say to that, Janevik?'

As so often before, he seemed to clam up and couldn't get a word out. He wriggled and squirmed as he felt a dull feeling of nausea rising from within, and before he knew what was going on he leaned forward and was sick, and once again liquid was streaming out of him, but this time from a more respectable orifice.

'I couldn't say anything, I couldn't defend myself against these …

accusations. The officer said fine, let's all go home, but on Monday morning I had to present myself in his office and explain, which I did. Later the three girls were summoned too, and it never got as far as a … case. But the damage was done, in such an open society as it was here then. A few weeks later some boys beat me up because I was such a dirty pig, as they put it, and as they left me lying on the ground, bleeding from my nose and mouth, they shouted: *Go to the cop shop and report us! They'll be pleased to see you again, you can be sure of that.*'

I could see how it hurt him to tell me this, and I can't deny that I felt sympathy for him. 'And that was all there was to it?'

'Yes.'

'Not entirely, judging by your expression.'

'No … some years later there were … there had been some attempted rapes, over by Florvåg. There was never any talk of full rapes and the victims couldn't give a real description of the attacker. But rumours started spreading that I was behind it and became so persistent that I was summoned to the police station once again – for a chat – as they used to say. But they had nothing on me this time, either, of course.' He stared at me with big, serious eyes. 'I wasn't guilty. Yet again!'

'No, I understand. And there's nothing you can say about Mette Misvær?'

He shook his head vehemently. 'No, no, no! How many times do I have to tell you? Nothing!'

I nodded. 'Well … your niece gave you the best reference in existence, so you're definitely held in high regard there.'

For the first time I saw a shadow of a smile on his face. 'Yes, Liv Grethe, she's … the sunshine in my life. Watching her grow from childhood has been my sole joy.'

'Your sister didn't have it easy, I understand?'

'No, the bastard she married, a guy from the Drammen area, they still have his name as a souvenir – Heggvoll,' he almost spat it out, 'jumped into another woman's knickers while Maria was pregnant with Liv Grethe, and she'd hardly got out of the maternity clinic when he upped and left her. What else could she do but come back here? Dad was dead, but Mum and I took care of them, and after Mum died, I helped them. But it was Maria who bore the brunt. After all, I only helped.'

'And the father has never shown his face since?'

'Never! That was how much he cared. While I, and I'm only an uncle, have … as I said…'

'So what's your life like now, Janevik? Are you still plagued by gossip?'

'No, it's died down now. Lots of people have moved away. The three girls … well, one of them lives up on the estate here and has teenagers herself now, but she always looks away on the rare occasions our paths cross. I think she's actually embarrassed by what she and her friends set in motion then. But … I have problems with my nerves, went to a psychologist for many years and eventually I was on disability benefit. Now I have a quiet, solitary life.' He looked down to the sea. 'Sometimes I take a boat out and do some fishing. Sometimes I go to Kleppestø – that's the centre here now – do a bit of shopping, have a cup of coffee in one of the cafés. I've even ventured to Bergen, but … I live alone, as I always have done. This is my childhood home and I'll die here when the time is ripe.'

We stood reflecting on that. I had no more questions to ask. I hadn't received any answers that I could build on, so in that regard the trip had been a waste of time. Another shot in the dark, from a darkened firing range, twenty-five years ago. It wasn't even worth checking the target. I knew the answer anyway. I doubted I was close.

However, I still couldn't free myself from my main preoccupation. Somewhere out there in the gloom was someone who knew something, and I had no intention of giving in yet. There were still lots of people to talk to. There were still some side roads to go down, on the trail of what everyone feared to find out, which nobody knew as yet – except for one person, maybe two.

With this in mind, I plodded back up to the main road, got into my car and drove back to Bergen. On Askøy Bridge I met the rush-hour traffic coming out. That is what happens when you have a bridge. You instantly become a suburb of the nearest big town, with the advantages and curses this brings. Which tipped the balance depended on the island. I didn't see much more than a line of white headlights in front of me, as regular as the drumstick beat of a seasoned drummer in Bergheim one Saturday night in the sixties, when The Stringers, The Harpers or some other Bergen band was playing at a dance for the kids out there, oblivious of what might happen on the country road as they were travelling home, late that same night.

25

As soon as I was back on the mainland I drove to a lay-by off to the right of the road. I took out my phone, rang Haakonsvern and asked to speak to Svein Stangeland. After a short wait he came to the phone. I said who I was and he grunted.

'Let's get straight to the point, Stangeland. I think we need to have another chat.'

'Oh, yes. Why?'

'It turns out you weren't actually at your cabin on the day little Mette Misvær went missing.'

I was met with a silence at the other end, so long I wondered if we were still connected. 'Hello! Are you there?'

'… Yes.'

'Do you agree that we need to talk?'

'Only if you insist.'

'So let's say I do. I'm not that far from Loddefjord now. Can I meet you at work?'

'No,' he said at once, so quickly that he felt he ought to explain. 'After 9/11 it's more difficult for outsiders to get in here than it is to steal a plane. I'll come out. We can meet … at Vestkanten, the café on the first floor – in half an hour.'

'OK.'

He rang off without another word. I sat musing, then pulled back on to the main road and drove through the tunnel towards the round-about that sent traffic in every direction of the compass, one of them to Loddefjord.

Vestkanten was the name they had given to the renovated version of the mall that had once been called Loddefjord Market. It lay like a stranded chunk of concrete at the bottom of the valley and really didn't invite passers-by to drop in, unless they were already going there for a reason. I drove into the rear and parked under a roof, the shortest possible distance to the entrance. In the mall, I found myself in a world the sun never reached, but there was eternal light from the ceiling, the walls and inside the packed shops. It was a place you could easily get lost in, but I found my way to the café on the first floor I hoped he had meant. I ordered a cup of coffee and a bun and sat down at an unoccupied table with a view of the concourse outside. I should at least catch sight of him when he appeared.

It was around 2.30 when he trudged slowly up the sloping walkway between the two floors. His gait was lumbering and without much energy, but perhaps it had been a hard day at the main Royal Norwegian Navy base, what did I know?

I waved my hand in the air to show him where I was sitting. He spotted me, nodded and made a beeline for the counter to get a cup of coffee before he came over, placed the cup on the table between us, shoved back his chair, slumped down and looked at me as if I were an overgrown fly in his cup. His thin, dark hair was possibly even flatter on his scalp than the last time I saw him, and the rash around his mouth seemed angrier, with dry white flakes over the irritated skin.

'Thank you for talking to me,' I said.

His eyes emitted a cold gleam. 'What did you want to say to me?'

'What I told you on the phone. It appears you weren't at the cabin that day.'

'Yes, I got that bit. Who have you been talking to?'

In my mind's eye I saw his wife on the school playground with her coat wrapped tightly around her in the chilly weather. 'I'll keep that to myself.'

He grimaced. 'In which case I'll keep what I know to myself too.' He made to leave, saw his coffee, stayed and took a quick swig.

'Then you give me no option but to go to the police.'

'To the police! It's no bloody secret to them. I told them back then.'

'Oh, yes. And what did they say?'

'They'd take note, they said. I never heard any more.'

'So … where were you?'

He looked past me. As though he was deliberating. 'I had a meeting.'

'Oh, yes. Who with?'

'What business is this of yours, Veum?'

I leaned forward. 'It's my business in the sense that I've been commissioned to find out what happened to Mette Misvær the day she went missing. Therefore I will not leave a stone unturned. You are one of the stones – and the fact that you were not at the cabin that weekend.'

'I was! I went back … afterwards.'

'After what?'

Again he went quiet. Perhaps he was one of those people who need a little extra time to make up their mind.

All the easier for me. Sometimes provocation was an effective tactic. 'A rendezvous?'

He blushed. 'What are you getting at? Who do you take me for?'

I shrugged. 'Perhaps your neighbours' games rubbed off on you … I did eventually find out about them.'

He glared at me. 'So now you know what made Synnøve and me leave?'

I nodded.

'And how does that tally with the suggestion you just came up with?'

I angled my head. 'The circumstances could be different. You could have met someone…'

'I hadn't met someone, as you put it, but…' He gulped. 'Alright then! Things weren't going well between me and Synnøve at that point. We seemed to be going round each other, without saying anything. It wasn't working. And there were so many others who… were breaking up. I … I was at a showing that Saturday.'

'What kind of showing?'

'A flat! Somewhere else to live. But I didn't want to tell Synnøve, of course. So that was why I just said I had a meeting. Something to do with work. She didn't have a clue. But when this Mette stuff came up I had to tell her. So that she wouldn't think…' He looked away, as if the thought of what she might have wondered made him uneasy.

'And then she said…?'

'Well, what did she say? We had a heart-to-heart. Talked things over. Everything fell into place. It – moving out – was never a topic of conversation again.'

I looked at him. The provocation had helped, but was he telling the truth? 'And you can verify this, can you?'

'Verify … that I was looking at a flat twenty-five years ago? Are you out of your mind, man? But … I did tell the police, as I said, at the time, they must have checked it out, because I didn't hear any more.'

'Are you telling me you weren't at home at all that Saturday?'

'No.'

'Can you swear on that?'

'What would I have been there for?'

'Mm, that's the question. So … if anyone had tried to ring you that day – at home I mean – you wouldn't have answered the phone.'

'No, my dear man, I wouldn't have. Have you got any more intelligent questions?'

'It wasn't a question. It was a statement.'

Like two experienced synchronised swimmers we raised our cups of coffee at the same time, staring furiously at each other. Neither of us liked what he saw and we didn't try to conceal it. We emptied our cups, got up and each went in our own direction, me back to my car, him back to work and then to Synnøve and whatever the rest of the day would bring them and their hitherto apparently perfect relationship, with just a tiny scratch on the surface.

26

I found Dankert Muus in the garden this time too. He was cutting dry twigs from a tree and with big branch loppers in his hands he looked no less dangerous than the last time.

Nor was the look he sent me the friendliest. 'Veum! Again? Don't tell me you've solved the case!'

'No. If only…'

He leaned forward heavily. 'So what's the reason for you coming here a second time and disturbing me while I'm gardening?'

'I'm chasing bits and pieces.'

'Tell me something that would surprise me, Veum.'

'You mentioned yourself that you investigated registered sex criminals – or minor offenders. One of them was called Jesper Janevik.'

His eyes narrowed. 'Yes?'

'He was in custody for twenty-four hours, I've been told.'

He maintained the same expression and repeated himself, a little louder this time: 'Yes?'

'I've just left him.'

'Yes … what led you to his door?'

'Well, his name cropped up, as I said. But … why did you decide to arrest him?'

'It was … We thought there was a good chance we had the right man.'

'Because…?'

'He had a record and he'd been seen up there.'

'On the actual day?'

'No. He had an alibi and then he was released. We put a tail on him for a while, but nothing was ever … nothing ever turned up. Nothing of any consequence anyway.'

'And what was his alibi?'

'A family gathering. A niece's birthday – photos were taken. His sister vouched for him and later we were sent photos of Janevik with the little girl on his lap.'

'With a date?'

'No, this was before that was possible, at least not on the equipment that was used. But there was nothing else that pointed in his direction – apart from the business on Askøy. Indecent exposure or whatever it was.'

'Great. Something else, Muus…'

'Ri-ght?' He sent me a sceptical look.

'Cecilie Lyngmo said she had a strange feeling there was something funny about the atmosphere in that co-op. Something she couldn't put her finger on. Did you experience anything similar?'

He snorted with contempt. 'Veum … I've always based my investigations on facts. Never on intuition.'

'In other words, you never noticed it?'

'Veum … I believe I told you last time: we checked out every single one of the neighbours carefully. We went through every single house, from cellar to attic. We found nothing. *Nada, nichts*, Veum!'

'So you never heard about what some of them call the New Year games?'

He yawned. 'Eh? New Year games! Which ones, if I may be so bold?'

'From what I understand it's a form of wife-swapping. New Year's Eve 1976, around nine months before Mette went missing.'

'Wife-swapping! You mean…?' He gesticulated with his arms. 'You can have mine, if I can have yours?'

'Sort of.'

He still looked a bit taken aback. 'No, I have to admit … we didn't get a sniff of that. But … what's this got to do with the Mette Case?'

'Yes, that's the question a lot of people have asked me over the last few days.'

'And what do you answer?'

'Well…' I stretched out my arms. 'What was it old Ibsen used to say? I only ask, answering is not my call.'

'That sounds like an excellent description of you, Veum.' The old grin was out again. 'Bursting with questions, but hardly ever any decent answers.'

'I have one more…'

He rolled his eyes and went chop, chop with the big branch lopper in the air. 'Can't you see I'm busy?'

'One of the neighbours, Svein Stangeland, a civilian worker at Haakonsvern: he and his family were supposed to be at their cabin that weekend, on Holsnøy, unless I'm much mistaken. However, it transpires that in fact *he* was in Bergen. To see a flat, he says. Does that ring any bells?'

Muus stared into the air. 'Yes, now you mention it. We were informed and I think we checked it out with the estate agent as well. He had been there.'

'Hardly for hours though?'

'No, probably not.' He looked at me pensively. 'Do you have reason to believe he had anything to do with the disappearance?'

I shrugged. 'Not yet. But I've mapped most things out and this was a little side road I'd missed earlier. I was also told about a phone that kept ringing in one of the houses. Did you study the phone calls up there that day?'

'This was long before mobile phones, as you know. In those days no one was very interested in checking calls like they do today. It's far more difficult now to deny you've been somewhere if there's been activity on your phone – either calls or messages.'

'Of course. Everyone knows that, but nevertheless…'

'No, Veum, I can't remember that we did much investigating of phone calls.'

'Well … I'm afraid that's the last of my questions.'

'Don't be afraid. I think you're doing very well.' He nodded with a good-natured expression on his face. Although irony glinted in his eyes.

'I'd better be getting on.'

'You do that. And Veum…'

'Yes?'

'Don't come back until you've solved the crime. And I'm afraid that means: never.'

'Never is a word I've never learned to use, Muus.'

'That's twice in one sentence.' He stretched up with the lopper and brutally severed a little twig. 'Hah!' he said with a look of triumph. 'Caught in the act!'

'Thank you – and the same to you.' I nodded and strolled away. I knew this. The Muus that roared had never been like other policemen. Somewhere he had a screw loose, and it wasn't that small, either. Now he was taking it out on the closest vegetation; once it had been whoever strayed across his path.

From Fredlundsveien I drove in slow motion back to Bergen town centre, where, as usual, the traffic at this time of day was like a serious bout of constipation in the digestive system, for which no one had pre-scribed the correct medicine.

When at last I was at home I found Bjarne Solheim's telephone number and rang him on the off-chance he was there. As I had suspected, he was still in his office.

'Bobby still on his beat?' I said.

'If you knew how much paper we have to deal with, Veum. It's good to put in an hour at the end of the day to get rid of it.'

'I can sympathise.'

'I don't suppose you got in touch to express your sympathy, though. Have you dug up anything on the robbery?'

'Nothing cast-iron, but there are a couple of things I'd like to ask you about.'

'Fire away.'

'First of all … the owner of the jewellery shop was very keen to know if I was from his insurance company. Do you suspect any skulduggery?'

'Schmidt? Not on the face of it, no. What sort of skulduggery?'

'Well, I wondered if he'd made a very high claim for the goods that were stolen during the robbery … Or he may have had something special hidden in the safe that he didn't want to divulge.'

'You're not suggesting … what are you suggesting?'

'I'm not sure. But let's imagine, for example, illegally imported items that might be converted into cash without paying any duties.'

'No, we … That's an aspect we hadn't considered.'

'Have you got a list of the employees there?'

'Yes, we get one purely as a matter of routine. We check out whether anyone knew of any special procedures, when most money was in the shop, where the most valuable watches were, that sort of thing. Not everything was taken. The robbers took mainly the most expensive watches.'

'Exactly. You couldn't send me the list, could you?'

It was a while before he answered. 'And for what purpose?'

'I talk to a lot of people. You never know what can come up.'

'Well … I'll consider it, Veum. Perhaps raise the matter with my colleagues. Have you got an email address?'

'I have.' I gave it to him and went on: 'I had a little chat with the two women who were customers in the shop when the robbery took place.'

'Why?'

'In fact they have a tangential connection with the case I'm working on at the moment.'

'Uhuh.'

'The younger of the two, Liv Grethe Heggvoll said she thought words were exchanged between Nils Bringeland, the victim, and one – perhaps more – of the robbers, before he was shot.'

'Yes, I think we picked up on that as well.'

'But she didn't hear what they said.'

'No.'

'Could Bringeland have recognised one of them? Did they remove their balaclavas before they ran off?'

'No one said they did. According to our witnesses they were wearing them as they crossed the street, boarded the boat that was waiting for them and then escaped.'

'But is it possible?'

'You think we should comb Bringeland's circle of acquaintances, do you?'

'That's really for you to assess. Have you got any further with the hypothesis that one of the robbers might be a woman?'

Solheim's voice sounded a little desperate when he answered. 'Veum, we've got enough cases on our hands. This robbery is three months old. Of course it's still on the pile, but actually nothing new has emerged since you were last here – day before yesterday, wasn't it?'

'Yes, but … There's just one more minor matter I'd like to discus with you.' He waited quietly. 'Earlier today I went to Sotra, in connection with a case. There was a car behind me the whole way, and after I'd finished talking to … some people there, it was parked close by. I drove behind it and took note of the number. The occupants of the car didn't appreciate that. Two unpleasant individuals, to be frank. Then I jumped back into my car to avoid a direct confrontation, but … I couldn't ask you to check whose name the car is registered in, could I?'

He sighed, but immediately sounded a bit more cheerful. 'Are you going to report them? What if you have a secret admirer, Veum?'

'If so, they wouldn't be driving round in an Audi with tinted glass.'

'No? No, perhaps not.' I heard the sound of busy fingers on a keyboard. 'You said you had the number?'

'Yes.'

I gave him the number and heard him key it in. Then a soft whistle.

'Looks like you'd better watch your back, Veum.'

My stomach region instinctively reacted. 'Right.'

'I don't know if you've heard the name Flash Gordon?'

'Popular cartoon character in my youth, otherwise no.'

'Well, he seems to have made his mark in criminal circles over the last couple of years, so unless you have contacts in the underworld, I …'

'Not on a daily basis.'

'Gordon Bakke. The car's registered in his name. Would you like his home address as well, perhaps?'

'Like? Not really, but …'

'Anyway, he's central. In Klostergaten.' He gave me the number as well. 'And would you like to know why they call him Flash Gordon?'

'Love to.'

'Because he strikes with lightning speed, they say. And strike is the operative word. He uses his fists and occasionally his feet. He's well trained in some oriental martial art and is supposed to be a nightmare to confront. I'd recommend you keep several arm-lengths away. Eye-witnesses say he just whirls through the air – and they end up on their backs. Those that confront him.'

'So why don't you lock him up?'

'We do! He's been inside. Several times. But he always gets out again. That's how it is with our clientele. We never get rid of them entirely.'

'And what's he registered as in GLEI Norway?'

He chuckled. 'A heavy.'

'Really?'

'No. To be honest I don't think he's registered anywhere except with us. But as I said … I'd recommend you keep out of his way.'

'And there was another guy with him. Big, solid. Hoodlum type.'

'Description fits so many, but I think he often operates with someone known as Thor the Hammer.'

'Yes, that's right. He called him Thor.'

'Heavier-handed than Flash Gordon, but effective in his way too, of course. Where did you meet them, did you say?'

'Sotra. Not so far from Ågotnes. I was talking to the owner of a garage out there, Tor Fylling.'

'Really? Is he still in business?'

'Erm … What do you mean? Tor Fylling?'

'Yes, he's in our files somewhere too. Not that we've ever had anything on him.'

'… On him … What sort of thing?'

'Well, I suppose it'd be receiving stolen goods. A few years ago he came under the spotlight in connection with what we saw as the organised trafficking of stolen cars. Several insurance companies were involved then.'

'And Fylling's role was … ?'

'A kind of necessary middleman. He took in the cars, re-sprayed them, made other cosmetic changes and then they passed along the system. He was never the one to deal with re-registering or that kind of thing. That's why we never got anything on him. But we caught the big fish and I think actually Fylling kept a low profile after that.'

'Right, that's news to me. He came onto my radar in connection with the Mette Case. He was one of the neighbours in the co-op.'

'I see.'

'When was this car case, more or less?'

'Early nineties. 1992–3 and to some extent in '94.'

I jotted down the years in my notebook although I couldn't see what connection there could be with what I was doing. 'This Gordon Bakke, to come back to him.'

'Yes?'

'Has he ever been done for sexual offences?'

'Not that I know of. I'll have to check up on that though, but right now I don't have the time, Veum.'

'Thanks for your help anyway. So far.'

We ended the conversation on a friendly note and promised to get back to each other if we came across anything useful.

I took a soup packet from one of the kitchen drawers, mixed the contents with water and made myself a thick tomato soup, with a tin of tomatoes and two hard-boiled eggs, and cut three slices of bread, which I ate with the soup. On the other side of the table I placed the unopened bottle of aquavit, like a message of doom: *Thus far and no further*.

I still hadn't finished the day's work, the next item on the programme was another trip to Solstølen. And now they had more to answer for, most of them.

27

I parked in Solstølvegen, crossed the street and opened the gate to the co-op. As I turned right towards Maja Misvær's house I had what felt like a shock. For an instant or two I was afraid I was hallucinating, but even after rubbing my eyes, closing and opening them, the result was the same.

There was a little blonde girl sitting in the sandpit in front of the house, busily shovelling sand into a plastic bucket as she sat chatting to herself. Subconsciously I thought: so she didn't disappear after all? Or was this a ghost? A figment of my imagination? A mental echo?

The young man leaning against the wall beside her with a plastic cup in his hands watched me with curiosity as I approached with, I imagine, an astonished expression on my face.

I nodded towards Maja Misvær's door. 'Fru Misvær ... she's in, I trust?'

He shrugged and said in a friendly way: 'No idea. We live next door...' He motioned towards the girl. 'We don't have a sandpit and Maja said we could use hers.'

'Yes, of course. I'm sure she'd think that was nice.'

'She hasn't got any small children herself any more ... and no grand-children either,' he continued chattily.

'No, I know.' I didn't want to ask him if he knew about Mette. Perhaps he didn't, in which case I didn't want to make him anxious. Instead I turned to the little girl and said: 'What's your name then?'

'Miranda,' she said, looking up at me.

'That's a grand name. And how old are you?'

She counted with her fingers. 'Four.' And then she added: 'And a half. My birthday's on 15th August.'

I nodded to the man I assumed was her father. 'No flies on her, I can hear.'

'Streets ahead of us, I can tell you.'

I nodded and smiled, then rang the bell at Maja's. She opened the door, poked her head out, acknowledged the young man, smiled a little sadly to Miranda and said: 'Come in, Varg. I'll put some coffee on.'

'Bye, Miranda,' I said to the little girl, nodded again to the young man and followed Maja into the house.

She turned suddenly to me. 'How lovely that is! Someone using the sandpit, I mean.'

'Yes, it is.'

'Have you got anywhere?'

'I'm still collating information. Something new has cropped up, but perhaps we can...' I glanced at the sitting room and she nodded several times.

'Yes, yes, of course. I'll just put some coffee on, as I said. If you'd like some.'

'Yes, please.' My stomach was almost coffee-brown anyway.

I went into the sitting room. Once again I was drawn to the two photos on the sideboard. The picture of Mette was the same as the copy I had. The picture of her brother at his confirmation reminded me that I would also have to talk to him.

When Maja returned from the kitchen with a tray of coffee cups and a plate of biscuits I said: 'I found Håkon's address. In Ålesund.'

'Yes, that's what I told you. He lives in Ålesund now. He played a few seasons in the team up there, but now he's probably over the hill.'

'What does he do?'

'Well ... because of football and all that, he's not really had any proper education. But I think the club has helped him a bit. I'm not quite sure.'

'Don't you have any contact?'

She looked down. 'No, not that much. He wanted to live with Truls after we got ... divorced. And later things just stayed as they were.'

'But he came to see you?'

'Yes, when he was small. But as an adult he doesn't...' She looked around the room. 'It's as if ... he doesn't like it up here, simple as that.'

'Do you think that's a hangover from what happened to his sister?'

'That would be natural, wouldn't it?'

'Yes.'

'But now I have to...' She got up and went towards the door. 'The coffee. It must be ready.'

While she was out I sat looking at the photo of Håkon. The thick blond hair, carefully combed for the photo, the strong eyebrows, the distant look in his eyes and the sad downturn of his mouth. It was obvious I would have to go to Oslo to speak to Truls Misvær. There was a strong argument for me going to Ålesund as well.

She returned with the jug of coffee and filled the two cups. We each sat on our side of the table, in the same places as the last time I had been here. She looked at me. 'Something new, you said.'

I cleared my throat. 'Yes, not as far as Mette's concerned, except that I've gone into the case with a lot more thoroughness than the police did. But ... you'll have to tell me about these New Year party games.'

Her eyes widened. 'How so?'

'The last time I was here you called them a kind of party game. In the meantime I've found out what sort of games they were.'

She blushed visibly. Her eyes sought the table. She took her coffee cup and lifted it to her mouth, but she couldn't hide the trembling of her hand. She put the cup back down and assumed a kind of defensive position. 'I don't need to tell you then!'

I looked at her. 'No, we don't need to go into any depth, but I've been informed you spent parts of the night between 1976 and 1977 with your neighbour across the yard, Tor Fylling. Can you confirm that?'

She tossed her head vehemently. 'I didn't engage you to poke your nose into my private life, Varg!'

'No, but in cases like this ... If you only knew how many links there could be. You know that my background is in child welfare. There are so many children I've seen moulded by their parents' lifestyles, actions or attitudes! There are so many wayward children I've had to pick up for the same reason, into their late adolescence and even older.' I cast a glance at the children on the sideboard. 'Trauma runs deep and they're anchored to the bottom, Maja. They lie there chafing, all their lives, unless someone dives down to release them.'

She met my gaze with an almost child-like defiance, but ice crystals glittered deep within, where tears were long frozen fast.

'So I suggest you let go a little, at least. It'll stay between us anyway. I know all about the set-up. Terje Torbeinsvik's suggestion, which no one apart from Svein and Synnøve Stangeland objected to. The drawing of lots, which ended up with your husband going home with Vibeke Waaler while you went with Tor Fylling. I met Fylling earlier today, by the way, on Sotra. Do you ever see anything of him?'

She shook her head. 'Not after he moved out.'

'But before?'

She swallowed and looked down.

'You knew each other before, too. From Landås.'

'We lived in the same block in Mannsverk, yes,' she said drily.

'And then you lived here for three or four years … How was it to be suddenly … intimate with him?'

She bit her lower lip. 'It was … fine. Tor was a man's man, fixed cars at home and at work, went to football matches wearing fan regalia, had a beer too many once in a while when he was on the town with the boys, and the way he dressed … well…' She gave a weak smile.

'He was a Striler lad with ambition, Torbeinsvik is supposed to have called him.'

'You know … you can hear when someone comes from Sotra to Bergen.'

'But you said that it went … fine?'

'I don't want to talk about this, I said! All I will say is that, privately, alone, he was considerate and gentle. We didn't feel that we were doing anything wrong. I mean … the others were doing the same in the other houses.'

'Not all of them.'

'No, Svein and Synnøve weren't, but…'

'More than them. At least one of the other couples, if I can call them that, chose to sit up chatting all night.'

'Who did that?'

'Well, perhaps I don't have to say?'

She reflected. 'OK … but…'

I completed her sentence. 'You and Tor didn't.'

'No.'

She stared into the distance. Her cheeks were red now, but not as much as before.

'Were there any repercussions?'

'Repercussions? What do you mean?'

'I was thinking that there must have been some special – what shall we call them? – homecomings in the morning. In all the houses. When the men strolled back to their wives. Perhaps met them in the yard? What do you think happened then? Do you think they exchanged experiences? Winked at each other? Or do you think they looked down … or away?'

She shrugged. 'What do I know?'

She remembered Truls came home. She lay in bed after Tor had left, warm and content, so content that she was on the point of falling sleep again, when suddenly Truls was in the doorway, as nicely dressed as when the party started, but with a different gleam in his eye. When he began to undress, with his back to her, she saw scratch-marks down his back, and with a shock she realised what had happened – not only had she been satisfied with a passion and warmth, the like of which she had not experienced for a long time, but Truls had also sampled something new and different in bed with Vibeke Waaler, no less, who played Lady Macbeth at Den Nasjonale Scenen and whom they read about in newspaper interviews at regular intervals. It was her nails that had scratched his back, like the dagger tips of the same Lady's murder weapons, and Truls had been between her thighs and not Terje…

Truls turned round and looked at her, with a foolish smile on his lips. Then he came over to the bed, clambered on top and lay close to her and at once they felt an immense desire, both of them, so immense that they made love again, but with each other this time, more intense and passionate than for many years … Afterwards they had slept in each other's arms and they lay like that right until Mette toddled in and woke them, sleepy-eyed, at ten the next morning. They couldn't get Håkon out of bed until late in the day.

She looked at me and said: 'Truls came home happy at any rate, and nothing dramatic happened … between us. Later we never talked about it. Life would carry on. The children would…' Her voice cracked. 'At school, in the nursery.'

'And Tor?'

She shrugged.

'I can see there's something you're not telling me.'

'Yes, of course. But I don't have to tell you everything … This has nothing to do with what happened to Mette!'

'Sure?'

'He came to the door a few times when he was alone and Truls was away. You know in the co-op we always knew who was at home and who was away. He said…' She lowered her voice, as though this was something that concerned no one else but herself. 'He said he fell in love with me that night. Couldn't we do it again? Meet somewhere out of the way. He could drive me there, he said. We could find somewhere quiet. But I said it was impossible. There was no reason for me to go away with him, and anyway … Well, perhaps I didn't feel the same as he did. And after a while he understood and gave up. Later we bumped into each other as usual, in the yard, shopping, places like that.'

'And Helle?'

'Well, she'd been with … Nils, hadn't she? That was actually the good thing about it. We were all in it together, so no one could start … gossiping.'

'Nevertheless it ended in divorce for every single one of you. The only ones left together are those who didn't participate, Svein and Synnøve. Does that tell you something?'

Again she shrugged. 'It might well have happened anyway.'

'Do you believe that?'

She looked me straight in the eye. 'It's impossible to know, isn't it?'

I sighed. 'Yes, but … the next question I have to ask you is this: do you think – I'm not saying it was like this, but I have to ask – do you think Tor Fylling could have done something to Mette … to avenge himself after you rejected him?'

She opened and closed her mouth several times before answering. 'Tor … doing something like…' Tears were in her eyes. 'No, I could never imagine … he would never do anything like that.'

'He was at home that day. Alone.'

'Yes, but … the police. They looked everywhere, in all the houses.'

'That very first day?'

'Yes, I think so. That evening. And they didn't find her, anywhere.'

'Would you dismiss the possibility?'

'I said … It's the same as I said before. Nothing is sure. It's impossible to know. But … I cannot believe that. Have you got any evidence pointing to that possibility?'

I shook my head. 'No, I haven't. But did you know he's been under suspicion for other criminal activity?'

'Who? Tor? What for?'

'Being a fence. Receiving stolen property, cars.'

'I can't believe that!'

'No? Not that either?'

'Where've you got that from?'

'It's how it is in cases like these, Maja. You have to lift every single stone and look underneath. Do you understand? Nothing is left to chance, no question is left unanswered. And then, sometimes, this is what you find.'

She nodded.

Again her eyes filled with tears. 'But I've told you, Varg. This has been what happened with Mette. We couldn't get it out of our minds. It was impossible to concentrate on anything else – at least for me. That was why they left me – both Truls and Håkon. I had only one thing on my mind.' She put her finger to her head and tapped her temple again and again. 'Mette, Mette, Mette! What happened to Mette? And that's what I've asked you to find out, Varg. Not all this other stuff. After Mette went missing that September day my life changed. One hundred percent. Nothing else had any meaning. Nothing else has had any meaning since then. Can't you grasp that?'

She stretched across the table, grabbed my hands and squeezed. 'Find out for me, Varg! Find out what happened! I can't stand this anymore!'

I returned her squeeze to reassure her, but I didn't dare promise any more than I would do what I could. 'In the next few days I'm going to Oslo,' I said. 'Perhaps directly from Ålesund. I have to talk to both Truls and Håkon.'

She nodded. 'I understand. No stone unturned ...'

A little later she accompanied me to the door. I stood outside until she had closed it behind me. Miranda and her father had gone now. It was perfectly quiet out here. But behind the illuminated house fronts there were still some hidden secrets, still some skeletons in cupboards that needed to see the light of day. And I knew who I was going to talk to first.

28

The woman who opened the door when I rang at Terje Torbeinsvik's was in her mid-thirties; she had short blonde hair and a face with clean-cut, regular features. She was dressed as practically as was natural for a mother of small children, in jeans and a tight blue-and-red patterned jumper. I said my name and was about to ask if her husband was at home when he appeared behind her.

He shot me an irritable look. 'It's for me, Britt.' He nodded to the side. 'We can talk in my office, Veum.'

Britt Torbeinsvik looked a little surprised. I smiled disarmingly at her and said: 'Jehovah's Witness.' Then I followed Terje Torbeinsvik into his office.

He slammed the door behind us. 'What is it now? I thought we were finished last time we spoke.'

'This case won't be finished until someone finds out what happened to little Mette.'

'And why do you come here raking up the past? For Christ's sake I'd … You'd be better off asking Tor Fylling where he was at the time!'

'Tor Fylling? He was at home, wasn't he?'

He looked triumphant. 'He definitely didn't open the door when I rang the bell to talk to him … about something. And he wasn't in the garage either. I went out and looked.'

'But … when was this? Did you see Mette too? In the sandpit?'

He shrugged. 'I … don't remember. Don't know if I'd registered she was there. There were always children out playing at that time. Or else they were inside eating or whatever they were doing.'

'I assume you told the police this when you were questioned?'

'I did! Was there anything else you wanted to plague me with on an evening like this?'

I ignored his tone. 'Several of the neighbours have told me about what you called the New Year games … on New Year's Eve 1976.'

His eyes hardened. 'I see. And was that … ?'

'Yes? Carry on, Torbeinsvik.'

'Was that supposed to have anything to do with what happened to Mette?'

'It definitely tells me something about a co-op with a relatively liberal view of morality, if you ask me.'

'I think I told you the last time you were here, Veum. You give the impression of a hopelessly old-fashioned moralist.'

'Aha. It's possible you may be confusing that with the child welfare officer in me.'

'Possibly! What we did that evening … was a kind of party game. It didn't create any problems afterwards.'

'It didn't?'

'No.'

'Well, one of the couples left the party before the game began. Those who remained all got divorced later, every single couple. Some wooed their partner for the night, others … did other things.' Before he could interrupt I continued: 'And you yourself … happy with your work that night, are you? Good job for you the statute of limitations for rape is ten years, eh?'

His lips twisted in contempt. 'So Randi blabbed, did she?'

'Not only her. And only after pressure. This is deep in every single person who took part, Torbeinsvik.'

'Not in my case!'

'No, you were the one who took the initiative. And your wife was in on it.'

'Vibeke … ?'

'Yes.'

'No, not at all. Anyway, she had nothing to complain about.'

'Now I don't know where you're going.'

'No, and it's got nothing to do with you, either, Veum.'

I nodded to the door. 'And you and your present wife, do you practise the same sort of free love? As free as butterflies?'

He glared at me.

'Butterflies die after a day or two, you know. They don't have a long life. And that was how it was with the marriages here too,' I said.

'This still has nothing to do with Mette. Have we finished now?'

'Maybe.' I got up. 'Let me put it like this, Torbeinsvik. You're on my list. If you could rape a neighbour you could certainly have a go at a little girl as well, if the need became too great.'

He shot from his seat and came right up to me. His mouth smelled and some drops of saliva hit me in the face as he hissed: 'Once and for all, Veum. I didn't rape anyone! It was a game. And … the rest I'll choose to ignore. I could bloody drag you in front of a court for that sort of accusation!'

I held his eyes. 'Yes, you do that! Then you'll have the public's attention on all your doings out here.'

He opened the door and almost shoved me into the hall. His young wife appeared again. She looked at us with alarm.

Once again I turned directly to her. I raised my hands in the air. 'Paradise on earth and he refuses to listen to me!'

Then Terje Torbeinsvik pushed me out and slammed the door behind me. I could hear their voices inside, both slightly falsetto, then I ambled down the steps, past the small patch of garden and into the yard.

At the gate to the road I met Helle Fylling on her way in. She was wearing a dark cape and had a big knitted hat pulled down over her head, which meant I didn't recognise her until we were face to face.

She came to a halt. 'Oh … You.'

'Yes,' I said. 'Me. And now I know a little more about the so-called New Year games than you wanted to tell me when last we spoke.'

'Is that so?' She didn't move. Then she added: 'But I don't have anything to complain about in that regard.'

'No?'

'No! And I don't have a guilty conscience, either.'

'Is it correct that you and Nils Bringeland just sat chatting?'

She gawped in amazement. 'Who told … ? Oh, right. He told Randi?'

I nodded.

'Well, there you go! No complaints. We had a nice … chat.'

'But you could have ended up with someone else, couldn't you?'

'Yes, and so? I didn't…'

'You didn't…?'

'I don't go to bed with anyone!' She started walking to her house.

I raised my voice. 'You could have had Terje Torbeinsvik, for example.'

She stopped. 'Oh, yes? And where are you going with this?'

'Well … I've been told he wouldn't take no for an answer.'

She stood with a thoughtful expression on her face, as though trying to recall who had ended up with him that New Year's Eve. 'Really? Sad for her then. I have to…' She didn't continue.

'Yes, what were you going to say?'

'Erm, this doesn't … You're investigating the Mette Case. What's this got to do with that?'

'Well, it's too early to say. But I cast a wide net. Carry on.'

'I … Some months after New Year Nils came to me … in the street. We bumped into each other by chance.' She told me their conversation:

'Helle! Something's come up. I don't know how to deal with it.'

She looked at him. 'What are you talking about?'

'New Year… You know…'

She smiled wryly. 'Yes, Nils, I know.'

'Joachim had an outburst yesterday. We were having an argument, about a note he'd received at school and then it came: "You two don't care. We saw what you were up to on New Year's Eve!"'

'What!'

'Yes, I was gobsmacked. New Year's Eve, I said. What do you mean? And then he told me … "Håkon came over after we were supposed to be in bed. We were upstairs when we heard someone come in and after a while we went down and saw … Mum and…" He almost threw up, Helle. "… Mum and that Torbeinsvik doing it and … yes, doing it … you know what I mean."'

'No! He saw Randi and Torbeinsvik … making love?'

'Those weren't the words he used, but … yes. And what was I supposed to say? I had to tell Randi, of course, but what could we do? How can you try and explain that? And at the same time … you and I, we did nothing, Helle! We behaved … properly…'

'Yes, we did…'

'So, what you're telling me is that Joachim Bringeland, who at that time must have been seven or eight, and Håkon Misvær, who was five, saw what Joachim's mother and another man in the co-op were doing. And so they wondered, naturally enough, what was happening in the other houses. Do you think they …? No, they couldn't get in anywhere else.'

'Apart from Håkon's house, no. The doors would have been locked.'

'At Håkon's, where the mother would have been … with your husband?'

I struggled to visualise all this, tried to follow some threads in the weave that now appeared before me. But the image of the two boys got in the way. Now I would definitely have to speak to Håkon – and probably with Joachim again as well.

Helle Fylling stood looking at me. 'Yes, not that I believe this had anything to do with what happened to Mette, but it's a terrible thought. I mean … they were just children!'

I cast a glance at Torbeinsvik's house. Had I only known this ten minutes ago…

'Did your husband tell you – afterwards – what he and Maja had done?'

She sent me a measured look. 'No, he didn't. We simply didn't talk about it.'

'Well, that seems to be a standard answer. No one talked about it afterwards. So at least you all had the wit to be ashamed.'

She shrank visibly in front of me. 'Yes, it wasn't something we … Even if Nils and I … Hm.'

'But that might explain … No, well, what do I know?'

'What were you thinking?'

'All the divorces. Nothing is more fatal to a marriage than something both partners know, but neither will talk about.'

She whispered: 'Yes. Mm.'

'Another minor thing, Helle … Your ex-husband, Tor. In fact, I paid him a visit yesterday. I met your son and daughter-in-law too. Afterwards I heard … Did you know he was under suspicion for what might be termed criminal activity?'

She opened her mouth and closed it again. 'Criminal! Tor? What on earth could that be?'

'Receiving stolen goods. Re-spraying, re-building stolen cars and selling them on.'

'Receiving stolen goods? Cars? I think someone's got their wires crossed.'

'You don't know about any of this?'

'I never had anything to do with his work, but … I refuse to believe this. He's never been accused of anything. He's never been taken to court.'

'No, the cleverest ones never are.'

She tossed her head. 'Even if Tor and I split up long ago I … you can tell that one to the marines!'

'Thank you. I doubt there are any marines in Sotra, but that's where I'm going.'

She snorted. 'You won't get anything out of me as far as that's concerned!' Then she walked towards her house and this time it was for good.

I didn't have any more questions to ask her anyway. She had given me more than enough to chew on as it was: Joachim, Håkon and … any others?

29

I parked my car outside the hostel in Jonas Reins gate, where I had looked for Joachim Bringeland a couple of days before.

The entrance looked as if Tiny had taken my criticism seriously. At least it looked a little tidier and there was a strong smell of detergent, so strong that it seemed as if they had sprayed the whole area with it, neat. The music from upstairs was a little more muted, as though someone had introduced a new regime on that front as well. But when I knocked on the door to what was called 'OFFICE. RECEPTION' no one answered.

I tried a foray to the floors above, but none of the doors was marked with a name. If anyone answered they just looked at me, lost, when I asked if they knew where Joachim Bringeland was. Some of them obviously didn't understand Norwegian. A couple of them were so fried they barely knew what their names were, let alone where they lived, and in the last room the music was so loud when the door was opened that the stubble-faced tousle head who stared at me couldn't manage to understand what I was asking. So I gave up.

Back on the street, I stood thinking what to do next. Another trip to Nygårdsparken, in the darkness, had little appeal. But the last time I looked, Little Lasse lived near here, to be more precise, in Hans Tanks gate.

I left the car and walked a block south and a stone's throw east. Through an arched passageway I came to some rear stairs leading to a cellar. There, behind a window with such poor illumination that only a dim reflection reached the yard, Little Lasse had his place 'so deep down in the ground' it was doubtful even the old evil spirit of Robert Johnson's song would ever have accepted an invite.

The window was covered by a filthy yellow curtain, which twitched warily to the side after I had tapped on the window. Little Lasse peered out through the crack, nodded when he saw who it was, and immediately afterwards the cellar door was pushed open, heavy and slow as it clearly was.

Lasse grinned. 'Varg the Wolf is out hunting?'

'I never rest. Have you got a moment?'

'Yes, I'm not exactly busy. The lady of the house has gone home.' He ushered me inside. 'Pull the door to after you.'

'Cellar flat' might well be what an estate agent with an enfeebled conscience would call this in an advertisement. If the client came from the Kalfaret side of Bergen, or thereabouts, they would have called it a 'hole', though nothing more vulgar. I was generous enough to refer to it as a refuge. Even at the Sally Army shop, Fretex, they wouldn't have taken the furniture, and the cans of beer I saw appeared to be empty.

Nevertheless, Lasse managed to find an unopened can in a plastic bag he kept under a low table. 'Would you like one, Varg?'

'Not tonight, thanks,' I said, my mouth dry at the mere sight. 'Driving,' I added, without much conviction.

'You're only walking distance from home, aren't you?'

'So are police officers.'

'Well, as you like.' He lifted the can to his mouth and drank straight from it. 'I'll have one anyway.' After swallowing another mouthful he looked at me from an angle. 'So there are other reasons for you dropping by, I assume.'

I nodded, took a couple of banknotes from my wallet and put them on the table between us. 'An advance.'

He eyed them and nodded, but didn't touch them. 'And the small print?'

'I'll tell you now. This morning I went on a little drive.' I told him about the trip to Sotra to pay a call on Tor Fylling, about the Audi with the tinted glass that hung on my tail, like a customs officer behind a suspicious tourist bus, the confrontation with the two guys in the Audi and it turning out to belong to Gordon Bakke, known as Flash Gordon in select circles.

'Plus Thor the Hammer, I take it.'

I nodded. 'Others have made the same suggestion.'

'I'd be wary of Flash Gordon, if I were you, Varg. He doesn't seem so menacing when you see him, but he's a vicious bastard, and if someone's put him on your tail you'd better watch yourself when you're out and about.'

'Funny. Bjarne Solheim, at the police station, expressed it in exactly the same words.'

'There you go. But you wanted to see Tor Fylling?'

'Yes, about an old neighbour actually, to do with the case I'm working on. It had nothing to do with what I gather might be some sort of work as a fence.'

'Yes, I've heard his name mentioned in that connection, but not with the baubles those I deal with steal. It was cars mostly.'

'So you can't see a connection between Flash Gordon and him?'

He shook his head and took another swig from the can of beer. 'But there's something else you might be able to use ...' He immediately took the two banknotes from the table, as though it was only now he realised he had earned them. 'You remember that robbery in Bryggen before Christmas?'

He had my full attention, probably more so than he was aware. 'Yes?'

'The owner, a certain herr Schmidt ... he has used Flash Gordon's services on other occasions.'

'Right! Such as ... ?'

'Well, again this concerns the types I deal with. A couple of times the guys I meet in the park have been to his shop and have pinched a watch or two and legged it. Herr Schmidt never bothered to ring the cops. No, he was more interested in setting an example. So he phoned Flash Gordon instead. Flash Gordon turned up in the park, did a round and woe betide the poor bugger who couldn't return the goods ... He got such a beating that no one would contact the cops either, only the hospital.'

'So in other words ... if this Herr Schmidt had received a call from a private investigator who, he suspected, was working on the robbery case, on behalf of his insurance company for example, then he would contact Flash Gordon to get him to keep an eye on who said investigator was visiting?'

'Exactly. And if said private investigator was the person I think he is, then there's even greater reason for him to … as I told you…'

'… Watch his back when he goes out at night?'

'Even in broad daylight, I would say.'

'But you move in these circles … Are there any rumours doing the rounds about who was behind the robbery? The police have obviously drawn a blank.'

'No, in fact there aren't, Varg. Either they're pros, in which case they were long gone a few hours after the robbery, on their way to Oslo or Gothenburg; or else they were pure amateurs, and unless they've left a trail of evidence behind them they'll be almost impossible to track down.'

'I'm listening to an expert here, I can see.'

He grinned. 'One has picked up the odd thing over the years, even if one doesn't always stay on the right side of the law.'

'Not to mention the intake of certain beverages…'

'You could put it like that.' He raised the can in a silent toast, put it to his mouth and drained it. Then he hurled it into a corner of the room, where it joined others of its ilk.

When I set off walking ten minutes later I followed his advice and kept a good lookout. But there were no tinted Audis, neither there, nor in Jonas Reins gate, and no one tailed me through town and up to Skansen, either.

There I made my last move of the day. I rang Truls Misvær in Oslo, told him who I was and about the assignment his wife had given me. He didn't sound overly enthusiastic, but agreed to meet the next day, for lunch at twelve in Theatercafé.

Next I rang the National Theatre and asked if it was possible to talk to Vibeke Waaler.

'No, she's on stage,' the woman on the phone said.

'So she is in Oslo then,' I said, as if to myself. 'Inevitably, if she's doing a play,' the woman said acidly.

'And in the morning?'

'She's rehearsing a new play.'

'So if I pop round tomorrow morning there may be a chance of meeting her?'

'I doubt that, but you can try.'

'Would you be so kind as to pass on a message to her? Write that a private investigator by the name of Varg Veum would like to meet her and it's about the Mette Case, from the time when she lived in Bergen.'

This seemed to whet the woman's curiosity: 'The Mette Case?'

'Yes.'

'She'll get the message alright.'

'Thank you.'

Finally I booked a return air ticket to Oslo for the following day and crossed my fingers it would be worth the expense for Maja Misvær and the bother for me.

I went to bed without having tasted a drop of alcohol the whole day. Labour dignifies the man, as the saying goes. That undoubtedly applied to private investigators too, as long as they held a steady course and focussed on the next day's needs. And watched their backs. Do not forget that, I told myself as I sank into the most surprisingly pleasant sleep I'd had for ages.

30

Oslo in March can be anything from the first glimpse of spring to the last bitingly cold day of winter. I had been lucky on this occasion. It was beautiful spring weather all day.

I got off the Airport Express train at the National Theatre stop and took the escalator up to the Earth's surface again, where I was blinded by sunlight as I emerged at the rear of the large theatre building. It was situated magnificently between Stortingsgata and Karl Johans gate, like an outrider for the Royal Palace further up the hill and with the old university edifice as a loyal attendant on its left. At the opposite end of Spikersuppa, the pool alongside Karl Johans gate, stood Stortinget, the Norwegian Parliament. Thus, within a very confined area there was Parliament, the Symbol of Royal Power, the Temple of Knowledge and the Citadel of Dramatic Art; you could hardly display the capital city in a more concentrated fashion. You didn't have to go far down side streets to find those who really ruled either: the Supreme Court and Finance.

The staff entrance to the National Theatre was down in the cellar from Stortingsgata. Behind a counter sat a nice lady, she flicked through some pieces of paper in front of her, but was forced to conclude with an apologetic smile that, no, there was no message from Vibeke Waaler. As I refused to accept this as a final answer, she made some internal calls, which culminated in her telling me that Fru Waaler was rehearsing on the Amfiscenen stage, but she would be finished by two if I wanted to try again then.

'Right, does that mean you can give her a message saying I'll be back then?'

'Yes, we could do that. Of course, we can't guarantee Fru Waaler's

time, but…' She smiled a little condescendingly, as though Fru Waaler
had admirers at the door every single day of the week, from early till
late, and I was hardly among those at the head of the queue.

Somewhat disconsolate, I trudged out into the sunshine again. The
sky was high and blue above the capital, like the backdrop to a cheery
1940s comedy with Lillebil Ibsen and Per Aabel in the main roles. At
five to twelve I was standing by the entrance to the Theatercafé waiting
for Truls Misvær. At twelve sharp a man arrived, wearing a grey suit
and a light-coloured coat, alert and slim with fair hair casually border-
ing his collar, as if ready for a quick visit to the closest fitness centre.
We looked at each other enquiringly, swiftly introduced ourselves, and,
after handing in our coats, he led the way to the inner rooms, nodded to
the waiters, as if in familiar surroundings, and went straight to a window
table facing Stortingsgata, where we had almost complete privacy.

'I had it reserved,' he said in polished, elegant Bergensian, showed
me to a seat on the opposite side of the table and sat down with his back
to Stortinget, so that he was facing in the right direction if celebs such
as Erik Bye or Wenche Foss should pop their heads in. A waiter was
quickly at our sides, handing us a menu. Truls Misvær cast an experienced eye over it, ordered the house's Caesar salad, and I was unoriginal
enough to follow suit. With the food he ordered a glass of red wine for
himself, but I was thinking of my car at Bergen Airport and my general
condition and chose a non-alcoholic beer. Once this was done, he
leaned back in his chair, regarded me as if I were a potential business
partner and said: 'So who are you, Veum, and what are your qualifica-
tions? What makes you think you can find out what the police gave up
on twenty-five years ago?'

In broad strokes I filled him in on my background, from my time in
child welfare up to the present day, without mentioning the adversities
I had struggled with over the last three years, and the resulting financial
and private difficulties.

When I had finished he looked at me sceptically. 'And you, a one-man
band with no access to computer systems, registers or whatever else
there is, are going to find something – I repeat – the police gave up on

years ago?' He raised his arms aloft. 'Maja's crazy to invest her money in this!'

'You've lost all hope, in other words?'

'Hope of what, Veum?' he snapped.

'Of finding out what really happened to Mette on that September day in 1977.'

He stared back stiffly. 'Yes, I'm afraid I have. Nothing would make me happier, of course, if Maja – if we were finally to have an answer – but to be frank … I doubt you're the right man to give it to us.'

'Well,' I said, shrugging. 'All I can say is that I'll do my best to unearth more.'

'I mean … the police hauled in everything that lived and breathed with regard to potential sex offenders. One was even in custody for a few days…' He looked to me for a response.

'Yes, I've spoken to him. Jesper Janevik.'

He nodded, although he didn't look particularly impressed. 'They found nothing. We searched everywhere around, they scoured Nordås-vatnet, they spoke to all the neighbours.'

'Yes, on that subject. Were the relations between neighbours there a little special?'

His eyes appraised me. 'In what respect?'

I didn't get an answer because the waiter arrived with the salads and drinks. Misvær nodded to acknowledge the fast service, sipped his red wine, motioned for us to start and set about his salad at a speed that suggested he was only minutes away from being expected at a conference and there was no time to lose.

Between mouthfuls I said: 'I was thinking about the way you entertained one another, let us say, on New Year's Eve 1976.'

He snorted. 'You've been muck-raking, I can hear.'

'According to my sources, you carried off the main prize that evening.'

He cast an involuntary sideward glance across the street to the National Theatre. When he met my eyes again, I nodded assent.

He opened his fork hand. 'What do you want me to say? Has this got anything to do with Mette?'

'God knows, but it says something about the moral climate in which she was growing up.'

He looked thoughtful, and for a second or two it was as though his eyes became turbid, then he concentrated on the salad again. 'Do you know why it's called Caesar salad?' he asked.

'No idea. I doubt Julius Caesar invented it.'

'No, he didn't. It was in the 1920s, an Italian restaurant owner called Caesar who lived in San Diego but had his restaurant in Tijuana, on the Mexican side of the border, to avoid prohibition restrictions.'

'And what's that got to do with the New Year party games?'

'You're not very quick on the uptake, are you. The idea was to change the subject.'

'Yes, I can understand that you don't like talking about it. Did you know that you were being watched?'

For a moment he stopped stuffing his face. 'Watched! Vibeke and … By whom, if I might ask?'

I kept him waiting while I swallowed and drank a mouthful of beer. 'You know, Misvær, that even if you don't want to talk about it, I know most of what went on that night already. I know who was where, I know what happened in most of the places and – I've just found this out – I know that Joachim Bringeland and your son, Håkon, watched what went on between his mother and Terje Torbeinsvik.'

Now he was visibly shaken.

'And I'm not ignoring the possibility that it made them – how shall I put it? – curious? You know boys at that age … they may have gone back to your and Maja's house to see if something similar was happening there.'

He had put down both his knife and fork now. He held his throat with one hand, ran his index finger around the inside of his collar, as though it were too tight, and scanned the room to make sure no one else could hear what we were talking about.

'And it was of course,' I concluded, not without a certain satisfaction at the way I had tripped him up.

He stared at me, his eyes black now. 'Vibeke and I … we … She came from … Perhaps it was the theatre circles, perhaps it was just her.'

'The theatre circles?'

'Yes, aren't they famous for being a little more … liberal? She told me about an incident, one that had taken place only a few days before.'

'Before New Year?'

'Yes. She said … it was after the performance. She was playing Lady Macbeth that winter. She had been leaning over her make-up table – with her dress pulled up – and was … erm, taken from behind … by one of the witches.'

'One of the witches?'

'Yes, well … the witches were played by men in that production.'

'I see.'

'And then there was a knock at the door, and without waiting … in came Terje, her husband, and caught them in the act, if you know what I mean.'

'Yes, I understand. This has happened before.'

'Yes, I suppose it has.'

'And what happened then?'

'Nothing! That's what I'm trying to tell you. Nothing happened. It became a good story. Terje laughed. Vibeke laughed. The guy playing the witch … yes, he started laughing too. And then they all got on with their own business and that was the last of it. Terje drove Vibeke home – he was there to collect her – and since … Do you understand what I'm trying to tell you? They had no inhibitions. It was typical that they came up with this game, or whatever we should call it.'

'Well. Every one of the couples joined in, except one.'

'Yes.' He looked down, started fidgeting with the rest of his salad. 'So you think Håkon and Joachim … that Håkon saw Maja with … well, it would have been Tor.' Then it was as though something seemed to dawn on him. 'Perhaps that's why he wanted to be with me when we split up a few years later?'

'Why not? He'd seen his mother in action. You were frolicking with Vibeke at her place.'

'Yes.' He evinced a wan smile. His face was beginning to assume a normal colour again. 'Yes,' he repeated. 'That was quite an experience, that was. She was worth...'

As he didn't complete the sentence, I pursued the point. 'She was worth what, Misvær? The divorce? What happened to Mette? What...?'

'What happened to Mette has nothing to do with this!'

'No? Are you sure?'

For the last time he put down his cutlery. The plate in front of him was empty. 'What could the connection be?'

'That's what I'm trying to find out. I'll certainly have to talk to your son about this.'

'To Håkon?' He looked at me darkly. 'He lives in Ålesund.'

'Yes, I know.'

'He does something with the football club. AaFK. He was a pretty promising player once himself, but then his form went. He was mostly on the bench at FC Brann. Then he got an offer from Wiggen – the coach at Ålesund – to go there, but it didn't work out, either. No wonder though. He was too old to kick-start his career, if I can put it like that.'

'So he's not active anymore?'

'No, but he's still connected with the club. Ground staff ... something like that.'

'And he's never talked to you about ... what they saw that night?'

'Never! Do you think I'm sitting here and putting on an act?'

I waited. 'No, I don't think so. In that area you probably don't have the same talent as your old flame across the street.'

Again he glanced in that direction. 'She's not ... There was never any repeat, unfortunately. And not long after, she left Bergen and came here.'

'Which you did too.'

'Yes, but ... ha! No connection. I moved only a few years ago, and I haven't seen Vibeke Waaler anywhere else but on the stage – from the auditorium – for the last twenty years. Have you spoken to her?'

'Not yet. But I have arranged to meet.' I shot a glance at my watch. 'Shall I pass on your regards?'

'No.'

'No?'

'No,' he said. After a short pause, he added: 'You just go, Veum. I'll take care of this...' He nodded towards our empty glasses and plates.

'Thank you.'

He shrugged. 'One expense less on Maja's bill?'

'That's one way of looking at it.'

Without exchanging any more pleasantries we parted company. Truls Misvær beckoned to the waiter for the bill. I crossed the street in a further attempt to gain an audience with Lady Macbeth.

31

It was the same nice woman sitting behind the counter at the staff entrance. She recognised me at once and confirmed that Vibeke Waaler had said she would meet me. Then she called on the internal intercom, received an answer and not long afterwards the protagonist herself came through a glass door to the left of reception. She shook hands with an expression of curiosity and said: 'Come with me, Veum.'

She must have been around fifty, but, like most actors, she was in impressive shape, at least as far as her exterior was concerned. No one would call her beautiful, but she had a strong, clear face with a striking though elegantly formed nose, sensual lips with a seductive smile never far away, and direct blue eyes that held you in a somewhat disconcerting way. It wasn't hard to imagine her in big roles, Lady Macbeth back in 1976, when she wasn't even thirty, later Hedda, Ellida Wangel and the Queen in *Hamlet*. Now they were rehearsing a new British play, she told me on the way to the dressing room. 'Authentic language, good dialogue, an interesting role.'

She moved with a confident sensuality, dressed in tight, faded jeans and a clinging black jumper with a deep V-neck, emphasising her youthful voluptuousness. Her hair was casually pinned up on her head and was her only colourless feature: run-of-the-mill blonde; but I suspected that she wore a wig on stage and that was why she wasn't taking her own hair very seriously at the moment.

I followed her down the corridor, up a staircase to the floor above and into another corridor. When we reached her dressing room she held the door open for me and stood at the side until I had passed, as if to test one element of nearness. Once I was inside and waiting she paused for a few seconds before indicating one of the two chairs and gesturing for me to sit down. She sat down on the other, by the mirror, crossed her legs and leaned forward with her eyes fixed on mine.

'Now I'm intrigued,' she said in a deep, melodious voice that instantly reminded me of radio, a play, in which the femme fatale had just made her entrance.

I quickly looked around. I had been in actors' dressing rooms before, and this was no different, even if it was the National Theatre. It looked a bit poky. It was a single dressing room and there wasn't much space to romp around. The mirror behind her was lit up all the way round. On the walls hung pictures of stage roles, some of herself, some of colleagues – in which case they were always signed. I recognised several of Norway's biggest stars over the years. On clothes hangers along one wall hung garments, perhaps for the new play, because they were very modern and apparently unworn. On a hat stand there was a dark-green cape and a large velvet hat in the same colour with a long red feather, perhaps a souvenir of a Shakespeare performance, *As You Like It, Much Ado about Nothing* or something like that.

'I'm glad you had time to talk to me.'

She smiled sweetly. 'What wouldn't one do for attractive men?'

'Well … As I tried to tell you on the phone last night, this is about what we know as the Mette Case.'

'Yes.' She nodded and immediately looked serious. 'It was a terrible story. But have there been any developments? Is that why it's being taken up again?'

'It's not officially being taken up. I'm a private investigator, and Mette's mother, Maja Misvær, has asked me to review the case.'

'Maja … Yes, I remember her. Very sweet, but … a little tense, maybe?'

'Nowadays definitely, but you mean in those days as well, don't you?'

She was still looking me straight in the eye. 'Yes, I think I remember that.'

'You had – let me get straight to the point – a … what shall we say? … an experience with her husband…'

She sat looking at me, as though she hadn't quite understood what I was going on about. 'Ah, you mean … the New Year…'

I nodded.

'Who on earth told you about that?'

'Well, a number of the neighbours – your former neighbours, to be precise.'

'And what's that got to do with Mette?'

'Mm, everyone asks me that, and they're quite right to, but there's something about the whole set-up at Solstølen ... A female detective who was on the case at that time ... she said she felt there was something under the surface which never quite became visible. And I'm wondering if it wasn't precisely this. These self-styled New Year games. A consequence of ... what shall I say? A lack of moral restraint? An imbalance? Something that triggered something else that led to ... Mette's disappearance?'

'"Something is rotten in the state of Denmark", she quoted solemnly.

'It was your husband who suggested this activity, I gather.'

She waggled her head coquettishly and looked at me cheerily. 'Yes, it was. But ...' Her face turned grave. 'It came like a bolt out of the blue for me – when he suggested the game. But of course I'm used to putting on an act, I mean from a professional point of view, so...'

'You knew nothing beforehand then?'

'No.' Her eyes were pensive. 'It was probably a way to get back at me.'

'Get back at you? What do you mean?'

'Well ... we both had a liberal view of who we would allow ourselves to go to bed with. But ... it wasn't always easy to accept when something happened.'

I quickly licked my lips. 'Truls Misvær mentioned an incident in the theatre. With one of the witches.'

Again she had a distant look in her eyes, as though she didn't understand what I was referring to. 'Oh, you mean...' She laughed a dry, autumnal laugh. 'Yes, Terje might well have been a little put out that time, but ... he got over it.' After a short pause she added: 'So Truls told you about that? Well I never. Did he also tell you that Mette wasn't his child?'

Now it was my turn to be distant. 'What was that? Mette wasn't his ... but they had Håkon, who was older than Mette. Who could ... ?'

Ironic smile. 'How should I know? Maja would be the right person to ask.'

'But Truls … must have had a suspicion?'

She gracefully shrugged her shoulders with the same wry smile.

'When did he tell you this?'

'That night. After we'd … enjoyed ourselves, as much as we could, it was time to cuddle up and relate confidences, wasn't it?'

'Maybe.'

'And that was when he told me. *But how can you be so sure?* I remember I asked him. *Surely you were together, conjugally, during that period too?* Yes, he said, but still … it was obvious who she was like. *Who?* I asked. But, no, he wouldn't say. He didn't mention any names. Later I remember looking at her, the little girl. But you know. Children. I wasn't that interested in children, not then, and they were always so well wrapped up … you know … Bergen, rain, sleet, wind and lousy weather … I wasn't that curious anyway. I mean Truls Misvær was a one-night stand and never qualified as anything more.'

'You set the bar high?'

'Higher than him anyway.' Now the ironic invitation in her eyes was obvious. But she was an expert at subtexts, it was her stock-in-trade.

'And him? Was he as sure as you?'

'What are you referring to now?'

'Well … if he thought the experience was wonderful perhaps he might have wanted more, later?'

'Do you mean, did he come scratching at my door at night like a tom-cat?'

'That sort of thing.'

'No, he didn't. I think he knew what was what when he left.'

'The man you were married to then, Terje…?'

'Yes?' She rolled her eyes. 'One of my biggest mistakes, it has to be said.'

'Oh, yes?'

'Yes, not the only one. I got married a couple of times afterwards too, but … Terje was a bit bohemian and quite romantic, at least to a young actress straight from drama school and at Den Nationale Scene. Well, we didn't meet there, but at Wessel, after a performance. And bed beckoned. It often did in those days. I was young and frisky and fancy-free. Hungry for life, you could say. And then, wham, we were married. Yes, I think it probably happened under the influence. But we stuck it out with each other for a few years, didn't have any kids, thank God, and in 1978 I cast off. I'd had enough offers from here by then. First of all I was at Det Norske Teatret for a few years, then I went to the National in 1982. In fact, I haven't exchanged a word with Terje since.'

'Not one?'

'No, what would we talk about? We didn't have any children, the house was his – designed and paid for by him. How is he?'

'Well … he's got a new wife and … two small children, I think.'

'Small?'

'Actually, I haven't seen them.'

'Took him a few years to get a new one, then.'

'Possibly. What I wanted to ask you … it may seem a bit intimate, but … that New Year's night. Can you remember who Terje ended up with?'

She didn't seem very interested. 'No, to tell the truth, I can't. Who was it?'

'Randi Hagenberg.'

'Oh, right. Next door. And?'

'He … she didn't really want to and he … was pretty brutal with her. Some might say he raped her.'

She looked more displeased now. 'Oh, really? Well … if you can't stand the heat etc.'

'Was that behaviour … standard for him?'

'You mean, was he prone to raping?'

'Yes.'

'He didn't rape me, anyway.' Another little wry smile and a subtext that was not hard to decipher: *It wasn't necessary …*

'And he never showed any predilections for … children?'

She mouthed a round O, a sign of theatrical surprise. 'Oh, you were thinking about …' She continued undeterred. 'No, he never told me to get undressed or put a ribbon in my hair when we went to bed. He was exclusively interested in adults. Actually, he was much too absent-minded to be interested in anyone apart from himself. I think he regarded me primarily as a trophy, someone he could take from Wessel to show the boys, and next day he would be back, wearing my stocking garter around his wrist, metaphorically speaking.'

'Doesn't sound like you think much of him.'

'If I'm honest, Varg … cute name, by the way – you're the first person I've ever met with that …'

'Mm? If you're honest … ?'

'I don't think much of any men. I've simply had too many of them.' She suddenly made the grand gesture, as though she were on the stage and reciting lines. 'Give me the great minds – Shakespeare, Goethe, Ibsen – they're my men. Not the likes of you. It is to the great minds I have dedicated my life and I flourish here, in these corridors.'

For a moment, a form of sadness fell between us, as though we both instantly saw that life was not like this: a stage where you needed a loyal prompter at all times to move safely from one wing to the other without being exposed to whistling from the stalls or a boorish lambasting in the newspapers the following day.

Then she said: 'But now I need my rest, Varg. I have a role to play this evening. I'm afraid I didn't help you much.'

I stood up. 'No, perhaps not, but thank you for receiving me and telling me what you did. About Truls Misvær's dubious paternity, I mean.'

'Take it for what it is,' she said, getting up, and opening the door. 'I'd better show you the way out.'

'Thank you.'

Afterwards we didn't say much more than goodbye and I strolled into Stortingsgata again, puzzled. On the pavement I took out my phone and tapped in Truls Misvær's number. He answered after a couple of rings.

'Veum here.'

'Right! What is it now?'

'I've just met Vibeke Waaler.'

'Uhuh. And so?'

'She said … she told me that you'd told her Mette was not your child.'

The other end went quiet, so quiet that finally I had to say: 'Are you still there?'

'Yes.'

'Well, what have you got to—'

'Yes, I'll tell you what I've got to say, Veum. This is none of your business. It has nothing whatsoever to do with anything!'

'It's definitely got something to do with Mette.'

'It has nothing—'

'So who was the father?'

'None of your business!'

'Can I ask Maja?'

After a short pause came the sarcastic answer: 'Yes, she would probably be the right person to tell you, wouldn't she.'

Without adding anything further he broke the connection, and I didn't try to ring him again. It wouldn't have helped, of that I was sure.

Instead I did as I had planned all along: I rang Thomas and asked if he and Mari were receiving guests. They were.

They had a new flat in Grünerløkka and although there were a few months to go to the birth, Mari was suitably podgy around the middle. They seemed happy and excited, both of them.

I spent a relaxed afternoon with them, then Thomas drove me to the central station and the airport express.

It was pitch black by the time I parked in Øvre Blekevei. I should perhaps have been on my guard, but I hadn't noticed an Audi with tinted glass parked anywhere. As I rounded the corner to Telthussmauet they appeared from the darkness and walked towards me, Thor with his big, heavy hammer, Flash Gordon bouncing on his toes like a devious Loki from Norse mythology beside him.

32

If we had been in the Wild West, I would have drawn my Colt 45 and pointed it at them. But this was Bergen and I was no spring chicken. Instead I drew my Nokia, dialled 112 and spoke quickly into it: 'This is Varg Veum. I'm ringing from Telthussmauet. I have a man who would like to talk to you. Gordon Bakke, address Klostergarten number ... er, what was it again, Gordon?'

He stopped immediately, four or five metres away. I remembered the advice I'd been given earlier and kept an eye on his legs. Thor the Hammer kept walking, then he hesitated, stopped and looked at his pal.

I held up the phone in front of them, like a miniature shield. 'I've got them here, Gordon. 112. What was it you wanted to tell the police?'

His dark eyes glinted. I saw the psychopath in him stop and waver: What should he do? What were the chances of getting away?

I moved the phone back to my ear. 'Hello? Are you there?'

A gruff voice answered: 'Yes? What's all this nonsense? Who's ringing, did you say?'

'Varg Veum. There's an old friend of yours here. Gordon Bakke. Some call him Flash Gordon, but he doesn't look very flash right now. He has a companion they call Thor the Hammer. I'm not sure about his surname. I'm not sure they bother about such things in the zoo.'

'I hear you. Varg Veum. Address ... ?'

'Telthussmauet.'

Flash Gordon made up his mind. He signalled to Thor the Hammer. 'Come on. Let's go.'

I said on the phone: 'Just a minute. It looks as if they may have changed their minds.'

Flash Gordon gave me the finger and looked at me with such

narrowed eyes he seemed to be squinting. 'Don't think we've done with you, Veum. You think you've been smart, but there'll be other opportunities and then you won't get away so easily…'

'Yes, but now they know who to look for afterwards, Gordon. Now they've got your name, and Br'er Bear's too, and at 112 they'll have logged your names for all eternity.'

He pulled a face and ran a finger across his throat, an unmistakeable sign of his intentions. Then he and Thor the Hammer went in a circle around me and up Fløygaten, which explained why I hadn't seen their car. Thor the Hammer looked at me with crestfallen eyes, as if somebody had pinched the food from right in front of his mouth.

'Hello! Hello!' I heard from my mobile.

'Yes, hello,' I said. 'This is Varg Veum.'

'Yes, I got that!'

'The situation appears to have resolved itself, but please log the conversation and file it for possible future use, if you should get a call from a detective at Bergen Police Station.'

'And why would they ring us?'

'In case these two come back. They were on the point of physically attacking me – if not worse.'

'Then I'd recommend you send in a report.'

'I'll consider that. Thank you anyway for your help.'

'Not at all.'

We rang off, and I continued down the alley and unlocked my door. After hanging up my coat I flicked through what was in the post box – two bills and local supermarket advertising – switched on the computer and went through the day's emails. Surprisingly enough, there was a message from Bjarne Solheim, with an attachment. *We agreed you could see this, Varg. Don't forget – this is confidential!* The attachment consisted of a list of names – employees of Schmidt, the jeweller, from 1960 to the present day, including summer temps. One of the names on the list stuck out from the others. Now I had another question for Tor Fylling, who shot to the top of the list of people I was going to visit the next day.

33

When I turned into Fylling Bil Dekk & Karosseri at ten o'clock the following day the place seemed totally dead. Even if the weather was good it had been cold overnight and there was rime frost on the fields, like stardust across the countryside.

None of the cars had been sold since my last visit and no one came out to try and palm one off on me either. There were no sounds coming from the garage, and the windows behind the curtains on the first floor were dark and lifeless.

I got out of the car, walked over and felt the door. It was locked and a security services sticker, frayed at the edge and therefore perhaps invalid, warned me not to attempt to gain entry.

I took a few steps back and looked up and down the front of the house. No signs of life; but it was a Saturday, so perhaps they were the late-breakfast types at the weekend. I went for a walk around the building and, sure enough, on the right was a little set of steps up to a side door with a bell and a sign, which said: *Marita and Einar Fylling.*

I pressed the bell and from where I stood I could hear it ringing on the first floor. But no one came to open up, no one opened a window upstairs and there was no indication that anyone was at home.

I went back to the car, took out the map and found a route to where Tor Fylling lived. It was five minutes back into town, in the direction of Kolltveit. I drove slowly towards Kolltveit while following the map. As I was about to turn right an Audi with tinted glass swerved into the main road in front of me, so suddenly that I had to jump on the brakes to avoid a collision. The Audi turned towards town in the left-hand lane until it straightened up, but not so fast that I couldn't recognise the number. It was Flash Gordon and Thor the Hammer, still out seeking adventure.

I made no attempt to follow, I turned right and up the steep hill they had come down, with a great deal more on my mind than a few seconds before. I crested the hill with a view on all sides, then went down into a hollow, where there was an old white farmhouse surrounded by bare trees, with the foundations of a demolished factory to the south and a run-down henhouse that looked as dead as the garage I had just left. It must have been many years since any poultry flapped their wings around this farm and the local hawks must have had to search for other hunting grounds years ago.

Nevertheless there were more signs of life here than at the last stop. Two cars were parked outside, both considerably newer models than the sale items on the garage forecourt. One was a shiny Mercedes, a 2001 model; the other a not quite so well-tended Opel Vectra, two or three years old.

I turned in and parked the car. No one came out to welcome me. I got out and closed the door behind me. Still no reactions from inside the farmhouse.

I felt an acute need for something to strengthen my resolve and instinctively put a hand into my inside pocket, where I sometimes kept a hip flask, but all I found was my wallet, and that was lean enough as it was.

I approached the house with care. The front door was in a little porch on the eastern side of the building. There was no sign of a door bell, and when I knocked no one came to open up.

I tried the door. It wasn't locked. I stepped inside. In the dark hallway there was a worn, dirty rag rug on the floor, and a staircase up to the loft on the right. I stopped and listened. From deeper inside the house I could hear some indefinable sounds, voices it was difficult to understand and a scraping noise, as though something was being pushed along the floor.

I walked towards the sounds, careful not to make my presence known. I came to a door that had once been white, and to a limited extent still was, though not exactly dazzling. The door was ajar, and now it was possible to hear what was being said.

A woman I recognised as Marita said: 'Give me a compress! He's bleeding like a pig.'

'Shit!' said someone I thought was her husband. 'I'll bloody smash those crooks!'

I hesitated for a few more seconds. Then I gently pushed the door in, so gently they hardly noticed.

Within a few more seconds I had an overview of the situation. Tor Fylling lay stretched out on the floor with a pillow under his head. His mouth was open and horrible gurgling noises were coming from his throat; it would be wrong to say that he looked particularly well. It was a long time since I had seen a man who had been given such a beating. His face was swollen, his eyes were glued together, and in his gaping mouth I could see several teeth were missing. He was almost unrecognisable. One arm lay in an unnatural position across the floor and the way he was moaning suggested he was in great pain. Around him the furniture lay scattered in all directions, and the scraping sound I had heard from outside must have been when they pushed a broken chair – possibly used as a weapon – away from his head.

When Einar Fylling finally noticed someone standing in the doorway, I coughed and said: 'Have you rung for an ambulance?'

Marita looked up from the floor, where she was holding a compress to Tor Fylling's head. 'Bloody hell! Oh, for f—' The choice of language revealed that none of them had attended Sunday School much in their childhoods.

'Veum's the name … Well, have you?'

Einar Fylling charged towards me. 'I'll fucking smash you!'

I retreated, but not quickly enough, and I met the door frame. He grabbed my jacket, pulled me back and hurled me sideways into the room, at some distance from where his father lay.

'Hey, hey, hey!' I shouted. 'I've done nothing!'

He came towards me again, fists raised and ready to strike. 'Oh, no? Who the hell put them on to us, then, eh? Only ten minutes after you left, they turned up!'

'Who?'

'Flash Gordon and a sidekick!'

'But they were tailing me!'

He punched the air in front of me, initially to mark his territory. 'So you admit it?'

'Let's say I know who they are and they're not on my guest list either.'

He came closer. I assessed the situation. He was a tall, strong lad, if a bit cumbersome in his movements. His wife followed us closely from where she was sitting beside Einar's father.

I nodded in his direction. 'He's going to die unless you get some medical help.'

'You're going to die too, Veum.'

'Einar!' Marita said.

'Will one more or less make any difference?'

This time he punched to hit, but I did the Ali shuffle and feinted. To my left there was a window. If I could smash it I had a way out. But then I would have to act fast. Again he came towards me and I lost my balance as I tripped over one of the overturned chairs. I fell headlong and his punch sailed past, but the next second he was by me, pulling at my ankle and twisting it, forcing me to move with it. I banged my forehead hard against the floor and saw stars. Then he pulled me in, my forehead banging against the floor again and again.

Marita screamed: 'Einar! What are you doing?'

'I'm going to finish him off. He's in on it, isn't he? Of course he bloody is!'

At that moment a new voice was heard, unclear and poorly articulated, as though it came from an oral cavity stuffed full with cotton. 'E-e-einar? Ma-rita?'

All three of us stared at Tor Fylling, who had half-raised his head and was looking around. There was a faint gleam in the narrow crack between his swollen eyelids. In the end his gaze found me too. 'Ve-um?'

Although my position was extremely uncomfortable I tried to sound as unaffected as possible. 'That's me. And you should go and see a doctor, Fylling. The sooner the better. But these kids refuse to ring casualty!'

'Ki-ds?' He looked around. 'You mean … ?' Again he looked at Einar. 'What happened? Who came in here?'

'Didn't you see them?'

'No…'

'But we had visitors today, don't you remember?'

'Visitors?' Fylling slurred.

With an immense burst of energy I wrenched my foot out of Einar's hands and stood up again. Then I signalled with raised palms that I wasn't going to do anything drastic – like running off or launching a counterattack. Einar glared at me, as if to say: *Just you try it.*

Then Marita spoke up: 'You must remember, Tor! The two that came on Thursday, right after him over there. They gave us until today. If not … and when you didn't appear at the garage as usual we drove here and found you like this.'

'And the henhouse is empty!' Einar said.

'Empty?' Fylling stared at him, puzzled.

Einar rolled his eyes. 'He can't remember a bloody thing.'

'No,' I said. 'That's a sign of serious concussion. Or shock. He's got horrible injuries and that arm's broken. I mean it! Marita, talk to him! He needs to see a doctor.'

Marita raised her face and looked at Einar. Neither of them said anything, but a combination of despair and hesitancy shone from their eyes.

I tapped my pocket and took out my phone. 'I can do it.'

Einar Fylling was breathing heavily as he watched me. Then he shifted his gaze to his father, who had closed his eyes again. A faint rattle came from his chest.

I said: 'This is an emergency!'

Then I keyed in 113. Neither of them protested. When I got through, I gave a brief rundown of the situation and tried to explain as well as I could where we were. I was told an ambulance was on its way. The woman on the switchboard continued to ask me questions: had we made sure his airways were free, did any of us know any first aid and could we perform chest compressions?

'I'm not sure that'll be necessary,' I said.

'Is he breathing?'

'Yes, but he's making gurgling – perhaps I should say rattling – noises.'

'That'll be his lungs. Has he got any external injuries?'

'Yes, lots. He may well have broken ribs.'

'Then you need to be very careful with compressions. Do CPR. Give him mouth-to-mouth. Two breaths in, then a break, then two more and carry on until the paramedics arrive.'

We rang off, and I said to Marita: 'One of you has to give him mouth-to-mouth.'

She looked down at him. 'Mouth-to-mouth? You can see the state he's in.' Her expression suggested she was going to be sick. Then she looked up. 'Einar! He's your father…'

He shifted his weight from foot to foot like a punch-drunk boxer at a dancing-school ball for the first time. 'Mouth-to-mouth?'

'Oh, my God. It won't kill you. Has he got syphilis or what?'

Einar shook his head in bewilderment.

I shoved him aside first, then Marita, leaned over Tor Fylling, opened wide, placed my mouth around his and breathed in. Once, twice. His mouth tasted of blood and vomit. Once, twice. I felt his bristles against my lips and saw coagulated blood around his mouth. Once, twice.

Marita sat holding the compress to his head, her eyes glazed. Einar started moving around the room. For a moment I wondered whether he would have another go at me, but actually he was clearing up, as though to make room for the paramedics when they arrived.

It was close on a quarter of an hour before we finally heard the sirens approaching. Once, twice…

As the ambulance came to a halt in the yard and the sirens were switched off, Tor Fylling made a sound. A spasm ran through his body and he tried to force open his eyes. In a faint, unclear voice, he mumbled: 'Veum?'

'Yes, it's me. Help's on its way, Fylling.'

'Mette was mine,' he said. Then he gave up trying to focus and his head slumped back.

34

The paramedics quickly placed Tor Fylling on a stretcher, got the basic information they needed, then lifted it up and made their way out. To make sure I wasn't left alone again, I followed them out, got into my car and stayed close behind them on to the main road. In my rear-view mirror I saw Einar standing alone in the yard watching us go. Marita went with the ambulance. On the main road I pulled in at the kerb, rang the number of Bergen Police Station and asked for Bjarne Solheim. He was off-duty. I asked if they could give me his private number, they refused. I had Helleve's number, so I rang him instead.

'Varg? Do you never give it a rest?'

'I think I've solved a case for you, Atle.'

'Oh, yes? Which one, might I ask?'

'The Bryggen robbery in December.'

'Right!'

'If you've got Solheim's number I recommend you grab a few hefty guys and come out here to Sotra. Then you'll definitely catch one of the perps. The other two are on their way to casualty.'

'Casualty! For Christ's sake, Varg! I hope it wasn't you who...'

'No, no, calm down. It happened before I arrived.'

I gave him the edited highlights and told him the registration of Flash Gordon's car. Helleve promised to set up a search for the Audi and to get under way as soon as possible. I sat in my car, keeping an eye on the turn-off in case Einar tried to make his escape this way. But nothing happened, and half an hour later a patrol car from Bergen pulled in right behind me. Helleve, Solheim and two armed, uniformed officers stepped out while the driver remained behind the wheel.

I got out, pointed to the turn-off and explained the situation.

Helleve eyed me with concern. 'Was he armed?'

'I didn't see any weapons. But he was pretty much out of control.'

They devised a quick plan, got back into their car and turned up the steep side road. Without asking, I followed them.

In the yard they parked across the road so that it was impossible for anyone to pass. The two armed officers jumped out on either side and took up a position behind the car. They were wearing bulletproof vests, helmets, and visors over the top part of their faces. I sat watching.

Helleve and Solheim waited for a second, then they got out of the car as well. Helleve cast a resigned expression in my direction. All four of them walked towards the house. The driver remained behind.

The two armed officers stood either side of the front door. Helleve and Solheim stayed close to the wall. One officer kicked open the door. After a short pause for thought they went in holding their weapons at the ready.

I opened the car door and sat listening. Not a sound. Helleve and Solheim conferred. They took a decision and followed their fellow officers into the house.

I got out of the car and gently closed the door behind me. Through the windows I could see them moving around inside, apparently to no avail. Through the open door I saw one officer go into the loft with his gun raised. Straight afterwards he came back down and stood in the doorway looking out while talking to his colleagues in the house. I left the car and walked over, just in time to meet all four of them coming out.

'Nothing?' I asked.

Solheim shook his head. 'Just overturned furniture and a trail of blood on the floor.'

I nodded towards the decrepit henhouse. 'Try there.'

Again the two armed officers advanced first. Helleve and Solheim hung back, and Helleve gave me a firm signal to do the same.

The same procedure was repeated by the henhouse. One officer kicked open the door, so hard it came off its hinges and slammed down on the floor inside. Then he rushed through and to the right. The second officer stood outside with his weapon poised.

We heard a call from inside. Then all went quiet.

The officer outside peered through the opening. Then he turned and waved us over.

Helleve and Solheim formed the natural vanguard. I brought up the rear, like an overgrown follower of a street band. We stopped by the doorway and looked inside.

The place had been trashed. The brooding boxes had been smashed and thrown around and there was a stench of mummified chicken shit and rotten woodwork. In the middle of the floor sat Einar Fylling like a monk in meditation, bent over, with a vacant gaze and a doomed expression on his face. An abandoned refugee on the quay after the last boat has gone, another animal not allocated a place on the ark.

We filled the doorway, blocking out the light, and he slowly raised his head and looked at us, no sign of recognition of me or the others.

I said over Helleve's shoulder: 'Is this where you hid the booty?'

He gaped at me and nodded.

'Is it all gone?'

'All of…'

Helleve turned to me. 'That's enough, Veum. We'll handle this.' Upon reflection he said: 'But you'll have to come to the station with us. We need your statement too.'

One officer gave his weapon to Helleve, then he and Solheim together pulled Einar to his feet, clicked cuffs on him, led him to the patrol car and pushed him inside. Helleve, the second officer and I followed like a contemplative funeral procession coming out of the chapel.

Both the farmhouse and the henhouse were cordoned off, then we drove away in separate cars, not breaking the speed limit once between Klokkarvik and Police HQ on the corner by Allehelgens gate and Domkirkegaten. After we arrived they checked Tor Fylling's condition. He had been taken to Haukeland Hospital, they were told; Marita was on her way to the station as well.

While Solheim questioned Einar Fylling in an interview room, Helleve and I went to his office, where he performed a formal interview with me too, though in a more cosy atmosphere, over a cup of coffee or two.

I told him about my confrontation with Flash Gordon and Thor the Hammer the night before, and like a delayed tidal wave washing in over me I realised that if I hadn't reacted as quickly as I had, I might have found myself a victim of the same brutal treatment as Tor Fylling. I also explained to him that they had tailed me to Fylling's the first time I went there and that, from other sources, I had learned Flash Gordon had done jobs for Schmidt after thefts from his jewellery shop.

'We'll have to talk to Schmidt,' Helleve said, nodding as he typed on the keyboard in front of the screen.

'And I really hope you can haul in Flash Gordon and Thor the Hammer. I wouldn't like to meet them outside my place again.'

'We'll do our utmost, Varg. Trust us.'

'What's Thor's surname, by the way?'

'Hansen, I think. Nothing unusual anyway.'

'Well, well … But back to the case. Solheim sent me a list of former employees at Schmidt's, including summer temps. I reacted to one of the names: Marita, who's married to Einar now. I had observed with my own eyes that the garage was in trouble and so I went out there again. The rest you know.'

'But when you first went to the garage it was for a very different reason?'

'Yes. The Mette Case, which we talked about yesterday. Tor Fylling was one of the neighbours at that time.'

Helleve shook his head. 'Ever heard the expression: Even a blind squirrel finds nuts?'

Suddenly we heard loud voices from the corridor and I recognised one of them as Marita's. 'That bastard got what he deserved! I was only fifteen and doing a summer job, and he was always trying to get me in the back room and grope me … all over the shop! He even opened his safe and showed me the fantastic watches he kept there. Each of them worth half a million, he said, and I could have one if I … would relax with him. Fifteen years old!'

'OK, OK,' I heard a female officer say. 'Let's take this step by step. Come here with me and...'

A door was closed and their voices were gone.

I looked at Helleve. 'That was what I thought. She had first-hand knowledge of what was in the safe. That's why they targeted it. But, Helleve ... there's a question I'd very much like to ask ... the detainees.'

Helleve sent me a patronising look. 'Not you, Veum. We might be able to ask it for you. What's the question?'

'It's important for you too. It's about the murder in Bryggen. What happened? What was said between the murderer and the victim? You see, the victim was also a neighbour of the Misvær family at the time their daughter went missing.'

'Sounds like a strange coincidence, if you ask me.'

'That's precisely why.'

'OK. Come with me.'

He led me to an office where we could see the adjacent interview room through a one-way mirror. Solheim was inside, a laptop in front of him and another officer at the side, Einar Fylling sat opposite, slumped across the table. Between them was a microphone.

'You stay here,' Helleve said in a low voice, left the office and entered the interview room. He took Solheim into a corner of the room, whispered, got a thumbs-up, then went back to the table and sat down while Helleve stood behind him with an expectant expression on his face.

I could hear their voices as well as if I were in the same room.

Solheim focussed on Einar and said: 'A man was shot as you left the scene of the crime. What happened?'

Einar looked up, shook his head. 'It was ... self-defence.'

'Self-defence?'

'He ... he tried to grab Dad. He said he recognised him.'

'Recognised your father?'

'Yes ... All I know is what Dad told me afterwards. He had to, he said. He recognised him. He said his name. It was self-defence.'

'Your definition of self-defence is questionable, but we'll make a note of that ... Your father was recognised by a casual passer-by and then fired a shot to prevent this information from going any further. Would you agree to that formulation?'

Einar nodded slowly. Then a light seemed to go on for him. He suddenly looked around. 'Shouldn't I have a … solicitor?'

Solheim glanced at Helleve, who nodded. Then he said: 'Yes, perhaps you better had.' He leaned closer to the microphone and said in a loud voice: 'The time is 15:26. We are taking a break.'

Einar was offered something to drink; he chose coffee and the officer went to get it for him. Solheim waited until he was back with the coffee and the officer stayed with him while Solheim came into the corridor to join Helleve and me.

He nodded. 'You got your explanation there, Veum.'

'Yes. Does it mean Tor Fylling will be charged with murder when he's back on his feet?'

'In principle, he was charged today. And when he's well enough to stand trial we'll ask for imprisonment. In the meantime we're expecting a report from the hospital.'

I splayed my hands. 'Well … what would you do without the help of the man in the street?'

Helleve smiled genially. 'Blind squirrel, as I said.'

Solheim looked from him to me. 'We'll handle the rest of this case though, Veum.'

'By all means. For me it was no more than a side track. However, it did take me a step forward.'

'Really?'

'Yes.'

But I didn't tell them what Tor Fylling had divulged before they carried him out. It had nothing to do with the robbery in Bryggen. I would have to visit Maja Misvær, though, once again.

35

The sun was going down when I parked outside Solstølen Co-op that Saturday evening a week before Palm Sunday. The red of the sunset between the scattered clouds lay like an open wound over the mountains on Sotra, with Mount Lyderhorn to the north-west like a tusk.

In the yard, where I was now a regular visitor, I took stock. There were lights on in all the houses, the distant sounds of a variety of activities, the impression as everyday as it could be, house fronts so normal you wouldn't imagine anything secretive could be taking place behind them.

I had called in advance to give warning of my visit, and it wasn't long after I had rung the bell that Maja Misvær opened up and let me in. She was clearly excited. I had said I had some news, but I didn't say what.

She showed me into the sitting room. The television was on. She threw a quick glance at the screen, then turned to me and said morosely: 'I always watch children's TV at this time of day.'

'I see…'

'Yes, I know it's stupid of me, but … I can't stop myself. I sit here with a lump in my throat thinking: 'Mette would have liked this. She would have laughed. Now she would have crawled into my arms because it was a bit scary. That kind of thing.'

I looked around. The photos were on the sideboard as before. Nothing had changed. She had set the table for two, with coffee cups, cutlery, plates and a dish of apple cake. In a little bowl I saw whipped cream.

Almost bashfully, she said: 'Yes, I assumed you would want … something.'

'Thank you. It looks good.'

She inclined her head towards a chair as a sign for me to sit down. After I had settled she poured the coffee, sat down on the sofa and pushed the apple cake towards me. I helped myself, placed the cream and spooned a bit to taste.

'Mmm...'

'Do you like it?'

'Perfect.'

Her smile spread across her face. 'Thank you ...' Then she helped herself.

For a while we sat eating in silence. She had turned down the volume, but the images on the screen flickered past. It was an animated film of some kind or other, animals jumping about in a setting that was definitely somewhere in the country, the romantic view that by and large only survives today in contexts such as TV and film: red barns, lush trees, happy domestic pets. No pollution, no rundown henhouses and no passing gunmen in action.

'You had some news, you said.'

'Yes. Last time I was here, two days ago, we talked about Tor Fylling.'

She nodded, and I saw her skin redden from her neck up to her cheeks.

'Today he's in Haukeland Hospital, badly injured.'

'Oh, my goodness!'

'When he gets out he will be charged with the murder of Nils Bringeland in Bryggen last December.'

Her eyes grew. 'What! Was he the man who...?'

'To cut a long story short ... it was Tor Fylling – and some others – who carried out the raid on the jeweller's and on their way out collided with Bringeland, who somehow recognised Fylling, said his name and was shot for that reason.'

She shook her head. 'Tor shooting Nils because he ... But ... this had nothing to do with Mette...'

'No, and there was no reason to believe it did, was there?'

She shook her head again. 'No, no, of course not.'

'Last time, I told you I'd found out Tor was involved in criminal activities, but you didn't believe me.'

'No, and I still think it's odd.'

'But now he's in hospital, beaten up by some criminals – we might call it a showdown – and Einar…'

'Einar!' She had tears in her eyes. 'Little Einar?'

'Well, little Einar launched a brutal attack on me earlier today, and he's no longer little. But he's confessed that it was his father who fired the gun and he's charged with robbery, along with his wife, Marita.'

'This is just incredible, Varg! And you found this out as a result of … of…'

'Yes, as a result of you asking me to find out what happened to Mette in 1977.'

She looked at me without saying a word.

'But before Tor was taken to hospital he said something to me, which I would like you … to comment on.'

'Oh, yes?' She seemed frightened, but I could see in her eyes she had guessed what was coming.

'He said … "Mette was mine". That's what he said. Only those three words: "Mette was mine".'

Her whole upper body trembled. She lifted her hands to her face and hid her eyes behind them. She said, in such a low voice I could hardly hear: 'Did he say that?'

'Yes. Is it true?'

She still had her eyes hidden. Then she slowly took her hands away and looked at me as though she were down a tunnel and peering out at the sun. I nearly waved back to show her where I was. In the end she whispered: 'Maybe.'

'In other words … you and Tor Fylling were already having an affair when you lived in Landås?'

She shook her head vehemently. 'No, no, no! Not an affair. It was a … one-off.'

'You slept together … once? And you hit the bull's eye, if I might put it like that?'

'Bull's…?' Confused, she looked at me.

'Yes. You became pregnant at the first attempt?'

Again she flushed from her neck upwards. 'It wasn't an attempt! It was … an accident.'

'Alright. People call it so many things. But … Håkon was older. How can Tor Fylling be so sure he was Mette's father? Had Truls and you stopped … your conjugal rights?'

'No, but … we were having a break.' She searched for the words. 'It … it was terrible – embarrassing. Humiliating. Truls had a hernia operation at Christmas 1973. He wasn't much in the mood for … you know … until it had healed properly, and that wasn't until late February the year after. And the pregnancy with Mette passed without any problems. Everyone said afterwards I was well gone when we moved in here in October 1974, and she was born on the 25th. Simple arithmetic. It must have happened in January – or at the latest in early February. I tried to tell Truls it was the latter, and in the end he accepted it. I assured him there could be no other explanation. But he … I don't think he ever believed me a hundred percent. The seeds of suspicion were always there.'

'But did you tell Tor?'

'No, but I think he was also counting on his fingers that autumn, and one day … Truls was away, I was fiddling around with some flowerbeds, Mette was asleep in her pram beside me. He came over, peeped into the pram and said: *She's mine, isn't she?*

She had responded angrily. What could she say? Deep down, she knew, of course:

'No, no, how could you believe such a thing?'

'I can work it out too, even if I'm only a simple car mechanic … From January to October is nine months, and it was in January we … You told me yourself Truls hadn't touched you for over a month and that was why you gave in so easily, but … anyway…'

He had walked over to the pram, rolled back the cover and looked inside.

'So?' she had said, breathless.

'I can see … she reminds me of my sister when she was small.'

'Your sister?'

'Yes.'

She met my eyes again. 'I never admitted it in so many words, but he could probably read me. She was as good as hairless when she was born, but … as her hair began to grow … they were the same fair curls that he had – back then anyway.'

'So, in other words … even without a DNA test you're sure he was right?'

She nodded and shrugged at the same time, still not completely ready to admit the connection.

'So when you drew lots at the famous New Year's Eve party and got each other, it was a kind of reprise?'

She looked at me and blinked, as if facing a gale-force storm. 'Yes…'

'Perhaps you talked about it too? When you were lying there … afterwards?'

He had sat up, resting on one elbow, stroked her body, down to her stomach, patted her gently and said: 'Let's make another one, Maja…'

She had met his eyes. 'Not this time, Tor. I'm on the pill now.'

'… Yes, I as good as admitted it then.'

'And how did he react?'

'Well…'

He had leaned forward, found her mouth and kissed her tenderly and long, and later they had made love again, the second time that night. She had later thought back to it so often, if for no other reason than to think about something else…

'And what about … later? Did he return?'

Something suddenly happened to her face, something she could no longer restrain. It was as though her boundless fears came to the fore, first in her eyes, then round her mouth, only to spread across her face until it became a stiff mask, a plaster-cast mould of the unhappiest face I had ever seen, a face where her guilty conscience shone through, from an intense, internal fire, burning white and as difficult to look straight at as the sun. I turned my head away, looked to the side, pulled myself together, straightened up again and asked the question I couldn't not ask: 'Not … that day, Maja?'

She nodded. When she did finally say something it was in an almost inaudible voice: 'Yes, that day...'

She had been standing in the kitchen watching him walk across the yard. She went to the front door and let him in. He looked at her and read her eyes. With a little smile he led her inside and there – behind the sitting-room door – he had kissed her passionately and taken her standing up, she with her back against the door and her gaze directed through the sitting-room window at the wide-open Saturday-still countryside ... She had clung to him, wrapped her arms around his neck, pushed against him and given him all she had, suppressed emotions and allayed desire, sighs and groans and tender caresses...

Afterwards they had sunk to their knees on the floor as they gasped for breath, as if after a long run over rough terrain. They had looked at each other with a mixture of shame and pleasure. Then they had carefully disentangled themselves, got up, tidied their clothes, stroked each other's cheeks and gazed deep into each other's eyes before he had quickly walked through the hallway and out. She had gone to the kitchen window to watch him leaving. It was only when he had let himself into the house across the yard that her eyes had sought the sandpit. And that was when she saw. Mette wasn't there any longer.

36

She leaned forward, banged her head several times on the table, as if it were a form of penitence. And then she started sobbing – such intense, racking sobs that I had to get up from my chair, move to her side of the table, take her in my arms and hold her tight, so tight that she couldn't hurt herself, so tight that the sobbing finally subsided, as it always does if you wait for long enough.

At least what she had told me gave me the answer to one of the two open questions: Why Terje Torbeinsvik hadn't found Tor Fylling when he was looking for him the day Mette went missing. Moreover, it was perhaps in Tor's house that the phone had rung and rung and no one had answered it…

In the end she looked up at me, still with her guilty conscience shining through her face. 'Can you understand how I've felt since then? Can you understand why it's been an obsession for me … for all these years? While Tor and I were at it, someone came and took Mette … out of my hands so to speak. Can you understand that I blame myself for what happened? Truls never forgave me.'

'But … did Truls find out? '

She looked at me in horror. 'No, no! Are you out of your mind? I've never told anyone! The only person who knew was Tor, of course, and even he … We never talked about it, and – believe me, Varg – we were never together again, not in that way. That was definitely the last time.'

'But then all that … We have to go back to the unintended pregnancy. Could that have anything to do with Mette's disappearance? Could your husband's suspicions have been so strong that he…' I searched for words, to express what I wanted to say in the most considerate way possible.

She looked at me aghast. 'What? Surely you don't think...?' She swallowed several times before she could continue. 'Truls always had a slightly distanced relationship with Mette. Perhaps because he suspected ... He had a very different relationship with Håkon ... still has. But he could never have done anything to Mette. Not even if he'd known. Not even if I'd admitted it. And Tor ... he ... I saw how he was always watching her. When we had communal dos with the children, for example. Very often he chatted to Mette or helped her if it was something practical. On a couple of occasions I even remember ... I happened to catch Truls's eye ... he was watching them and was ... almost jealous.'

'Truls was jealous of Tor?'

'Yes ... I don't know, but ... maybe.'

'But not so much that he could have done something to Mette, even if he felt sure she wasn't his and he might therefore not have such warm feelings for her...'

'Of course not! And anyway, he was away the day it happened. At football training with Håkon. Have you forgotten?'

'No, I haven't. If I can contact Håkon I'll go up to Ålesund in the next few days to talk to him.'

'Yes, you were in Oslo. How did that go?'

'Well ... I met Truls. But he didn't have much to add to the realities of the case. He said nothing about what we've talked about, for example.'

'That's good!'

'But there's another matter that's come up and I'm afraid I'll have to ... ask you about it.'

'There's more?' She was clearly nervous.

'First of all, I'll have to ask you ... did you notice anything about Håkon after New Year's Eve?'

'Are we back there?'

'Yes.'

'Notice? What do you mean by that?'

'Did he behave differently? Did he confront you – with what you'd both done?'

'Confront? God, no. He was five. He had no idea what was going on? He was asleep in bed.'

'You're sure? Sure he was asleep, I mean.'

'Yes. I'm sure he was.' She looked absolutely terrified now, and I could see the questions I had asked churning round in her head. 'Have you heard anything to the contrary?'

'Yes, I suppose I have. Joachim, the neighbour's son, who was three years older than Håkon, told his father that he and Håkon hadn't gone to bed at all that night, but were in Joachim's room and were doing something or other when they heard Randi, Joachim's mother, and Terje Torbeinsvik come in. Well, they didn't know it was Torbeinsvik, of course, but they crept down to watch...'

'What? Did they see them?'

'In full flight, you might say.'

'Joachim and Håkon...'

'Yes.'

'But that means ... Why would he ...? Neither Truls nor I...'

'No, the only other house they could get into was probably this one and it might well be – this is in fact one of the questions I have to ask Håkon – it might well be that they came back here and caught a glimpse of Tor and yourself.'

'We were in the bedroom. We had the door shut.'

'Sure?'

She stared into the distance.

'Hundred percent positive?'

'No...'

'In other words, it's a possibility.'

'Could ... could that be the reason he went with Truls when we split up three years later? I mean ... in that case he only saw me, not ... oh, my God! Just the idea of it.' Her face was scarlet now and tears were rolling from her eyes.

'My social welfare experience tells me it could well be the reason.'

'Oh, God, no! I had never imagined this.' She was sobbing aloud now, tears streaming down her face. But there wasn't the same intensity as the first outburst. Even for her there was a limit to how many tears could fall, and it seemed as if her guilty conscience had been a stronger trigger than the shame she felt now.

But at least Mette was asleep, I told myself. *The sleep of the innocent.*

While she had cried herself out I took a last swig of coffee. On the silent screen the children's programme had changed to a film, obviously aimed at slightly older children. The voiceless heads were in a different world, far from ours, with a massive glass wall between them and us, preventing sound from escaping.

At length she took out a handkerchief, dried her eyes and looked shyly in my direction. 'Sorry … that was just so overwhelming. The thought of it.'

I nodded sympathetically.

After a while she said: 'Do you know … You must be the first guest I've had here for many years. At least on a Saturday night.'

'Are you usually on your own?'

'Alone with my thoughts, yes. You can probably understand how it's been, from what you've found out.' Her eyes went to the sideboard and the two photographs. Then she said, in a slightly stronger voice: 'I haven't had one … I haven't been with anyone – after Truls moved out.'

'Not … And we're talking what here…?'

'We're talking about all the ways you can imagine, Varg. I've lived like a nun, in complete celibacy … and I haven't missed it. Not for one second! I was weaned off it in the most brutal way you can imagine.'

'Yes,' I said neutrally, trying to imagine myself in her shoes, not entirely successfully. 'Has it been … a very different life?'

'I would have happily thrown away all those years if I could have had Mette back! If she'd been here with me … all the time. That's all that counts. You'll have to keep searching, Varg. Even if I have to spend all the savings I have. I can't bear it any longer. I've got to have an answer!'

I didn't delve any further and we had another piece of the apple cake and drank our coffee. Fifteen minutes later I left the house. She would probably spend this Saturday evening alone as well, in her chosen celibacy, with no other guests at her door but her painful thoughts. And she would never be able to shut them out. They would always come visiting, bidden or unbidden.

37

There was one more woman I wanted to speak to before the police did. Sølvi Heggi had told me she and Bringeland lived in Åsane, somewhere between Morvik and Mjølkeråen. I drove home and flicked though the telephone directory. Her address was in Saudalskleivane. I knew where it was.

I phoned and she answered after five or six rings. 'Yes?'

'Varg Veum here. I don't know if you remember me?'

'I do indeed. It's not so easy to forget a name like that.'

'I've got something to tell you – about Nils and why he was shot.'

'Why?' Her voice had a touch of steel.

'Mm, could I come over?'

She hesitated. 'Can't you say it over the phone?'

'Everything can be said over the phone, but I often prefer face to face.'

'OK, fine. I'm here on my own with a glass of red wine, so … just come.' Another woman sitting alone on a Saturday evening; but with Sølvi Hegge there was an undertone that suggested long-term celibacy was not a natural option, however fresh her widowhood.

'I'll be there within the hour.'

'See you,' she said, and rang off.

While I was on the phone I thought I might just as well call the number I had jotted down: Håkon Misvær in Ålesund. No one answered, but I left a message on his answerphone, gave my name, told him I had to speak to him urgently and asked if he could ring me.

It had been a long day and I had eaten only a couple of hot dogs earlier and then the apple cake at Maja Misvær's. I cut two slices of bread, added some ham and stuffed them down, then threw off my clothes, stepped into the shower and stood there for five minutes letting the hot water run and run over my body, partly bruised after my morning tango with Einar Fylling. Fifteen minutes later, with clean clothes on and a moderately clear head, I got into my car and drove to Åsane.

Saudalskleivane rose steeply towards Geitanuken, one of the finest vantage points in this whole part of town. Sølvi Heggi lived in a detached house, quite high up, and when I had parked the car and got out I was struck by the impressive view of Byfjorden and Herdlefjorden. Out there lay the islands, Askøy and Holsnøy to the north-west, and even further north, Radøy and the Lindås peninsula. On the fjord I saw the express boats from Sogn og Fjordane on their way to Bergen, evidently the last trips of the day. Up here people stayed indoors.

My phone rang. I fished it out, studied the screen, didn't recognise the number, but answered at once. 'Yes? Veum here.'

The voice was thin and a little high-pitched, like a patient chatting while waiting to see the doctor. 'This is Håkon Misvær. I'm ringing from my mobile. You wanted to speak to me?'

'Yes! Thank you for calling back. It's about … your sister, Mette.'

' … Yes?'

'I'm a private investigator and your mother commissioned me … You know, of course … it's almost twenty-five years since she went missing, Mette, that is, and now your mother's asked me to review the case a final time before the statute of limitations comes into effect. Do you follow me?'

'Yes.'

'And so I'm talking to everyone.'

'I have nothing to tell you. I was only six years old.'

'Yes, I know, but it's unbelievable what you can turn up by talking.'

'OK.'

'Can you set aside some time for me if I come to Ålesund on Monday?'

'I'm working.'

'Where?'

'At Kråmyra. The football pitch up there.'

'Can you spare me a few minutes?'

'Yes…' He didn't sound particularly keen, but he didn't object either.

'I'll ring you when I've passed Vigra. Can I get you on this number?'

'Hopefully.' Then he rang off and I saved his number in my directory. I locked the car, opened the gate and walked down the path to the house where Sølvi Heggi lived.

It was built in the seventies or eighties I guessed, with a whitewashed base and vertical cladding on the main floor. I rang the bell and not long afterwards Sølvi Heggi opened the door and welcomed me. 'Come in…'

She was more casually dressed at home than she had been at the office in Bredsgården, wearing cord trousers, flat shoes of the slip-on variety and a grey-and-black patterned blouse that hung loose over her hips. From what I could see she had put on discreet lipstick, perhaps for the benefit of the visitor, unless she was the type of woman who was forever touching up her appearance, out of habit.

I followed her through a porch into the hallway, where she indicated an open wardrobe with space on the pole and I hung up my jacket. I started to remove my shoes, but she stopped me: 'No need.' Then I traipsed after her into the big, tastefully furnished sitting room with tall, broad windows looking out on the same view from the road. There was art on the walls, books on the shelves, quite a large sound system and a television of older vintage in a corner. It was a room in which I could feel comfortable.

In a corner, the one with a view of the fjord – at least if you craned your neck – were a sofa and a table, set with two glasses and a carafe of red wine. One glass was half-full.

'My daughter's staying over with a friend. So I'm here alone.' She looked at me archly. 'May I offer you a glass?'

I coughed. 'I'm driving.'

'You can allow yourself one glass.'

'Well…' All of a sudden my throat was drier than a temperance preacher's on the booze cruiser from Denmark. 'One then.'

She smiled pleasantly, ushered me to the sofa, filled my glass and her own before seating herself a short arm's length from me. Her face became serious. 'You said you would tell me *why* Nils was shot?'

'Yes. Obviously it was pure chance that he happened to be passing by, but once there it turned out the assumed main robber was a close acquaintance of his – from their schooldays – and somehow Nils recognised him. It might have been something he said, it might have been the way he moved, at any rate there was something he reacted to. Nils said his name. It might have been shock or sheer desperation, but the robber recognised Nils and shot him – dead. In other words ... now he's no longer a chance passer-by but was potentially a central witness in the case.'

'Goodness!' She was taken aback. 'That changes things – a little anyway.' Then she took a deep breath. 'But I don't know if it makes the grief any easier to bear.'

'No.'

'Tell me some more. Who was this man he recognised?'

I told her as far as I was able about Tor Fylling, Einar and Marita, Marita's summer job in Bryggen, the probable background for the robbery and how I had unwittingly put Schmidt's henchmen, Flash Gordon etc, on their trail.

'But why did they follow you?'

'I went to the jeweller's after I'd spoken to you the other day. Schmidt suspected I was conducting an investigation for his insurance company and probably concluded I might lead them to the potential perpetrators. Gordon Bakke clearly knew Fylling and about his activities – receiving stolen goods among other things – and assumed, correctly as it happened, that he was their man. They beat him into such a state that finally he told them where he'd hidden the goods, which I imagine by now are safely back in Schmidt's hands.'

'Rotten to the core!'

'You can certainly say that, and of course I agree. Dubious methods. But also pretty effective once you're on the right track.'

'So what will the police do?'

'Interesting question. Shall we ring them and ask?'

She smiled, in disbelief. 'Can we do that?'

I smiled back. 'Not this evening maybe, but ... another day.'

'But ... this isn't the case you were investigating.'

'No, this was literally a side track.'

'How's that one going, then?'

'Not exactly a breakthrough, but ... bits and pieces have cropped up.
I'd like to ask you...'

'Ask away.' She raised her glass for a *skål* and I was obliged to follow
suit. The first sip of red wine tasted like velvet on my palate and I felt
the inside of my mouth narrow around the dark-red liquid. Then the
first mouthful slipped down my throat like the juice from a rare steak,
spreading warmth and unrest throughout my body, where an invisible
demon began to bang on his drum with a regular beat: More! More!
More...

She observed me with curiosity. 'That seemed to go down well?'

'It was terrible.'

Our eyes met and something deepened between us; it was a few
years since I had experienced such a rush. I looked away quickly – and
down. When I looked up again she was still there, with her eyes perhaps
a touch more sardonic now.

'There was something you wanted to ask me...'

'Yes. You told me about Joachim last time and later I met him ... in
Nygårdsparken.'

'Right.'

'I've heard from a secondary source ... Well, perhaps I'd better tell
you ... or ... did Nils ever tell you about some New Year party games
they played in Solstølen?'

'No...' She smiled. 'Games?'

'A kind of party game that ended up ... in wife-swapping. For a night.'

She opened her mouth in surprise. Between her front teeth I
glimpsed the pink tip of her tongue. 'No, he never told me about that.'

'But you said he told you something happened between him and
Randi, and that was the reason they split up.'

'Yes, but he never said what. Does that mean … they…?'

'Well, that's perhaps the point. According to my sources, Nils behaved exemplarily that night. He and the woman he drew in the lottery spent the night – at least if she is to be believed – chatting. Nothing else happened. Randi, on the other hand, well, she was raped, in her words, but…'

She nodded slowly, as though she hadn't quite understood what I was saying. 'So, put another way, that could have triggered the process that led to them moving apart?'

'Possibly. But there's another matter. Joachim and another boy from the co-op, Håkon, little Mette's brother, must have seen Randi and Terje Torbeinsvik – if the name means anything to you – at it; they also may have seen what was going on in the neighbour's house, where Håkon's mother had a visitor.'

Her jaw dropped. 'But … but … that's crazy, what you're telling me. They couldn't carry on like that with children watching!'

'Well, it wasn't intentional, of course. And so I'm back where I started. Joachim confronted his parents with this, later, and what I wanted to ask is … did Nils have a theory about how Joachim had ended up today in Nygårdsparken, and when did this all start? In 1977 he was only eight, after all.'

'No, I don't think he said anything. He was just sad and depressed by what happened, to Joachim, I mean. Several times he said words to the effect of: *We have a bad conscience, don't we? It's our fault. We did something wrong. We, the parents.* But that's natural, isn't it?'

'Parenting's a tricky business, but of course it's not the parents' fault, not every time. There can be other factors at play too.'

'But that they could even think of…' Again she smiled that strange, wry smile of hers. 'Sounds a bit exciting too.'

'What do you mean? The New Year games?'

'Yes…' Our eyes met over the edge of the glasses. Then she carefully put hers down on the table between us. We were sitting on different sides of the corner sofa, but so close I could have reached out and touched her. 'Not that I … What you've told me about Nils and the neighbour sounds right. Nils was a gentleman of the old school and a kind-hearted person, with great modesty. She chewed her lower lip. 'For as long as he lived I could never have dreamed of … going to bed with another man.'

I drained my glass. She took the carafe, leaned forward and asked: 'Another?'

'The car,' I said weakly.

'You can ring for a taxi, can't you?'

'I could.'

She filled my glass. 'Or stay until the morning…?'

I stayed.

38

On Sunday morning I woke up in an unfamiliar bed with what I assumed was a happy widow beside me, judging by the contented sighs coming from her lips. I lay staring at the ceiling and reflecting on how on earth I had ended up in this situation.

I could hardly consider myself a seduced youth, but it had definitely been her who took the initiative, first with her simmering eyes, then filling my glass of wine, which didn't stop after the first two, then shifting over to my side of the sofa and resting her head on my shoulder, only to turn face-on and lie heavily against me, reach up and place a gentle red-wine kiss on my mouth which, at that point, was in the process of finishing the story of what had happened to Karin three years ago.

'Oh, poor thing!' she had said, before we kissed. Whether it was Karin or me she meant, I never found out.

Lying there, I could feel the heat of her body and I said to myself: 'She's definitely not too young and we're both fancy-free, three months in her case; three years in mine...

'You must think I'm mad,' she had said in the semi-darkness afterwards. 'I don't throw myself at the first man to knock at my door, you know.'

'I sincerely hope you don't.'

'But isn't there a phrase, *carpe diem* or something? Seize the day, or night in this case.'

'Yes, a kind of ... nearness grew between us, didn't it?'

'You have no regrets?'

'I never have regrets. That is, yes, I do, but not on this occasion.'

'Sure?'

'Cross my heart.'

'*And hope to die, stick a needle in my eye,* we used to say when we were kids.'

'Mhm.'

We had made love like the experienced sea-lions we were, frolicked in the pool as well as we were able, yet with the meek self-confidence born of the fact that we had done this before and we knew most of what there was to know about this. When you are young you think physical love declines with the years. Naturally enough, it doesn't. You make love as passionately at fifty-nine as when you were seventeen, twenty-two or thirty-three. Less often, but better, as a well-known author said in an interview I had read once many years before.

She had tasted so strongly of soap that I suspected that she had gone straight into the shower after I had announced my impending arrival, to be prepared for all events, and when she came tears rolled from her eyes, but when I asked her if she was sorry, she whispered: 'No, it was so good ... You don't get better compliments than that at my age.'

Suddenly she opened her eyes and looked at me in shock. For a second or two it was clear she had no idea who I was or what I was doing in her bed. Then it dawned on her, she blushed becomingly and met my gaze with an immediate tenderness. 'Oh! Good ... morning...'

She lay half-across me and looked at the alarm clock, which was on my side of the bed. 'What's the time?'

'Around nine.'

She stayed on my chest, stroked my cheek and said: 'It'd probably be a good idea if you were gone by twelve. I'm expecting Helene.'

'Right.'

'But you must have some breakfast first.'

'Don't worry.'

'I do.'

She swung over, got out of bed on her side, pulled on a blouse before getting up and going to the bathroom. Straight afterwards I heard the sound of water.

We had a peaceful breakfast in her white kitchen; freshly brewed coffee, bacon and eggs, pickled herring from a jar and seasoned cheese.

I felt a strange calm in my body, as if this was really something we had done for years and we would continue to do for the rest of our lives.

Before I left, she accompanied me to the door. 'Will I see you again?' she asked, almost shyly.

'I hope so.'

'Will you contact me?'

'As soon as I've finished the case.'

'Fine.' She stretched up, kissed me lightly on the mouth, opened the door a fraction and let me out while she hung back discreetly, in case any of the neighbours should see us.

Driving back to Bergen, I was happy I didn't meet any police checks. My wine consumption the previous evening had been of such an order I wondered whether I would get through a breathalyser test without them pocketing my licence for a couple of years. I drove to a petrol station and bought two Sunday newspapers. There was a big spread about the arrest of the Shell Suit Robbers, and the police got all the accolades, though after 'a tip-off from a member of the public', as they put it. That suited me down to the ground. I had always preferred to keep a low profile as far as the press was concerned, so low that I would barely be visible after my death, if anyone was looking for material for a suitable obituary.

This time I had a good look around after I had parked, but I couldn't see any Audis with tinted glass. Nevertheless, I fell straight into the trap. I was totally unprepared for them breaking into my flat. As I slammed the door behind me and turned to the clothes stand in the hall I was embraced from behind by far less loving arms than those that had been holding me hours before, and out from the sitting-room doorway came Flash Gordon with a triumphant expression on his little rodent-face.

'Welcome home, Veum,' he grinned. 'Where the fuck do you spend your nights, you slippery bastard?'

39

They had put me in one of my own chairs, bound my arms behind my back, and tied a rope round my ankles and the chair legs and up the back in such a way that I couldn't move a muscle.

Thor the Hammer stood by the door staring at me. Flash Gordon had his face so close to mine that I could smell the strong throat pastilles in his mouth, mixed with nicotine. There was a small brown stripe round the corners of his mouth, and when he spoke droplets of saliva landed on my face.

'You should have boarded up your back door, Veum,' he hissed.

'Or got yourself a burglar alarm,' Thor said, grinning like a security company salesman who had just received a commission.

'What the hell do you want?'

'To get rid of a dangerous witness, since you ask so nicely.'

'And how will that help you? The police have had your names and numbers for ages. It's just a question of time before they haul you in.'

His eyes narrowed. 'That'll be after your time, Veum. We've been given orders by the highest authority, and there'll be cash in an account when we're out.'

'You...'

'And we always get out again!' he guffawed. 'Always!'

I could feel unease spreading through my body. Was this the plan? Was one last night of bliss what fate had dealt me? Was it already time to pay for the sweetness with pain?

I scanned the room. 'And who said I didn't have a burglar alarm?'

Flash Gordon smiled condescendingly. 'Veum, we came here last night. It hasn't gone off yet. Perhaps you haven't paid for it yet?'

'We're being filmed.'

For an instant, I saw a shadow of uncertainty sweep across his face. He quickly looked around, searched the corners of the ceiling, the book shelves, the windowsill. Then he turned his attention back to me. 'Good try, Veum. But I can't see anything. And they should have been here by now, shouldn't they?'

'Listen, Gordon ... You and Man Thursday over there. You've got enough lives on your consciences. Fylling has too. Schmidt as well, if you carry out his orders. Think about it. Premeditated murder. That's twenty-one years, with no concessions because of the records you have. And it's you who will pay the price. Schmidt will get off with a far shorter sentence, you can bet your bottom dollar on that.'

I glanced at Thor the Hammer. I detected some uncertainty there too and gave him another jab in the same direction. 'What do you think, Thor? Sick of living here among us normal people? Feel like a spell in Åsane until FC Brann have yo-yo-ed between divisions a few more times? Goodbye to all of life's pleasures, big and small?'

Flash Gordon made a dismissive gesture with his hand. 'Shut up, Veum! You saw the state Fylling was in. Do you fancy a bit of the same treatment?'

'He's got a point, Gordon,' Thor mumbled from the doorway.

Flash Gordon turned on his heel and snapped: 'And you shut up too! Have you got that?'

'Right,' Thor mumbled quietly, but not that amenably, judging by his face.

'What you can do, Thor, is go up to Skansen and get the car. Drive as near to the front door as you can make it so that no one will see the container when we move away.

'OK,' Thor replied, without stirring a muscle.

'It's quiet now. Let's put him in a sack, take him away and find a suitable place to drop him in a lake. Remember we get paid for this job.'

'The rest of your lives!' I shouted.

Flash Gordon slapped me so hard that my head was knocked sideways and my skull sang.

'I warned you, Veum.'

Thor the Hammer was still in the doorway, uncertain what to do. Flash Gordon ran across the floor to him and held out his hand. 'Give me your phone. You won't need it while you're out getting the car.'

They stood glaring at each other. For a moment I had hoped Thor would use his superior strength, fold Flash Gordon up, put him in his pocket and remove him from my life. But it didn't happen. Flash Gordon's eyes were too strong for him. He dug into his jeans pocket and handed it over to Flash Gordon while gazing at it longingly, as though he were reluctantly parting with an amputated body part.

Flash Gordon stuffed the phone in his pocket without a second look and nodded to the door. Thor the Hammer turned obediently and left. Flash Gordon came back to me with pinched lips and an ominous look in his eyes.

'That leaves just us two, Veum.'

From his inside pocket he took a small case. He opened it and removed a syringe. From the same case he lifted an ampoule filled with a clear, faintly yellow liquid. I stared stiffly at the medicine. Again I felt fear burn through my body, like a wild animal from another reality.

He looked at me with a little smile playing on his lips and held the syringe in the air while tapping it in an affected professional way. 'Just relax. You won't feel a thing. All that will happen is that you will fall into a deep sleep – and never wake up again.'

'Gordon! You're going to regret this.'

His eyes glittered malevolently. 'If you're worried about your neighbours, you can be reassured. You won't be left to pollute the neighbourhood. We'll find a suitable place to drop you into the sea.'

He put the syringe down on the table and came towards me again. I stirred uneasily, tensed the muscles I could in the hope I could loosen the ropes they had used, but there wasn't enough time and my muscles were too weak; it was no use. He went behind me. 'I just need to find a suitable vein, then …' He leaned over and I could feel his fingers fumbling around my wrists to fold up my shirt sleeve.

I clenched my teeth and felt my eyes fill with tears. My vision blurred and I focussed on the door, as though to force it open and get the world outside to come in.

Miraculously, it worked, with a loud slam, which made Flash Gordon jump in the air and snatch at the back of the chair. I was sent flying backwards across the room and lay staring up at the ceiling as a swift and orderly assault continued above me, around me and on all sides. I heard shouts, roars, groans, and only when strong hands grabbed the chair, put it back in a vertical position and cut the ropes binding me to it did I have any kind of perspective of what was going on.

I recognised two of the guys from the police raid in Sotra the day before. They had Flash Gordon in their control now, although he fought against it, cursing and swearing in a way that a full-blooded Satanist would have envied, his eyes positively snarling as handcuffs were clicked in place behind his back.

I had never seen the man who cut me free before. He was wearing a black leather jacket, a brown T-shirt and dark-blue jeans. His face was symmetrical and anonymous, he had dark-blond, shoulder-length hair, blue eyes and three-day stubble, and after he had released me, he held out his hand, shook mine and said: 'Moses Meland, undercover cop.'

'Moses?' I said.

'Your parents must have been equally imaginative,' he grinned.

'But we've never met…'

'No, we undercover guys prefer to stay in the background. But we have our uses, as you can see.'

'You were keeping my flat under surveillance?'

'Since the incident on Friday night, yes. And it paid dividends. Even though they fooled us by going in the back way. We saw you come home and when Thor Hansen burst out of the block an hour later we knew something was up. But there are others here who can tell you more than me. Come down to the station with us and we can take it from there.'

We followed the two uniformed policemen out of the house and up to Øvre Blekevei. Thor the Hammer sat in handcuffs in the back seat of the car, with an apparently relieved expression on his face. When they shoved Flash Gordon in beside him he couldn't hold his tongue. 'Idiot!' he hissed into Thor's face.

'Same to you,' Thor mumbled back.

Moses Meland grinned beside me and nodded to a Toyota Corolla as anonymous as my own. 'Let's go in mine to avoid the aggro.'

A quarter of an hour later I was in Atle Helleve's office.

He smiled apologetically. 'Sorry about the bother, Varg, but …'

'You could at least have told me you had my flat under surveillance.'

'We didn't want to make you even more worried.'

'Ha ha.'

'I mean it. But now everything's under control. The whole case is wrapped up. Schmidt's in one of the interview rooms talking to Bjarne. Doesn't seem to be a very cosy atmosphere in there. And now that we've got Gordon Bakke and Thor Hansen nicely installed on the lower floor, it won't be long before we have a complete overview of that bit of the op. I would guess everything that was stolen in December is back in place. Otherwise we'd hardly have found Schmidt in his shop late on a Saturday evening. Now we're waiting to have a search warrant signed and we can order him to open his safe.'

'Sounds good.'

'Marita's spilling the beans. She's giving us everything and you heard yourself what she said when she came in yesterday. Today she's gone into detail. Now that side of the case is probably too old, but we could have charged him with sexual abuse of minors, if we'd known a few years ago. Some of his actions could be defined as rape. But the most interesting thing she told us about was one evening after opening hours when the jeweller had invited her into the back room to show her something.'

'Which was … ?'

'He'd opened the safe and taken out a tray containing eight diamond-studded watches, each one of which, according to her, was worth around half a million kroner. And that was then. Eight times half a million – that makes four by my reckoning and a pretty good profit for a quick shift in the afternoon, plus what they earned in the shop. What do you think?'

'Well …' I was still dazed after the latest events of the day, both away in Åsane and home in Telthussmauet, and had difficulty concentrating.

'He'd put one of the watches around her wrist and said – still her words, Varg – she could have it if she would … erm, perform certain acts on him.'

'And she said … ?'

'She says she refused, but she blushes to her roots when she talks about it, naturally enough.'

'She didn't get a watch then?'

'Hardly. She wouldn't have wanted to wreak revenge for no reason. At any rate she was the one who suggested the idea to her husband and father-in-law when they first started talking about where they could get some quick money.'

'And did she tell you how they made their getaway?'

'Not in detail, but it was more or less as we thought. We've got the name of the boat owner as well. A guy who worked at their garage.'

'Yes, I think I know who it is.' I pictured the little guy with the asymmetrical moustache who had arrived as I was leaving the garage the first time I was there.

'He was waiting in the boat with the engine running while they crossed Bryggen and jumped in. They landed on the Laksevåg side where they had a car ready – probably one of the wrecks in their garage. That night they went back to collect the boat, which was probably moored at a mole somewhere on Sotra – we haven't got that far yet and she wasn't very precise with regard to places.'

'So, in principle, the case has been solved? Thanks to …'

'Thanks to a coincidence, yes. We'll mention your name to the insurance company. Don't be surprised if you get a little mark of their appreciation.'

'Thank you very much.'

We sat looking at each other. He seemed restless, as though he couldn't wait to have Flash Gordon and Thor the Hammer in his interview room as well. 'And what else have you got on? Are you still working on the other case?'

'Yes. Tomorrow I'm off to Ålesund.'

He got up quickly. 'I won't detain you any longer, then. You've probably got a bit to tidy up at home too.'

'Afraid so, yes.'

'Would you like us to get someone to drive you?'

'It's just as quick walking. Thanks for the offer anyway.'

Back home in Telthussmauet, I tidied up the sitting room. They hadn't made much of a mess. Most of it was caused by the police. I made a futile attempt at fixing the lock on the back door, where they had broken in. I ended up shoving a heavy dresser against it and decided to postpone the repair until I could afford it.

As happy as pig in clover, I filled a kitchen beaker full of aquavit, sat down in the good chair and slowly sipped it. This was all I could do. Medicine for unsettled red-wine tummies. I wondered if I should give Sølvi Heggi a buzz and tell her about the warm welcome waiting for me at home, but I decided against it. She had enough on her mind as it was. Instead I put on a Ben Webster CD and sat in the chair, as busy as an owl during the daytime, while Ben looped and swooped through *They Can't Take That Away From Me* in a way that brought me straight back to Saudalskleivane and the previous evening with no transport costs of any kind.

40

I caught the morning flight to Ålesund, landed on the island of Vigra in a gale, and took a taxi straight from the airport to Kråmyra Stadium via the two tunnels under the sea that, since 1987, had joined Vigra to the mainland.

The FC Aalesund ground was up the south-eastern side of Mount Aksla. For a stadium of a team aspiring to first-division football this appeared to be relatively modest, but was in fact an acknowledged Sunnmøre principle. You didn't throw money around for no reason. If you wanted to see a football match you had to stand outside in the westerly wind and rain.

There was a red clubhouse on the long side to the north. From there you could see across the fjord to Langevåg and Sula. At the top of the stand a man in dark-blue overalls bearing the club's logo and name in orange was scraping away the last traces of the winter with a robust snow shovel. As I approached I recognised Håkon Misvær from the confirmation photo I had seen in his mother's house.

He looked up and rested on the shovel while he waited for me to reach him. He had a blue-and-orange woollen cap on his head, pulled well down over his ears, leaving only unruly tufts of blond hair sticking out at the back. His thick eyebrows were arched, which made him look surprised more or less all of the time. His mouth was sullen, surrounded by a two-or-three-day growth of stubble.

'Håkon Misvær?'

He nodded.

I held out my hand. 'Varg Veum.'

He shook my hand limply.

'Is there anywhere we can go?'

'We can do it here.'

'Right.' I shrugged, unhitched my shoulder bag containing the little baggage I had and took out my notebook. 'As I said on the phone … your mother gave me this assignment.'

He nodded.

At the end of the stadium a group of young men in track suits were running up and down the concrete steps. I pointed. 'This year's team?'

Again he made an affirmative movement with his head.

'Aiming for promotion, I see from the papers.'

He observed me without speaking.

'You played here yourself, after leaving Brann, didn't you?'

'Yes, Bård Wiggen brought me up here. In Brann I was mostly on the bench. Or in the stand. Had a few run-outs.' He added bitterly: 'Fifteen games, zero goals. My club stats for Brann.'

'And up here?'

'Started ten games, came on as a sub twenty-odd times. Thirty-two games, one goal – against HamKam. Geir Hansen also took me on. But then it was over. Now Ivar Morten Normark is the manager. You can see him over there. Blond hair, on the side line.'

'But you still work here?'

He shrugged and looked around. 'Ground staff. I do odd jobs inside and out. Never do away trips. Spend my time in Kråmyra.' Then he looked down across the fjord. 'In a few years though we'll have a new stadium, down there. Perhaps conditions for us foot-soldiers will be a bit more endurable too.'

He was beginning to thaw now. Football has that effect, at least among those for whom it is their overriding interest in life. 'So what do you remember about the day your sister went missing, Håkon?'

We were quickly back into everyday life. He sent me a surly look, as though I had asked him an unpleasant question, and indeed it was. 'What do you think? I was six years old. That's very young.'

'You and your father were at football training?'

'Yes, there was a training pitch near Fana Stadium. A guy came running over and said there was a call for Dad in the clubhouse. I stayed on the pitch while he dashed off, but soon afterwards he came running back, took me out of training and dragged me up to the car. Then he drove as fast as he could home. And all he said was: 'It's Mette. She's gone missing.' Afterwards everything was chaos.'

He went quiet again.

'Anything else you remember?'

'Such as? It was a terrible mess, that year and the year afterwards. Mum was completely hysterical. All she talked about was Mette, Mette. Dad was … calmer. If there was anything, I would ask him, and the following autumn I started school. He took me and stayed with me during the first few days.'

'Your parents split up in 1979.'

'Yes.'

'And you moved out with your dad?'

'Yes.'

'Why?'

'I told you! Mum was … out of her mind. Dad, at least was normal, and after a few years he met Gudrun and we almost became a normal family again.'

'Did they have children?'

Sullenly, he said: 'Yes. I've got two half-sisters.'

A silence grew between us. At the end of the stadium the players had stopped the step-ups. Now it looked as if they were getting ready for a run. Håkon watched with wistful eyes. He would have much rather been there than in the stands with me.

'You had a friend, then, called Joachim.'

Suddenly there was something new and wary about him. 'Yes?'

'I've been told that on New Year's Eve 1976 Joachim and you saw something you shouldn't have.'

He paled visibly, and his voice vibrated as he said: 'Oh, yes?'

'It's not something that can be swept under the carpet. Many of us know about it.'

His face revealed some noticeably fiery-red patches. 'Joachim talked, did he?'

I made a gesture with my hand that could have been interpreted as 'yes' or 'no'.

He pressed his lips together, as if to show he was refusing to say anything.

Both Joachim and he had their bedrooms at the rear of the houses. Sometimes they opened their windows, stretched out and chatted, even after they had gone to bed. On that freezing-cold night Joachim had said: *They've all gone to the architect's house! Come over here and we'll find something to do.*

Håkon thought it was a great idea, had dressed and crept over to the adjacent house, where Joachim stood in the doorway waiting for him. Then they had gone up to his room, read comics – Joachim could already read, he couldn't! Afterwards they had played a board game: *The Missing Diamond.*

'Let's tiptoe downstairs and have a look,' Joachim suggested.

He had nodded.

Joachim carefully opened the door. They slowly crept down the stairs to the ground floor. There was no one in the sitting room, and it was pitch-black, but the door of Joachim's parents' bedroom was ajar, and they heard some strange banging noises – and someone trying to say something but not quite managing it.

Håkon had been frightened. What was going on? He looked at Joachim, who was two years older than him. His friend stared into the bedroom with mouth agape and eyes wide open. When Joachim tiptoed over to the door crack he followed automatically as if tied to him by an invisible rope – or possibly because he was too frightened to be left on his own in the darkness.

Joachim pressed his face to the door. After watching for a little while he waved to Håkon, who squeezed his head up against Joachim's to see.

Again he was frightened. He wanted to scream, but Joachim held a finger to his mouth to tell him to be quiet. He didn't quite understand what was going on inside. A woman he eventually identified as Joachim's mother was lying on the floor by the bed with a man on top of her. The man had pulled her dress right up and his trousers down to his knees. His white backside bobbed up and down while he held a hand over her mouth so that what she was trying to say only came out as half-stifled, muffled sounds. Only after they had watched for a while did he notice the hair of the man lying on top of her. It was ... the architect man. Torbeinsvik.

His bum was going faster and faster, up and down, up and down, but suddenly Joachim pushed Håkon away and pointed to the door before dragging Håkon after him. Close to the door he whispered: 'Come on! Let's get going before he sees us!'

'Him?'

'Yes!'

Before he knew what was happening they were outside on the stairs. It was freezing cold and they weren't wearing any outdoor clothes. Joachim pointed. 'Let's go to your house!'

Håkon nodded and together they ran over to the house. He felt the handle: the door was unlocked as he had left it.

'Did you see that?' Joachim said excitedly.

He nodded.

'They were doing it! Mum and ... that architect!'

'Were they?'

'Yes, but you saw it, didn't you? They were screwing!'

'They were scr—?' He didn't understand.

'Your mum and dad have done it too.'

He shook his head vehemently. 'Noo! Never!'

'So how do you think Mette and you got here? Did they buy you in a shop? Were you delivered to the door?'

'No, mum said ... something about a stork.'

'A stork! They're screwing, but they won't admit it. Because that's how it is...' He waggled his bottom, the way they had seen the architect's bum going up and down. 'In and out! In and out!'

'But she didn't seem to like it, your mother didn't.'

'No...' For a moment Joachim looked pensive. 'It wasn't Dad...'

They froze. From the house they heard noises like the ones they had heard at Joachim's. They looked at each other. Joachim nodded. 'Listen!' But Håkon just shook his head. 'Not here! Never!'

Joachim led the way into the sitting room. One of the lamps was on, and on a table there were two wine glasses, one with a drop left at the bottom, the other half-full.

Joachim pointed to the bedroom door. But this one was closed. They stood outside with their ears to the door and listened to the sounds coming out. It was a kind of groaning. 'Oh, oh, oh!' But it wasn't as muffled as at Joachim's, and they could clearly hear there were two of them, one voice higher-pitched than the other, and then the bed creaked, like when he and Mette had been jumping on it, early one Sunday morning while their parents had been lying half-asleep beside them.

Just like at Joachim's they speeded up, the groaning became louder and louder, until it culminated in what sounded like a half-strangulated scream, and then everything went quiet, only a faint mumble reached their ears.

They quickly tiptoed away from the door, as though they suspected someone was about to come out. They stood there bewildered. What should they do? There were no more houses they could go to, and they couldn't hide at Håkon's, not safely anyway. 'I'm going home,' Joachim said, making for the door. Håkon didn't protest. Straight afterwards he was alone.

But he didn't go to bed. He trudged up the stairs to the first floor. There he sat in the darkness, resting his head against the wall while keeping an eye on what was happening downstairs.

He had been sitting there half-asleep when he gave a start. What was that? Where was he? Suddenly he realised. He heard a rush of water in the pipes after someone had been to the toilet. Then he heard voices down below and recognised his mother's. It was too far away for him to hear what they were saying, but then they came into the hall, his mother only in her dressing gown and – that was … the father of Asbjørg and Einar, fully clothed. For a moment they stood together, close, by the door to the porch. He saw Asbjørg and Einar's father stick his hand up mum's nice dressing gown, which she had been given for Christmas a week ago, put his arms around her waist, pull her to him and then – they kissed! For a long time. He had sat upstairs, perfectly still, scared to death they would notice him.

But no one saw him. His mother said goodbye to Asbjørn and Einar's father; then she quickly came back in and went into the sitting room. Håkon got up and went into his own room, clambered up into bed, stared at the dark wall and slowly subsided into such a deep sleep that when he awoke he was no longer sure whether what he had seen was a dream or not. And he definitely didn't dare ask!

It wasn't until six months afterwards that he and Joachim spoke about it again, but that was because Joachim wanted to take Janne and Mette into the woods and try it themselves, Håkon with Janne, Joachim with Mette…

41

He glared at me sullenly. I had coaxed most of it out of him: what he and Joachim had seen at his friend's house that night and what he had observed from the stairs at home, a few hours later.

I said: 'There's a pathetic question that sports reporters always ask: How did it feel?'

He didn't answer.

'Most children can handle it if they catch their parents hugging or making love, so long as parents tackle it in the right way. But to see your mother being embraced by another man, right after you've seen Joachim's mother in action with another neighbour … You don't have to be a child psychologist to realise it must have been a traumatic experience, Håkon.'

He made a movement with his head, still unwilling to continue the conversation.

'Perhaps that explains why, as far as I gather, you still haven't committed to a regular partner…?'

No comment.

'And perhaps that explains why Joachim ended up on drugs and today is one of the most emaciated veterans sitting in Nygårdsparken.'

Håkon burst out: 'But it wasn't Joachim who did it!'

'Did … what?'

'That with Mette.'

'That was a bit too fast for me, but…' Gradually a new and perhaps even more unpleasant image began to form for me. 'You don't mean … that you copied the adults, do you? Children often do.'

He nodded, and he was off again.

It had been the middle of summer. Mette and Janne had been sitting in the sandpit playing. He and Joachim had been kicking their heels round the yard, bored. Nothing to do! Too cold to go down to Skjolda-bukten to swim and all the others in the football club were on holiday. What could they do?

Joachim had nudged him, looked him in the eye and said: 'Remember New Year's Eve?'

'Yes...'

'What we saw?'

'Yes...'

'I've been thinking ... We should try! It looked such fun, didn't it?'

'No.'

'Yes! It's fun. Loads of the boys at school have been talking about it. Screwing. All the adults do it. We just have to be big enough.'

'Yes, but...'

'We can take Janne and Mette into the woods and try it. Can't we?'

'Janne and Mette?'

'Yes, they're ... women. They've got holes.'

He stood gaping at him. Was his friend serious? Horrified, he turned away. What if anyone had heard them talking? Some of the adults?

But it was mid-July and the houses were all quiet. Just the mothers were at home and they were probably sitting and chatting and drinking coffee. The two girls were engrossed in their work digging holes in the sand for their small plastic animals. They didn't give them a look.

'Chicken.'

He wasn't chicken! 'Nooo!'

'Come on then!'

'But how will we ... get them to come?'

'We'll say ... we've got something nice for them.' Joachim grinned like one of the big boys. 'And we have, haven't we.'

'Yes...'

Håkon still wasn't convinced, but when Joachim grabbed his arm he went over to the sandpit, where he heard Joachim say that if the two girls came with them to the woods they'd get something nice from them.

'What?' Mette asked.

'Chocolate.'

She brightened up. 'I love chocolate!'

Janne looked more doubtful, but followed anyway when Joachim took Mette's hand, helped her up and set off for the gate with her. Janne and he wandered after them.

But it didn't work. Not for Janne and him. When they came to the gate and Mette and Joachim were already outside, Janne planted both feet on the ground and refused to move. 'Mummy and daddy said we should never go out of the gate.'

'But…' He looked over at Joachim and Mette, who were crossing the street now. 'Mette and Joachim have gone out.'

Janne had looked up at him with a defiant, sulky stare. 'Mummy and daddy told me. Never go outside.'

'But … chocolate…'

'We only have sweets on Saturdays. Otherwise we'll have holes in our teeth.'

'Yes…'

He could still remember the feeling he was left with when he saw Mette and Joachim strolling into the woods over the road. Should he run after them? But they couldn't both … with Mette!'

'So what did you do?'

'Nothing. Janne went back to the sandpit and continued doing what she had been doing, as though nothing had happened. As for me … I went up to my room. Found a comic and sat looking at it. Must have been a Donald Duck or a Red Indian comic: *Sølvpilen* – we used to read them all the time in those days. After a while they returned. Mette and Joachim.'

'A while? How long's that?'

'I have no idea. Not the foggiest.'

'And what happened then?'

'Nothing.'

'Nothing? And your mother … Wasn't she shocked when Mette went out?'

'No, they didn't notice. Neither her nor Joachim's mother. Because

Janne and her were together … or so they thought. And when Joachim came back asking after me, Mette was playing in the sandpit again as though nothing had happened.'

'But Joachim … must have said something?'

'No.'

'Surely you asked him?'

'No, I didn't want to say anything, and he just looked … embarrassed. Maybe it hadn't been so easy after all. Maybe he didn't know what to do when it came to the crunch.'

'And Mette didn't say anything?'

'No. She seemed happy and content, and there was nothing that struck you about her. She even had chocolate smeared over her mouth, so she got that anyway.'

'But … when you started telling me about this you said Joachim didn't do it. You were thinking about what happened in 1977, weren't you?'

He looked down. 'Yes.'

'Why?'

'Well … it struck me – several times – as everyone was searching for her, for days and weeks … I pictured Janne and me standing inside the gate. Mette and Joachim walking into the woods. But Joachim was eight years old! He could never have done anything … so nasty to Mette. I couldn't believe that.'

'So that's why you chose not to tell any adults?'

'Well…'

'Until now?'

'No.'

'And what do you think today, with all we know about child brutality? I mean, we hear stories on the news – from America and England … The same could happen here. Children copy adults, something they've seen in a film, a computer game, heard big boys talking about … and then they accidentally kill someone of their own age.'

He looked at me, desperate. 'But then surely they would have found her? Wouldn't they? He couldn't have hidden her!'

'You've thought the thought. Admit it!'

At once tears came into his eyes. 'She was so small. She wouldn't have understood anything. And she came back of course.'

'The first time, yes. But can you be sure he didn't take her many times? Or at least one more time.'

'No ...' he said at length, so low it was almost inaudible.

'Well ... I'll ask him, of course. I'll have to.'

'Don't say...' He didn't complete the sentence.

'That it was you who told me? I'm afraid he'll know. The alternative would have to be Janne. She's married and lives in England, by the way.'

He wasn't interested. 'Right.' Then he grabbed the snow shovel and lifted it demonstratively into the air. 'I have no time for this any longer. I have to do my job.'

I nodded. 'Thank you for everything you've told me. It's been very useful.'

'Don't tell Mum what I've said.'

'No, no. Not unless it's absolutely necessary.'

He threw me a sceptical glance, as though he didn't believe me, but feared I would go back to Bergen and tell her everything anyway, holding nothing back.

Then he nodded sullenly, took the shovel and went on his way.

For my part, I discovered I had lots of time on my hands before my departure. I followed a sign pointing to Fjellstua and ended up there, at the top of Mount Aksla with a panoramic view over the town, the fjord and the islands. From Mount Sukkertoppen to Okseblåsen, or whatever the narrow rock formation in the north was called. Afterwards I went down the steps to Byparken, crossed Hellebroa Bridge and arrived at the same eatery I had visited ten years ago, to see whether the klippfisk dish they served was as good as back then. It was.

With the taste from Sjøbua restaurant on my palate I caught the airport bus to Vigra, and from there the evening flight back to Bergen. From Flesland Airport I took a taxi directly to Nygårdsparken. The driver watched long after I went through the gates from Parkveien. He probably had his own ideas about what I was doing, and that was fine by me. I had no more time to lose. Someone had waited long enough as it was and we had never been closer to the answer than now. I could see them, walking together into the woods, Joachim and Mette, Mette and Joachim. Two small children on their way to … what? That was what I had to find out. It was now or never.

42

Wandering over Flagghaugen in Nygårdsparken after the onset of darkness was not something anyone would do with a light heart. On the other hand, it was much quieter there now than earlier in the day. Most of the druggies who had a fixed abode had already gathered all the ampoules they needed for the day, and they would hardly be expecting someone with a tempting wallet to appear so late at night. Others had rolled out their sleeping bags to spend the March night under the stars or under a rhododendron bush. I didn't envy them.

I peered between the bushes and trees, where I saw them sitting in huddles, and said gently: 'Joachim! Joachim Bringeland! Are you there?'

Only mumbled negative responses came back until, at the fourth or fifth attempt, a high-pitched voice squeaked: 'Try down at Tiny's. That's where he's staying for the moment…'

'So you haven't seen him here?'

'Not for a few hours, no,' came the answer from the rhododendrons.

'Thank you.'

I went down to Jonas Reins gate and tried the front door of Tiny's hostel again. This time the door marked OFFICE. RECEPTION was ajar … I knocked so hard that the door swung open. Through the crack I met the dark eyes of Tiny sitting behind his rickety desk with an open can of beer beside him and a half-eaten kebab installation, like a failed work of art, over today's edition of *Bergensavisen*.

He belched quietly and beckoned me in. 'Veum, wasn't it?'

'Yep,' I said.

'Jokken?'

'You have a good memory.'

'Never forget a fizog. Handy facility to have in this line of business, to know who you can trust and who you can't.'

'Are you telling me you can trust me?'

'I only said I remembered you.' He smirked and rubbed his mouth with the back of his hand. He hadn't lost any weight since I was last here, and God knows if he had changed his shirt in the few days that had passed. The one he was wearing was definitely the same filthy yellow colour.

'Is Joachim in?'

'He is – *I think*. He made an appearance an hour ago anyway, seemed pretty happy, so just go on up two floors and try the first door to the right. If he doesn't open up, try the door. If it's locked you'd better come down and tell me, and I'll give you a hand.'

I thanked him and followed his instructions. There was no need to do any fetching. Joachim was in. He didn't open up, in fact, but when I tried the door, it was unlocked and when I went in he was sitting on a chair with an elastic band around his arm and a used syringe on the floor beside him, his head lolling back, his eyes glazed and probably beyond all communication for the next couple of hours.

I checked his pulse, but it felt relatively normal. He was breathing regularly and when I touched him he could focus well enough to recognise me, so perhaps it wasn't going to take quite so long after all.

'Oh, it's you,' he mumbled before closing his eyes fully again, as if to avoid the sight of me.

'Yes, it's me,' I said, looking around.

The room was Spartan: an unmade bed, a low table, two chairs, a sink and a worktop with a hotplate. At the back a door led to what I assumed was a toilet, in the best-case scenario a bathroom, or perhaps just a rear staircase. Scattered across the floor were various used syringes, empty boxes, an overflowing ashtray someone had apparently tried to set fire to and a well-used pipe. On the floor beside the chair he was sitting in was a pile of newspapers and magazines. There were no pictures on the walls, no books, there was no stereo and there was no TV. Joachim Bringeland lived his life in a monotonous rhythm, within the outer limits of Bergen Shopping Centre and Nygårdsparken, making sporadic forays to Torgallmenningen, where his main aim was to beg enough capital for the day's dose and otherwise keep his head above water. It was difficult to see him as the eight-year-old, active, somewhat domineering friend who had tried to entice Håkon Misvær into the woods with his little sister, Janne, and who himself had taken Mette at least once in 1977.

On the hotplate was a well-worn coffee jug and on the table next to it a jar of instant coffee. I filled the jug with water from the tap over the sink, put the jug on the hotplate and switched on the electricity. It didn't take long to boil and I was soon able to serve us a mug each of gourmet coffee, Nescafé Gold-style. Gradually I managed to resuscitate him, pour coffee down him and establish a kind of contact. He swung his head and his eyes roamed, but every so often he focussed on me, as though he no longer remembered who I was or what I was doing there.

'I spoke to you a few days ago,' I said loudly, staring hard at him. 'About the Mette Case.'

That made him focus his eyes once again, and this time he held on, at least for a while. 'The Mette Case…'

'Yes, and now I know a great deal more than I did then. So now I want you to tell me word for word what took place between Mette and you that time in September 1977.'

'September…?' He thrust his eyes open. 'When she disappeared, you mean?'

'Yes.'

'N-n-nothing. I know nothing about it. I told you that last time we spoke … didn't I?'

'Yes, but you were lying.'

'Eh? Lying? Me? About what?'

'I could reel off all the things you didn't tell me. What you and Håkon saw on New Year's Eve 1976, for example.'

'Ha! So Håkon cracked, did he? Where the hell did you find the twat? On FC Brann's rubbish heap?'

'Somewhere else. And he also told me how you went into the woods with Mette one summer's day that year to try it yourself, as you put it.'

'He's got a memory like an elephant, hasn't he? I can barely remember where I was this morning.'

'A different place from here?'

'Oh, shut up!'

I followed his advice, for a while. He sat staring angrily into the air with the empty mug between his hands.

'More coffee?'

He nodded and passed me the mug. I took it to the hotplate, poured instant coffee and more hot water in, repeated the ritual with my cup and returned to the table. I gave him the mug, he nodded thank you, raised it to his mouth and drank a mouthful, which must have made the skin inside flinch with pain. But he didn't turn a hair.

He had gone into the woods with Mette. She held his hand, as though he were her father. He felt almost proud, but at the same time he had a feeling in his stomach – of tension, excitement, which he couldn't yet give a name…

She was wearing a blue jumper and light-blue trousers with braces, and her blonde hair shone in the summer sun. They hadn't got very far before she asked for the chocolate he had promised her. 'Just a bit farther,' he said. 'Over here.'

He had decided on the place earlier. Through the woods, down into a hollow with moss on the ground, and there … there he would do exactly what the architect man had done to his mother that night six months before.

'Here, Mette…'

She looked up at him in hope.

'But it's got to be a secret.'

She nodded enthusiastically. 'Yes.'

'Lie down on your back first. And close your eyes!'

She looked at him slyly, as though she liked such secrets. And she did exactly what he said, lay down on her back and screwed her eyes shut. He crept over to her, loosened the belt on his trousers and opened them at the front. He pulled her braces down over her shoulders and was placing his hands on her trousers to pull them down when it happened.

A steely hand grabbed him by the neck, squeezed and lifted him until he was hanging and wriggling in the air above the terrified girl, who had now opened her eyes and was watching what was going on, her mouth agape.

'What on earth are you doing, boy?' he heard a man's voice say in his ears, but he didn't dare turn around to see who it was.

He just whimpered in protest. 'I wasn't going to!'

Then he was hurled to the side, so hard that he fell against a tree trunk, hit his shoulder so hard he had bruises for more than a week afterwards, and fell to the ground. When he did finally dare to raise his eyes he saw the adult man bend down, pick Mette up and brush off all the debris from the forest floor. While he patted her softly on the head with one hand he took out something wrapped in pale-yellow paper and held it in front of her.

Mette looked up at him and the corners of her lips curled. Then she stretched out a hand and said: 'Chocolate!' She put one piece in her mouth and munched while looking up at the tall man and grinning with brown chocolate on her front teeth.

The man turned to Joachim, who was still sitting against the tree root where he had fallen, stunned and resting. The man glared at him and his eyes flashed as he said: 'Don't you ever do this again! If I catch you one more time I'll take you to the police and you'll be put in prison for the rest of your life, do you understand me?'

When he didn't answer, the man repeated himself, in an even firmer tone: 'Do you understand me?'

Then he nodded. 'Yes. I'll never do it again...'

'Good. So let's forget all about this, shall we?' The man turned to Mette again and stretched out a hand. 'Come on!'

Just as she had innocently followed Joachim here, she walked back hand in hand with the tall man.

Joachim sat where he was, as quiet as a mouse, until long after they had gone. When he returned to the yard a bit later and carefully opened the gate, Mette was in the sandpit playing with Janne, as though nothing had happened.

Finished with telling his story, Joachim sat with the cup of coffee to his mouth, perhaps wishing he could hide behind it. Nevertheless, a calmer expression had spread across his face now, as if getting the story off his chest after so many years had given him peace of mind.

Then he turned to me. 'But this was mid-summer. This was long before the day she disappeared. That day I was in my room all the time. I swear to you!'

I nodded thoughtfully. 'And this adult man, have you seen him since?'

'Both before and after!'

'Oh?'

'It was Langemann!'

'Langemann?'

'We called him that because he was so long. He was the pedo who used to visit Eivind and Else.'

'Jesper Janevik?'

'Yes…'

43

Jesper Janevik started to close the door the moment he recognised me on the step, but I was as fast with my foot as I had been on the previous occasion and placed it in the door opening. He stared at it, furious, as if intending to push it off, but from his mouth came only a deep groan of despair.

'Janevik ... This time we have to have a proper conversation. Let me in!'

'We had one last time, didn't we? Stop harassing me!'

'We didn't talk enough. There have been some fresh developments since then.'

We stood staring at each other. He was wearing the same dark-blue jeans as before, or at least the same brand, but his shirt was white and his vest, visible at the neck, black. There was a silvery glitter in his dark hair and his eyes were shiny and feverish. He looked as if he had slept badly since I last visited him, in which case it was not without good reason.

'It's too cold to stand outside. Either you let me in or I'll ring the police and ask them to get a search warrant.' I looked around and motioned towards the flowerbeds around his house. 'They'll dig up every bloody bed you've got!'

'No!' he whimpered, as though this was the worst calamity that could befall him. 'Not that, please! Come in then, if you absolutely have to.'

He hung back in the dark hallway. I pushed the door and followed him in. The air inside was cold and the morning light from outside showed me the way. He pointed to an open door, which led into a rather old-fashioned sitting room, in which the flower pots on the windowsill were the sole sign of life. A radio cabinet from the 1950s and a television from the 1970s, an inheritance from his parents, judging by the sight of them, occupied one wall and a corner. An empty coffee table, a sofa and three chairs, upholstered in the same grey-brown material with red patches under the arm rests, made up the remainder of the furniture. On the cabinet was the same photograph I had seen in his niece's house four days earlier: the father and mother in front of a dark Fiat, both well advanced in years, but proud of their new acquisition, which they would keep for the rest of their of their lives and then leave to their heirs.

I walked over, picked up the photo and held it in the air. 'Your father was proud of this car, Liv Grethe told me when I visited her and your sister, last Thursday.'

He glanced at the picture, then back at me. 'Yes.'

'You must have driven it yourself now and then?'

'No, never. It was Dad's.'

'Yes, but Liv Grethe said … After your father died it just stood in the garage. Your mother didn't drive. I suppose you do, though?'

He shrugged and nodded. 'Yes…'

'Don't say you never borrowed it.'

He squirmed. 'Once in a blue moon maybe.'

'Like that Saturday in September 1977, for example?'

'That Sat—' He kept blinking as if I was blowing at him, hard. 'No, no! What are you after …? Are you accusing me of …? Do you think I…?' Tears were in his eyes, so big and shiny they were like oil.

I persisted: 'That Saturday in September 1977, when you drove up to Solstølen and took little Mette, whom you knew after you saved her from an incident in the woods earlier that summer.'

He stared at me in silence.

'You parked in the street. You saw her alone in the sandpit playing. Probably you called her from the gate, showed her a bar of chocolate and asked if she wanted some … When she went over you gave it to her, lifted her up, carried her to the car and asked if she felt like a trip, that would be more fun than sitting along and digging sand, wouldn't it? And of course she thought so too?'

His face contorted, twitched, more violently and uncontrolled than before, as though he were on the verge of some kind of stroke. He was breathing hard, but chewed his lip so as not to let out the smallest sound.

'Isn't that true? Give or take a detail? Wasn't that how it happened?'

'No! Not like that...'

'How then?'

Again he stood staring at me. I could read in his eyes that it was only now he realised what he had said. 'I didn't mean...'

'You didn't mean to do it?'

'To say ... what I said.'

'But now you have.'

At once he burst into tears. He slumped down on the nearest chair, covered his face with his hands and sobbed loudly and painfully as his whole body quivered and shook. It was like watching a little child that has fallen and hurt themselves. But I had to remind myself – what had happened to the little child we were discussing was far worse.

With mixed feelings – sympathy and cold distance – I watched him, I didn't say a word, I didn't move. I just waited, as so often before, when I knew a breakthrough was imminent.

In the end his crying subsided. He was sitting hunched up in the chair, but lowered his arms and looked at me with the eyes of a wounded animal. 'I knew it! Knew I would be blamed yet again for something I haven't done.'

'I—'

'First the damned girls. Then the police. Then that dreadful policeman in 1977 – Dankert Muus. I still wake up in the night and see him before me. He was evil ... evil!'

'That may be a little exagg—'

'And then you come along, twenty-five years later, with the same accusations.' He hiccoughed and drew a deep breath. 'That isn't how it was. I've never been ... like that. It wasn't my fault she drowned.'

This went through me like a sliver of ice. 'Did she drown? Mette?'

He looked at me as if I were an idiot. 'Mette? I'm not talking about Mette!'

'Who then?'

'Liv Grethe, for Christ's sake!'

'Liv Grethe?'

'I told her when I went to make coffee that she had to keep an eye on her all the time. But she just lay there, half-naked in the sun. She was desperate for a tan. And then she fell asleep – or dozed off – or whatever it was that happened.'

'And now you're talking about … your sister?'

'Maria, yes. And when I returned with a jug of coffee, Liv Grethe wasn't anywhere to be seen.'

Before he had gone off she had been sitting and playing at the edge of the water. Her little blue bucket and red spade were still there, but she…

'Maria! What are you thinking of? Where's Liv Grethe?'

She had given a start, pushed her sunglasses up on to her head and looked around, befuddled. 'What? But she was here!'

'Well, she isn't now. She's gone.'

They had desperately searched everywhere. He had run over to the water, but the waves were washing in and out and the sea quickly became deep. He threw himself in, swam out, dived down, opened his eyes, looked around, paddled back up to the surface, took a deep breath and dived back down. It was only after – how long? he was never quite sure – fifteen, twenty, thirty minutes that he found her, at the bottom in her tiny swimming trunks, her hair floating up with the water, her mouth and eyes open, the pupils had long disappeared behind her eyelids. A little mermaid.

He swam down to her, so deep that his blood pounded like timpani in his head and his eardrums hurt, but he managed to get hold of her, grab her arm and pull her up, drag her shore-wards until he felt firm ground under his feet, stood up and waded back with the lifeless bundle in his arms, staring at his mother, his sister standing there, her stupid, pained face, stiffened into a grimace that would soon crack, soon dissolve into a thousand pieces, never to be the same face again, with a slow-working poison in her soul and brain that would leave its marks for the rest of her life.

'She was dead, you see? We did all we could, but there was no life left in her. And that was when Maria realised, when she broke down. I don't think I've ever seen anyone so desperate. Desperate? Hysterical! She howled and screamed, pummelled my chest and said it was my fault, everything was my fault! Now she had lost everything, first of all her husband, then her daughter, now she had nothing left to live for, she might as well jump into the sea herself. I had to restrain her, I had to hold her so tightly my nails were gouging her skin, but she kept hitting me – *your fault, Jesper, your fault, Jesper!* And then I said … Well, then, I told her.'

He paused. He stared at me blindly. He had been so deep into his narrative that he was finding it difficult to return to the present. His head sank further and he sat studying his hands, which opened and closed, opened and closed.

'So then you told her…' I repeated.

He nodded mutely.

'What did you tell her, Jesper?'

He shook his head and refused to say.

So I said it for him. 'You said you'd find another little girl for her, didn't you.'

'Yes.'

44

I didn't dare leave him while we waited for the police. Now everything was out in the open a new composure came over him, as though this was what he had been yearning for all these years: finally to be able to tell the truth about what really happened on that September day in 1977.

As soon as he had promised her, he knew at once what he would do. First he had taken Maria into the house, given her several Valium tablets from a bottle she'd been prescribed and laid her down on the sofa in the sitting room with a woollen blanket wrapped round her. She fell asleep almost at once.

'And the body, what did you do with that?'

The next thing to do was to go back down to the beach, take the drowned child to her house, and, after a quick think, bury her. The rose bed facing the north-east was the nicest spot. With a spade he buried her deep, moved the rose bushes to the side, wrapped Liv Grethe in a blanket and placed her in the deep grave. For a moment he stood with bowed head looking down at the round bundle. Then he picked a pale-red rose from the nearest bush, held it to his nose and smelled the bewitching perfume, and dropped it onto the tartan plaid. Then he shovelled the soil back in, placed the rose bushes over her and it wasn't long before everything was as it had been. No one could see a difference.

'And she's still there?'

He nodded slowly. 'It's the most beautiful rose bed of them all.'

We sat in silence, both of us, as the unreality of the situation gradually sank in.

I was the first to speak. 'And then … ?'

'This was a Friday…'

He had checked his watch. It was too late now, but the day after …
He spent the evening with Maria, sitting in the armchair next to the
sofa, where she lay as if in a coma, with the television on, but not the
volume, so as not to wake her up.

She opened her eyes a couple of times, looked around, met his gaze
and asked in a daze: 'Liv Grethe?'

'She's asleep.'

She was satisfied with that answer and soon went back to sleep.

The following day he drove the car out of the garage for the first time
in many months, got behind the wheel, filled up with petrol in Florvåg
before driving down to the terminal in Kleppestø and waiting for the
ferry to dock. During the crossing he stood on deck. It was a beautiful day with a few scattered showers, sunny intervals and late-summer
temperatures, although it was mid-September. Inside, he felt a strange
calm; everything was predestined, somewhere it was written in the stars
that this is what he would do.

In Solstølvegen he parked the car outside the fence, sat for a moment
and deliberated, then he got out of the car. When he reached the gate
it struck him once again. This was no mere chance. This was how it was
meant to be. She was in the sandpit – alone. And there wasn't anyone to
be seen in the yard between the five houses. No one else but her.

He took a bar of chocolate from his inside pocket, held it in the air
and said: 'Mette! Look what I've got for you …'

The little girl looked up, recognised him at once, got up so quickly
she knocked over the blue bucket she was filling and ran towards him
smiling. 'Hi!'

He broke off a bit of chocolate for her. She took it and put it in her
mouth in one movement while beaming up at him.

'Look what I've got for you today, Mette … My new car.'

She stretched her neck to look over the gate, nodding happily. He
scanned the houses, from one to the next, window to window. Not a
sign of life, not even in the house where she belonged. Then he quickly
leaned over, lifted her up, held her away from his body and said: 'Do you
feel like a little trip with Uncle Jesper?'

'Uncle Jesper,' she answered, and nodded. 'Are you my uncle too?'

'I certainly am. Come on!'

He whisked her off to his car, opened the door on the left, placed her on the front seat without fastening her seat belt, ran round the car, got in behind the wheel, twisted the ignition key and started up.

It had been so easy. That was all there was to it.

He drove carefully so that she wouldn't tumble forward if he had to brake suddenly. On board the ferry he sat in the car and gave her chocolate, got out to pay the ticket collector and then got back in, happy that he hadn't met anyone he knew. But who could that be? Who did he have anything to do with anymore on Askøy? And on a Saturday morning most people were going the other way, to Bergen; and those travelling this way were not Askøy residents but Bergensians on a day trip, maybe to do some fishing on the island of Herdla or out towards Hjeltefjorden.

He drove ashore, unnoticed, and continued to Janevika, equally unnoticed, where he put the car straight into the garage and parked it for good. He had never used it again and a few years later he sold it for no great profit.

During the trip Mette changed. At first she had been trusting and enthusiastic. When they arrived at the ferry she suddenly looked serious, as though she realised that now something was happening which she didn't understand. But when he consoled her with more chocolate she relaxed again – for the time being. When they arrived her lips started trembling. 'Where's Mummy? I want my mummy!'

At first he didn't know what to say. Then he said: 'Mummy's gone away, Mette. Now you're living with Uncle Jesper and … a new mummy. We'll make sure the nasty boy won't come and take you.'

She looked up at him, puzzled. Then she started to cry. 'Mummy! I want my mummy!'

'Come here, Mette. In here, you'll see. A nice lady's waiting for you …'

He lifted her up and carried her kicking into the house. Inside, Maria struggled to her feet and staggered around. 'Maria,' he said. 'Here I am with a new Liv Grethe for you … Look!'

He put the girl down on the floor in front of him. She stared at Maria. Then she threw herself round and clung to his leg. 'I want my mummy, my mummy, my mummy!'

Maria stood watching her, not understanding much more herself. 'Liv Grethe, is it really you?'

From that moment on they never called her anything but Liv Grethe. The first nights she cried herself to sleep, sobbing inconsolably, which changed into resigned sniffling. When they woke her in the morning she was startled, sat up in bed and looked round, disorientated, she had no idea where she was. But as the weeks went by she seemed to adapt to the situation. Gradually a kind of resigned calm fell over her, as though realising that her mum and dad and Håkon were gone forever, they had left her and would never come back. She began to forget them, there were longer and longer intervals between her asking after them, and in the end it was as though she had repressed her previous existence and had become ... Liv Grethe.

The house was isolated, hidden behind a tall hedge, and everyone knew Maria had brought her daughter with her from Østland. The bitterness of her marital break-up had meant Maria never sought contact with old friends, and from now on it was him or the mother who took care of the practical side, went shopping, that kind of thing. Later it was just him. No one reacted to the sounds of a child playing in the house. When, four years later, she started school, it was with Liv Grethe's birth certificate as her ID, and no one looked at that more than once. He didn't talk to Maria anymore about the past. He was never entirely sure if she had ever really understood that in fact she had a new daughter. But then he didn't really understand women.

The day he would never forget was the Thursday, barely two weeks after he had been up to Solstøvegen to collect her, when two police officers suddenly appeared on his doorstep on what they called a routine patrol. After a detailed discussion with him and conferring with the officers in charge of the investigation in Bergen they took him to Police HQ where he was confronted by Inspector Dankert Muus, who wanted to talk about his many visits to Synnøve in Solstølvegen, and not only that, Muus also brought up old cases from Askøy. It all ended with him being in custody for twenty-four hours before the defence lawyer he had been allocated had him released, as there wasn't a scrap of evidence against him; even the circumstantial evidence was thin. Later Maria was also summoned to an interview, although they got nothing sensible out of her, and he had given the defence lawyer photos of Liv Grethe, Maria and him, taken on her birthday the year before, the 17th September, as a kind of alibi for the same date the year afterwards. It was accepted because he never heard any more. Life continued as usual. The daily drama carried on. Except that one of the characters had been exchanged.

He met my gaze again. 'She became like a daughter to me, Veum. Maria was never the same again. Something had gone for ever inside her. It was me who took care of Liv Grethe, helped her with her home-work, gave her advice and accompanied her to school and so on. And I was a decent father. I never did anything to her. I did nothing wrong!'

'No? All you did was destroy a family, leave a mother, father and brother in total darkness, never knowing what had happened to their daughter and sister. All you did was steal a child.'

The look he gave me was dark and unfathomable. He didn't know what I was talking about. He hadn't done anything wrong.

45

The Head of Department, Jakob E. Hamre himself, accompanied by Inspector Annemette Bergesen and two officers, arrived at the old house in Janevika to make the arrest and carry out the first interview. The two cars swung into the drive in front of the house, and I met them at the door.

'Up with the larks for a Tuesday morning, Veum?' Hamre said with his usual sarcasm.

'Someone has to solve your cases for you.'

His eyes narrowed visibly. 'Spare me. We did what we could, but we hit a wall. I remember the case well, even though I was only a young officer at that time. Your stumbling over a solution almost twenty-five years later doesn't mean we didn't do what we could.'

'Muus was actually on the track when he had the guilty party in custody, but his defence lawyer, whoever it was, was smarter.'

His eyes went distant. 'I don't remember that. However ... where are you holding the man?'

'He's waiting in here.'

We went in, all of us. Jesper Janevik was where I had left him, with a somewhat bemused look on his face, as though he didn't understand what all the fuss was about after so many years.

'It provides an explanation for everything, though not the one we were all expecting,' I said.

'We'll handle this,' Hamre said, going over to Janevik, holding out one hand and introducing himself. 'Let's take this from the top,' he said in as friendly a voice as he could muster.

Through the window I saw Liv Grethe Heggvoll on her way down the path between the two houses. I quickly turned to Annemette Bergesen. 'Could you come with me? Here's...'

For a moment I didn't quite know what to call her, but Bergesen received an affirmative nod from Hamre, who said: 'Yes, it'll be good if we can speak undisturbed in here first.'

With the female inspector I left the room. We met Liv Grethe Heggvoll before she quite reached the house. She looked with surprise from the two civilian cars to Annemette and finally to me. 'Veum ... What's going on here?'

Bergesen answered. 'We're the police. Who are you?'

'The police!? I'm Liv Grethe Heggvoll. Is ... Has anything happened to Uncle Jesper?'

Bergesen looked into her eyes. 'Nothing to ... Nothing dramatic. Not to him.'

Again Liv Grethe looked at me. 'Would it be possible to have some kind of explanation? Veum?'

'That's not so easy. But ... let me show you something.'

I reached inside my jacket. Bergesen regarded me with suspicion as I pulled out the little envelope I'd had there since my second visit to Maja Misvær exactly a week ago. From the envelope I took the little photo of Mette, taken when she was two or three years old, and showed it to the woman in front of me.

She leaned over and looked at it. An amazed expression filled her eyes. She looked at me again. 'But that's ...'

'Yes,' I said. 'It's you, isn't it?'

'My goodness. I've never seen ... Where did you get it from?'

'Actually, this is rather a long story. Perhaps you and I and Inspector Bergesen can take a seat and go through this bit by bit. Shall we ... go up there?' I gazed at the road which she had come down. At the top of the slope we could glimpse the roof of the house where she had lived since September 1977. 'But it might be advantageous if ... well, the woman you believe is your mother is not present.'

'The woman I believe ...' She was open-mouthed and Bergsen glowered at me.

'Do you know what you're doing, Veum?'

'I think so.'

The young woman turned and looked up at the house she had just left. 'Let's do that then, if…'

Two hours later she was sitting in front of me, in floods of tears. Annemette Bergesen sat with her arms around her, but my impression was that she still hadn't fully taken in what I had told her.

At length I said: 'There's a lot left to explain, but … in fact I've got a job to do and I think it would do both of you good to meet.'

Through her tears she said: 'You mean…' Her eyes drifted over to the closed door to the sitting room, where Maria Heggvoll was sitting on the sofa and watching morning TV. Then they came back to me. 'My … mother?'

Bergesen sent me a serious look. 'Do you think this is right, Varg?'

I nodded. 'I'm sure. She's waited long enough and…' I looked back at the young woman. 'Yes, it's time.'

'Let me confer with Hamre first.'

I nodded. 'I'll be here.'

She left. When we were alone the young woman stared at me helplessly. 'I just can't understand it. I don't get it. That someone could…' She gazed out of the window towards the house where Jesper Janevik lived. 'That something like this could happen.'

I said dispassionately: 'They were lucky. External circumstances – out here – helped them. But it's not your everyday story, I can vouch for that.'

'No…'

She seemed more composed now, and we sat in silence, rapt by our own thoughts, until Annemette Bergesen appeared in the doorway.

She nodded to me. 'It's fine. They're in the process of getting a full confession. Hamre said it wouldn't do any harm. Not to the case anyway.'

The young woman burst out: 'But what will happen to him? To Uncle Jesper, I mean.'

'Too early to say,' Bergesen said in a matter-of-fact tone. 'After all it's a long time ago … what happened, I mean.'

The young woman moved her head in thought.

I looked at her. 'I can drive you there.'

Again that helpless look came in her eyes. 'But first I have to…' She gestured towards the closed door.

I nodded. 'Of course. But this isn't goodbye. The woman in there … It's too early to say how much she understood, so … don't say anything either. Nothing … about all this.'

Bergesen added: 'Yes, that's important. She'll have to be interviewed as well.'

'I see,' the young woman said. She took out a handkerchief and a little mirror and removed the most visible signs that she had been crying.

We followed her into the sitting room and kept in the background as she went to the woman on the sofa, leaned over to her and said: 'I'm going for a little drive, Mummy…' A half-stifled sob shook her chest. 'But I'll be back, don't worry.'

The elderly woman looked up at her, confused. 'Worry? Why should I worry?' The look she gave us suggested she didn't recognise any of us.

Then she shifted her attention to the TV screen as we went towards the door and left.

46

For what I assumed would be the last time for quite a while I parked my car in Solstølvegen. The young woman with short reddish hair and large blue eyes sat in the car beside me without evincing any indication of wishing to get out. Slowly she looked around, studied the houses on both sides of the road, shifted her gaze to the tree-clad slope opposite, considerably more built-up than it had been in 1977; then once again she ended up looking at me.

I nodded towards the low gate in the wooden fence that screened the Solstølen Co-op from the outside world.

She heaved a deep sigh. 'I don't recognise this place.'

'No, but give it time.'

We stayed sitting. I glanced at her. 'Shall we … ?'

She hesitated. Then a shudder went through her. 'Yes, we better had.' She didn't appear to be looking forward to this.

I opened the door on my side. She didn't move. I went round the car and opened the door for her. Only then did she swing her legs out and stand up. I closed the door behind her and locked the car with the remote.

I walked ahead and opened the gate. The yard was quiet, as it usually was in the morning. No one was playing in the sandpit in front of Maja Misvær's house. The young woman looked at it pensively and it was exactly then I saw the shadow of a memory in her eyes, a tiny glimpse of recognition.

She stood looking around, from house to house, and when she turned back to me there were tears forming in her eyes. In a voice so low it was barely audible she said: 'I've been here … I've seen this…' She looked down at the sandpit, where there was still a little bucket, a spade and some play figures. 'But I thought it was something I'd ... dreamed. A place that didn't exist in reality.'

I motioned towards the house behind the sandpit. 'Here it is.'

She followed my gaze.

'Shall I?'

She gave a brief nod.

Then I rang the bell and stepped aside, like a master of ceremonies introducing the evening's main guest to an impatient audience.

When Maja Misvær opened the door she looked at the young woman first, then at me, then back at the woman.

'There's someone I'd like you to meet, Maja,' I said, but I hadn't needed to say anything. From a distance of twenty-five years, in a moment of inexplicable magic, they recognised each other.

'Mette ... is that you?'

'Mummy...'

They fell around each other's necks crying, and even a fifty-nine-year-old private investigator, of the so-called hard-boiled variety, had to turn away, swallow the lump in his throat and quickly wipe away his tears before he moved back to the doorstep.

I met Maja Misvær's eyes and smiled in confirmation. Her rose wasn't dead after all. Someone had just picked it. But she had been there all the time, in a place where roses never die.

A few hours later I did as I had promised and drove Mette back to Askøy. Which she still called 'home' and where she had a lot of tidying up to do. I drove back to my flat, called Hamre and was told that this case would take its legal course, but the offender would initially be admitted to a psychiatric unit for surveillance – so that he wouldn't harm himself, as Hamre phrased it.

After the conversation with Hamre I sat staring into the air. Suddenly I felt empty. I had completed my assignment, I would be paid my fee, the month's supply of food and drink was secure, but had I become a happier person? Had I brought the dead to life?

The unopened bottle of aquavit was still on the kitchen table and behind it I saw the contours of an endless succession of blood relations, bottle after bottle. If I opened the first, the next stood at the ready, waiting, and then the next, and then the next … On the other hand … I could phone Sølvi Hegge and ask if she had anything planned for this evening. The choice was mine. The rest of my life was mine. All I had to do was choose.